WILD RIDES

WILD RIDES

Three gay novellas

ELIZABETH COLDWELL

Published by Xcite Books Ltd – 2012
ISBN 9781908262363

Copyright © Elizabeth Coldwell 2012

The right of Elizabeth Coldwell to be identified as the author of this work has been asserted by her in accordance with the Copyright, Designs and Patents Act 1988.

The story contained within this book is a work of fiction. Names and characters are the product of the author's imagination and any resemblance to actual persons, living or dead, is entirely coincidental.

All rights reserved. No part of this book may be copied, or transmitted in any form or by any means, electronic, electrostatic, magnetic tape, mechanical, photocopying, recording or otherwise, without the written permission of the publishers: Xcite Books, Suite 11769, 2nd Floor, 145-157 St John Street, London EC1V 4PY

Printed and bound in the UK

Cover design by
Madamadari

Contents

Ridden Hard   1
Stud To Go   55
Layover   145

RIDDEN HARD

Chapter One

IT WOULD NEVER HAVE happened if I hadn't told a lie.

Not one of the small personal lies we've all come out with at some stage in our life: 'I completely agree with you,' or, 'No, I've never had a lover with a bigger cock than yours.' Those are the lies that grease the wheels of our relationships and keep them running smoothly. Without them, no one would ever get laid.

No, this was a professional lie. Actors' résumés are full of them. We shave a couple of years off our age, add an inch or so to our height, purport to be fluent in French or able to carry off a number of accents, from upper-class English to downtown Glaswegian. Anything that might give us an advantage over all the other equally accomplished actors going for the same rôle. In my case, I claim I can ride a horse. In truth, I'd trotted along Clacton beach on the back of a donkey a few times when I was a toddler. Since then, nothing.

It never mattered. No film or TV show I appeared in ever required any riding ability on my part. Until I received the script for *Grail*.

My agent, Keira, sent me two scripts that week. One was for a film about rival football gangs, adapted from his own autobiography by a former hooligan who condemned all the violence he'd been involved in while describing it with lip-smacking relish. I would be reading for the part of the author's younger brother, who never quite managed to escape the gang's influence. I knew I could play the rôle in my sleep, but the project had the air of something the audience had seen too many times before. I was looking for a different challenge.

Grail, on the other hand, grabbed my attention like nothing had in a long time. A stripped-down retelling of the legend of King Arthur's knights and their search for the Holy Grail, the storyline had me gripped from the start. The part I'd been suggested for – Sir Bedivere, one of the knights who remained loyal to Arthur as his band of warriors gradually fell apart – was both meaty and sympathetically written.

It didn't bother me that there were a couple of nude scenes in the script. I've never had a problem with taking my clothes off for the camera, and I wouldn't quibble even when the part required me to do a full-frontal shot. It helps that I have one of those cocks which looks impressively big when it's limp, even if it doesn't grow much larger when it gets hard. We all know size doesn't really matter, but there is a warm glow of satisfaction that comes from being on the receiving end of envious glances in the showers.

'I've told the casting department you're pretty handy with a sword,' Keira said, when I rang and told her how much I loved the script.

That, at least, was true. I'd taken fencing lessons at drama school, and excelled at them. Two summers ago, I'd been part of the repertory company at the Globe Theatre, dying on the point of a sword in an adrenaline-fuelled production of *Romeo and Juliet* four times a week. *Grail* would call for me to handle a heavy broadsword, but I was sure I was equal to the challenge.

'And you've got no problems with horses, eh, Jamie?'

'Absolutely none.'

'Great. And from what I can gather, you've got the look they're going for.'

Sometimes, "the look" can be more important than your acting ability. I'm not one of your conventional pretty boy types. My jawline's too prominent for that, and my nose is crooked from where I broke it playing football at school. Fortunately, it seemed the director of *Grail* wasn't in the market for pretty boys.

'I shall keep my fingers crossed for you,' Keira promised before she put the phone down. 'I have a really good feeling about this one.'

The first audition was the following Monday. To help give the impression I was a world-weary knight, I stayed up till the small hours, so when I woke I looked bleary-eyed from lack of sleep, and I didn't bother to shave that morning. Nervous as I was, the audition went well enough that they called me back for a second reading a week later. By now, I knew I was down to the last three for the part of Bedivere, but the competition was strong. I wasn't as hopeful about my chances as Keira was, so when the call came to welcome me on board and let me know location filming would begin in the Czech Republic in two weeks' time, I was speechless. Even more so when the casting director added, 'You know what swung it for you, Jamie? The fact you were the only one of the final three who can ride a horse.'

I didn't know whether to break out the champagne or book riding lessons immediately. In the end, I decided I could bluff it. Everyone says when it comes to riding, it's the horse that does all the hard work anyway. So instead I rang Fin and asked him if he was free for a drink.

Fin was one of the first friends I ever made when I moved down to London and started looking for work. Five foot ten of pure Galway beefcake, with the wickedest laugh you could ever hear, I met him on a building site. He was the foreman, I was doing a spot of hod-carrying to pay the rent while I waited for my first acting break. Not only did we click as friends, but the fact he was openly bisexual meant we also struck up a relationship as fuck buddies, sharing each other's beds on the most casual but enjoyable basis.

We arranged to meet in one of his regular haunts, Tubby McNulty's, an old-fashioned Irish pub in Kilburn. You have to be in the right mood for the rundown old place and its raucous clientèle, but that night I most definitely was. While The Pogues blared from the jukebox, Fin and I sat in a dingy corner, knocking back celebratory pints of stout.

'So tell me more about this film, then,' Fin said, wiping a foam moustache from his full top lip. 'Would I know anyone who's in it? Any Hollywood A-listers slumming it?'

I shook my head. 'The most famous actor in the cast is the

one who used to be the two-timing anaesthetist in *Holby City*. Remember him?'

'Mmm. Big green eyes, nice arse.' Fin's tone was appreciative.

'Well, he's playing Arthur. There's a French guy playing Lancelot. Most of the rest ...' Draining the last of my stout, I reflected that most of the rest of the cast had the kind of face which would have the audience wondering where they'd seen them before. As did I. 'Can I get you another pint, mate?'

Fin shook his head. 'No thanks. Why don't we call it a night here and go back to mine?'

I knew exactly what he had in mind; it was a large part of the reason I'd arranged to meet him here tonight.

He lived over a betting shop on the Kilburn High Road, only a couple of minutes away from where we'd been drinking. Even that short dash through the steadily falling rain stoked my appetite to be in Fin's bed, stripped and ready for him.

We kissed as he fumbled to unlock the front door; hot, sloppy kisses that showed how much we wanted each other. Laughing, Fin pushed me up against the wall, scrabbling to pull my T-shirt out of my jeans.

'Slow down,' I murmured, not really meaning it.

'Can't,' he replied. 'Got to taste your gorgeous body. Got to have your big hard cock in my mouth.' When Fin was really turned on, he spoke like someone out of the filthiest porno you've ever seen. It was all part of his charm, as far as I was concerned, and my cock pushed at the fly of my jeans, aching to be in his grasp.

Somehow, we made it as far as the bedroom, leaving a trail of hastily discarded clothes in our wake. I didn't know whether he was sharing his bed with anyone else at the moment, and even if he was, it wouldn't have stopped me doing what I was about to do. Exclusive wasn't a word in Fin's vocabulary, which probably explained why our relationship had never progressed beyond the occasional fuck.

True to his earlier words, Fin pinned me down on the bed, slurping a wet trail the length of my body with his lips and tongue. When his mouth latched on to the head of my cock, engulfing me in warm wetness, I squirmed against the covers. Fin's blue eyes shone with amusement at the strength of my reaction. 'Ready for me, were you?' he chuckled.

I just groaned, wanting him to take me deeper. Nothing, in my experience, compared to the sensation of having my cock buried deep in a sucking, clutching throat. Coupled with clever fingers caressing and tugging on my balls, it was the quickest way I knew of making me come.

I tried to express some of this to Fin, but my words came out as garbled, helpless moans. Fin had taken charge of my pleasure, and it felt so marvellously rude to lie on his unmade bed in that shabby flat, while he brought me ever closer to a bone-shaking climax. I clung on to the threadbare padded headboard, dampening the fabric with the sweat from my palms. Fin had wormed a saliva-slick finger up into the tight recess of my arsehole, and that was all it took to send fierce, hot spasms of orgasm pulsing through me, my come jetting into his greedy mouth.

'Delicious,' he murmured as he rose, wiping a stray droplet or two from the corner of his mouth.

His obvious delight at my reaction was coupled with the knowledge it was his turn next. I loved the moment when the rôles reversed and Fin, so aggressive the moment before, rolled passively on to his front, presenting his taut, peach-fuzzed arse to me. Fin's lubricant of choice was baby lotion. The powdery scent that always brought him to mind whenever I smelt it mingled with the aromas of sweat and come as I uncapped the bottle and poured lotion liberally into my cupped palm. He sighed as I smoothed the lotion around and into his dark pucker. His arsehole seemed to devour my fingers as I pushed first one, then a second inside him.

'Christ, that's good.' He pushed his rump up at me, wanting more, clearly needing to be filled with something thicker than my fingers.

A strip of condoms lay among the clutter of items on his bedside table. I tore one open, surprised by the speed by which I'd got hard again, and smoothed it down over my shaft.

Fin groaned audibly as my cock skewered him. I could feel

the heat of his channel even through the latex sheathing me. For a moment I revelled in being so tightly clutched by him then I thrust in to the root. Sweat beaded on his back, matting the ends of his black hair to the nape of his neck. Sometimes we'd fuck when he had come straight off the building site, without time to shower the grime and stink of the day off him. That unwashed scent drove me to almost feral wildness, but tonight I was unbelievably roused just from the faint taste of salt as I nuzzled his freshly washed skin. I was high on the excitement of landing the film rôle and the adrenaline rush of good sex, and I plunged into Fin's welcoming arse over and over.

'Fuck me, you big fucking stud,' Fin begged, voice cracking as his excitement peaked. Beneath me, I felt him hold still, driven beyond movement, beyond words by his climax. His anal ring clenched tight around my cock. Much as I wanted to keep going, keep fucking that hot arse of his, the erotic clamping motion defeated me. For the second time that night, I found myself beached on the shores of pleasure, spunk filling the condom in sharp, draining bursts.

Afterwards, trotting naked to the bathroom to dispose of the used condom and trying to remember exactly where in Fin's flat I'd kicked off my underwear, I wondered why neither of us ever broached the subject of spending the whole night together. My encounters with Fin were so hot and sweatily exciting, yet they always ended the same way, with me standing on the High Road, waiting for a cab to take me home. Though even that was a step up from the days when I'd been so broke I had to make my way back to Archway on the night bus. The truth was we didn't have the kind of relationship that led to breakfast the next morning, followed by a long walk in Regent's Park to dust off the cobwebs. What Fin and I had was fun, but it wasn't anything romantic, anything permanent. I couldn't understand why I suddenly felt that might be what I really needed.

Chapter Two

TO TAKE ADVANTAGE OF the generous tax breaks the country offered to film production companies, *Grail* was being shot on location in the Czech Republic. That was the reason why, less than three weeks after my frantic fuck in Fin's messy bed, I was sitting in the back of a minibus as it rattled out into the countryside surrounding the picturesque little town of Ledeč nad Sázavou. The film's director, Marc Brannigan, was outlining what he expected from us that day.

'More than anything,' he was saying in his abrupt Brooklyn tones, 'I just want you to use today as a chance to get used to being on your horse.'

My stomach lurched. I tried to put it down to the way the bus was bouncing over the potholed road, but the truth was I just didn't want to get on the back of that horse.

The past couple of days' filming had gone very well. Though I'd told Fin he wouldn't recognise many of the cast, I knew a few of them from past projects, and we'd spent the first evening re-establishing the kind of friendship that thrives in the intensity of location filming, then fades as you move on to other jobs.

I'd also made a new friend, one unlike anyone else I'd previously met on set. Tom Stratford had been an army dog handler, working in Afghanistan with animals trained to sniff out explosives, until he'd lost his right arm when a roadside device had detonated unexpectedly. The injury finished his military career, but opened the door to a whole new world. Tom had the perfect qualifications for work as a stuntman – he was fit, athletic and ideal for rôles where a prosthetic limb could be fitted in place of his missing arm, then hacked off in gruesomely realistic fashion. It didn't hurt that he was easy on the eye too, with close-cropped dishwater blond hair and a sexy cleft in the point of his chin. When directors realised he could handle lines as well as stunt work, he'd found himself getting small speaking parts in historical epics. *Grail* was his biggest film to date.

Though we couldn't have been from more different backgrounds – Tom was public school educated, what I'd have described as Home Counties posh, whereas I'd grown up on a rough East London council estate and scraped through a handful of GCSEs at my local comprehensive – we struck up an instant rapport. He told me about some of the nerve-wracking experiences he'd undergone while on active service, leaving me in awe of his bravery. But he knew the one thing I was really curious about was how it felt to be minus an arm.

'It did take some getting used to, I'll admit,' he said with more than a measure of understatement. 'The prosthetic limb helps, but I've had to learn how to write left-handed and there are some things it's difficult to do unaided. But probably the hardest part was getting used to wanking with my wrong hand.'

'Seriously?' I was sure he was messing me around, but at the same time my mind filled with vivid images of Tom lying naked on his bed, left hand wrapped round his hard shaft as he brought himself to a sweaty, gasping climax.

He grinned, grey eyes twinkling. 'Yeah, but it's not all bad. It feels like someone else is doing it to me ...'

Cute as Tom was, I didn't rate my chances of an on-set hook-up with him. In the course of our conversations, he'd mentioned his conquests with women both before and after the accident, and I was usually pretty good at sniffing out men who were either over-compensating for their latent gay desires or curious to see what sex with a man was like. Tom didn't set any of those alarms ringing.

Not that I was desperate to meet someone new. If I hadn't walked away from my last encounter with Fin feeling so unfulfilled, I wouldn't even have considered it. But maybe I was reaching the age where I was looking for more than just a friend with benefits.

The minibus pulled to a halt, bringing me back to my surroundings. One by one, we piled out, looking round at the scrubby woodland, bare trees raising their twisted limbs up to the leaden sky. The financial advantages to working over here might be considerable, but spring was still some distance away and the temperatures were close to freezing. I shifted from foot to foot, trying to keep myself warm.

'OK, everyone,' Brannigan said. 'Listen up. We're going to get each of you paired up with a horse, and to do that, I'd like you to meet Andrej Berger. He's going to be your riding instructor, though I'm sure none of you are going to need his help, right?'

I nodded, hoping no one would notice how I was hanging back as the horses were led out of their box. It wasn't solely down to my fear of getting on the back of one of these big, softly snorting beasts. My first glimpse of Andrej had struck me dumb.

If I'd thought Tom was handsome, it was nothing to my reaction as the riding instructor approached. Lust isn't the first emotion you'd expect to hit you as you stand in a chilly wood, waiting for the fact you've lied about being able to ride to be exposed. But Andrej drew that emotion from me as no man had in a long time.

'Gentlemen, I'm charmed to meet you all.' His accent was clipped, with a slight rolling of his Rs, marking him down as a native Czech speaker. It didn't matter what he had to say, or that his syntax was occasionally fractured; I knew I could listen to him talk all day.

He pushed his sleek, shoulder-length black hair back from his face, exposing a broad forehead and high cheekbones. Slate-dark eyes glittered as he eyed us up and down. 'There are only a couple of things I need to tell you before we begin. Man has a relationship with a horse like that with no other beast. Never underestimate the intelligence of these creatures, or their strength. Treat a horse well and he will be your closest, most loyal ally. Treat him badly and–' Andrej let out a short, sardonic laugh. 'Well, all I will say is you will have me to answer to.'

Why did my mind flash to thoughts of Andrej brandishing a riding crop as I grovelled at his feet, promising to do whatever he wished? I wasn't into any of that kinky master and slave punishment stuff – at least, I didn't think I was, but the image of Andrej towering over me, powerful and dominant, wouldn't go away.

'And you are ...?' It took me a few seconds to realise I was being spoken to. I snapped back to the moment to see Andrej regarding me with an amused look.

I felt like a boy who'd been hauled to the front of the class for talking when he should have been studying, guilty and wrong-footed. 'Er – Jamie Desmond. I'm playing Bedivere.'

'Jamie. For you I have Smoke. I think you and he will get along very well.' He led me over to where the horses stood patiently with their wrangler, blankets over their flanks to keep them warm in the February chill. Half the time it seemed animals on set were treated better than the average human performer, but the American Humane Association had to be satisfied their guidelines were being followed to prevent any cruelty. As I looked at the grey stallion that was to be my mount for the duration, I wondered who ensured no humans were harmed in the making of this film.

Andrej's assistant, Iréna, an unsmiling blonde girl in tight-fitting jodhpurs and shiny black riding boots, fitted a saddle to Smoke's back. I patted the horse's neck, breathing in his scent and hoping I could form a bond with him. He was bound to be a good-natured animal; those used in films like *Grail* tended to have a decent temperament, as well as being trained not to react badly to the noise and chaos of a battle scene.

'OK, Jamie, on you get,' Andrej said, not unkindly.

There is no way I can do this, I thought. Then visions of flying back to England in disgrace, having been replaced in the rôle, flashed through my mind. Taking a deep breath, I cautiously heaved myself onto the horse, sure my clumsy manoeuvring as I made myself as comfortable as I could in the saddle and slipped my feet into the stirrups was obvious to anyone who actually knew how to ride.

Remembering something I'd seen in countless cowboy

films, I tapped my booted heels against Smoke's sides. Big mistake. In seconds, the horse was trotting down the rutted road, picking up speed as he went. Yelling and explosions might not cause him to bolt, but I'd managed it.

'Whoa!' I yelled, tugging at Smoke's reins, but nothing I did caused him to slow down even the slightest. Fear prickled through me, raising the hairs on the back of my neck and tightening my scrotum. There was only one way this was going to end, with me lying in a ditch, neck broken as I tumbled from Smoke's back.

The road took a sharp right turn ahead of us. Somehow, and I would never be able to explain in my panicked state how I did it, I managed to exert a measure of control over my horse, steering him so that we turned back on ourselves. Now we were galloping at speed to where Andrej, Brannigan and the other actors were gathered. I clung on to the reins for dear life, sure everyone was finding my predicament much more amusing than I did. As we approached, Smoke finally began to slow down. Andrej thrust out a strong hand, catching hold of his reins. The horse came to an abrupt halt, shaking its head and giving a little whinny. If I hadn't known better, I'd have sworn the damn animal sounded pleased with itself.

'Well.' Andrej addressed the group as I dismounted gingerly, feeling twinges in my thighs. 'I think Jamie has shown us what we should not do. I trust the rest of you have a better sense of how to behave when on your horse.'

'Yeah, take it steady,' I chipped in, starting to recover my equilibrium now I was back on solid ground. With any luck, Brannigan would believe I'd meant to go galloping off like an idiot. Andrej, I was sure, knew differently.

When the other actors began to walk their horses in a slow, steady line, under the watchful instruction of Iréna, Andrej kept me back.

'You don't fool me, Jamie.' His grip on my arm was sure, sending a lightning bolt of desire shooting through me. 'You know nothing about riding, do you?'

'Don't tell anyone, please,' I begged. 'If Brannigan realises I've lied to him, he'll kick me off the film.'

'Don't worry. Your secret is quite safe with me.'

A thought struck me, lifting my mood. 'You could teach me, couldn't you? Show me what to do.'

His expression was unreadable. 'Oh, yes, I will show you. Come to see me tonight, and your instruction will begin.'

That evening, I slipped off to keep my assignation with Andrej. In common with most of the cast, I was supposedly getting an early night, ready for my six o'clock alarm call, but once everyone was tucked up in their rooms, I let myself out of my room and crept down the corridor in my stockinged feet. We were staying in what had once been a boys' school, until it had been converted into hostel-style accommodation, and the place, though comfortable enough, still retained something of an institutional feel with its grey-painted walls and canteen-style dining room. I certainly felt like I was bunking off class, as I made my way down the fire escape at the back of the building, not wanting to run the risk of running into Marc Brannigan in the hotel lobby. He liked to enjoy a nightcap in the hostel's tiny bar before retiring for the night, and it would be just my luck if he caught me out of my room when I should be asleep.

Andrej had given me directions for reaching the stables where Smoke and the other horses were being kept, a brisk ten minutes' walk down the road from the hostel. Outside the main tourist season, the town was quiet, the winter chill keeping most people in their homes. No one who I passed on the way paid me the slightest attention, and I was confident that even if anyone got any bright ideas about trying to jump me and relieve me of my wallet I was more than capable of fighting them off.

The stables were set back a little way from the road, the earthy smell of horses and their droppings growing stronger as I approached the cluster of low wooden huts. Everything appeared shuttered and dark, the only light that of the full moon, and I called Andrej's name, softly at first, then a little louder. The only answer I received was a sharp whinny, one of the horses shuffling in its stall at my presence. Was the man playing some kind of trick on me? Had I come all this way for nothing? For a moment I debated whether I should leave. I did have a stupidly early start in the morning, after all. Then I felt a strong hand clap me on the shoulder.

Turning in alarm, raising my fists in an instinctive self-defence pose, I found myself looking into Andrej's unreadable eyes, darker than ever in the dim light.

'Fucking hell, you scared the life out of me!'

Andrej laughed. 'That was not my intention, I promise you. Now, come with me.' In his free hand he clutched a hurricane lamp. He used it to light the way as he unlatched the stable door and led me inside, into an area that, from its size and freshly swept earth floor, must be used for exercising the horses. Smoke, my mount from earlier, stood tethered to a wooden post.

'Firstly, let me thank you for coming.' Andrej set down the lamp. 'I was not sure you would. Obviously your desire to learn is strong. As is mine to teach you. But what you must understand is that my methods are like no one else's. You must do exactly as I say at all times.'

Again I couldn't shake the feeling there was another meaning to his words, one that had nothing to do with any attempts to improve my horsemanship. The impression was reinforced when Andrej came close to me. He smiled, as though at a joke whose punchline I didn't understand.

'The first thing we must do, Jamie, is get you to a place where you are completely comfortable astride your horse, where you know you can control him with the most subtle of movements and he will follow your bidding. Now, when man first learnt to tame these beautiful beasts, he had no saddle, no spurs, no crop. He rode bareback, and that is what I wish you to do.'

'OK.' I made to walk towards Smoke, still a little apprehensive about getting on his back, especially without the aid of stirrups to give me a leg-up, but reckoning it might be a little easier with him tied to the post.

Andrej stilled me, gripping my shoulder. 'You don't understand. When I say bareback, I mean you as well as the horse. Take your clothes off.'

I almost laughed at the suggestion, even as some deeply

buried part of me thrilled at the idea of having to undress in front of this gorgeous man. 'Are you serious?'

'You think I would joke about a matter like this?' He shook his head. 'You do not know me very well, though I think that will change as these lessons progress. Now, we do not have all night, and you have already wasted enough of my time today. Strip.'

The word sent a jolt of lust straight to my cock, making it twitch. Anxious not to displease Andrej any further, I removed my bulky padded jacket, tossing it to the ground. My sweater and T-shirt followed, pulled off over my head in the same motion. Goosepimples prickled on my skin as the cold air hit it, but I continued to undress, aware of my instructor watching me with impatience.

Unsure whether he wanted me to take off my boots, I turned to my jeans next, unbuckling the belt and making short work of the fly buttons. Pulling them down, I did an awkward little hop from foot to foot as I manoeuvred them off over my heavy boots. If Andrej thought I looked foolish, he kept his opinion to himself for once.

Standing in front of him, hoping he'd be satisfied by the speed with which I'd followed his instructions, I began to regret my choice of underwear. My tight white briefs did nothing to conceal the outline of my cock, visibly swollen beneath the thin cotton, or the damp spot of precome already forming at its tip.

'You call that stripping?' Andrej's tone was scathing. 'The rest as well, and be quick about it.'

This was crazy. The stable was freezing cold, and now he wanted to me to stand on the grubby floor in my bare feet, to say nothing of the humiliation of being bare-arsed naked while he was fully dressed. Yet if this was humiliation, why did my cock surge up even harder as I peeled off my briefs?

I dropped my underwear on top of the pile of clothes then stared at Andrej with a defiant look on my face. I wasn't going to be browbeaten by him, and I wanted to show him I had nothing to be ashamed of – at least, not in the cock department.

He returned my gaze with a smile. 'Very nice.' I wasn't sure if he was referring to my body or my willingness to obey him.

'At last you are ready to begin.'

Andrej dragged a heavy wooden block over to Smoke's left side. 'This is a mounting block. It makes it easier for you to get on a horse when you have no stirrups to aid you. Now, climb on to your horse, nice and slowly.'

He was right. Stepping on to the block did make all the difference. I threw my right leg over Smoke's broad back with relative ease, feeling the heat of his body against my bare thigh. His reins hung loose and I picked them up, gripping them with more confidence than when I'd mounted him this morning.

'Very good, Jamie.' Andrej was praising me for the simplest thing, yet I felt a thrill of pride that caused me to sit a little straighter. 'Now we need to correct your position. First, you need to find your balance. I want you to sit so your seat bones are comfortably in the middle of Smoke's back, with your legs hanging loose on each side. Make sure you do not slouch. Everything needs to be in the correct alignment. OK, you have done that?'

'Yes, sir.' I had no idea where the honorific came from, but it felt right to use it, rather than his Christian name. I didn't realise it, but the balance of our relationship had been shifting since the moment Andrej led me into the stable and, as every moment passed, I was relinquishing more control to him – and doing so willingly.

'So now we lead you round, letting you get used to the feeling of being on your horse. I will walk you forward, turn, halt Smoke then walk you back to the block. You are ready for this?'

'Yes, sir.' Andrej unhitched Smoke's leading rein from the post and urged him forward. Relaxing into the ride, keeping my shoulders back and breathing deeply as Andrej had advised, I felt myself moving with the horse, rather than fighting against him as I'd done earlier in the day. We walked to the far side of the exercise area then Andrej brought Smoke to a halt before leading me back to the mounting block.

'You are OK with that, I can tell.' Now his voice caressed my ear, rather than barking instructions into it. 'But I need to know that you are comfortable to do this on your own.' He dropped the leading rein. 'So, now you do just as I have done. You make Smoke go forward, turn him and bring him back. Use the reins to steer him.'

'I – I don't think I can.'

'You can. You will. I will be beside you. If there are any problems, I will take over control of Smoke. And I will not let you fall.'

My heart thundered in my chest. My palms were clammy. I couldn't remember the last time I'd been so nervous. Walking into any audition room in the world would be a breeze compared to this, I thought, as I gently urged Smoke forward using a combination of my bare heels and the reins. For a moment, I feared a repeat of this morning's catastrophe, with Smoke bolting into the darkness. Instead, he shook his shaggy mane then slowly walked in the direction I wanted him to go. Andrej kept a steady pace beside us, saying nothing. When I managed to turn the horse and take him back to the mounting block, I almost wanted to whoop with excitement.

'Now you do it again,' Andrej informed me. 'On your own, without me beside you. Walk Smoke a whole circuit. You can manage that.' It wasn't a question.

'Yes, sir.' I was so buoyed up by what I'd done so far, I felt I could handle almost anything Andrej asked of me.

He leant against the post, arms folded, watching as I rode Smoke with rapidly growing assurance. 'You do so well,' I heard him say. 'Next time we master the trot, then the gallop.'

My mind drifted to a terrible arty French film I'd seen years ago, on a date with some guy with whom I'd had very little in common but who I desperately wanted to fuck. He liked arthouse and sushi; I preferred action blockbusters and pizza. I made the error of compromising my tastes to impress him. I couldn't recall the name of the film – hell, I couldn't even remember the name of my date that night – only that it had stolen two hours of my life I'd never get back, but one scene suddenly came back to me with absolute clarity. For reasons that had nothing to do with the plot and everything to do with increasing the film's nudity quotient, one of the cast, brawny and very well-endowed as I now remembered, had gone riding naked on a horse in the early morning mist. A voiceover had described the sense of freedom and exhilaration he'd felt – though I'd picked this up only by following the subtitles, knowing hardly any French apart from the words for "please", "thank you" and "I would like a beer". I couldn't help feeling if I ever found myself galloping naked on Smoke's back I, too, would experience that same exhilaration.

'Good,' Andrej said, as I finally brought Smoke to a halt in front of him. 'That is enough for tonight, I think. You may dismount.'

I did so, feeling the muscles in my thighs and arse twinge as I climbed down onto the mounting block.

Andrej chuckled. 'For someone who looks like he works out, I think you are using muscles that don't get stretched in the gym too often, hey? I must warn you, Jamie, you will be sore in the morning, unless you take a bath when you get back to your room.'

He tethered Smoke, throwing a blanket over his back to keep him warm till he was led back to his stall. While he was occupied with ensuring his horse's comfort, I reached for my underwear, ready to start dressing now my lesson was over.

When Andrej turned and saw what I was doing, he snapped, 'Hey, who told you to do that? We're not finished yet, boy.'

My erection, which had wilted while I'd been concentrating on riding Smoke, returned with a vengeance the moment Andrej called me "boy". 'I'm sorry, sir,' I stammered, briefs falling from suddenly nervous fingers.

He strode over to me. 'I told you that you have much to learn. Not all of it is to do with riding a horse. Much of it concerns how to show due respect to the man who instructs you. I look at you and I see a boy who thinks he has it all. The acting ability, the body, the cock ...' As he spoke, his cool fingers closed round my shaft. I stifled a groan, excitement pulsing through me at his touch. 'But I sense there is something missing in your life. An area where you would also benefit from some instruction. Tell me, boy, have you ever been made to submit to another man?'

'No, sir.'

'Then you truly have much to learn.' His grip on my cock tightened slightly, and he began to stroke up and down my length with slow, subtle movements that had my spunk roiling in my balls.

My brain, fuddled by the way he wanked me so deliciously, struggled to process the word "master". Andrej wanted to take me into a kind of relationship that was utterly alien to me, and though I'd always told myself I wasn't into domination and submission, with a shock I realised I was more than willing to follow him there. 'Yes, sir.'

'By the time I have finished with you,' he continued, his hand never pausing in its back and forth motion, 'you will be sore, and not just from the strain of wrapping your thighs around a horse in full gallop. You will bear the marks of my whip. You know you have an arse that was designed to be punished, don't you, boy?'

All I could do was whimper. I was so close to the brink that only a couple more pumps of Andrej's fist would have me spilling my load.

'And you will obey my rules. When you arrive here for your lessons, you will strip in the yard and leave your clothes outside. You will not be allowed to put them back on until you leave. Do you understand?'

'Y–yes, sir.'

'If I want you to masturbate yourself for me, you will do it. If I want you to get down on your knees and kiss my boots, you will do it. You will not question me, and if I feel the need to deal with any aspect of your behaviour, you will take whatever punishment I deem fit and thank me for it afterwards. Do you understand?'

I tried to shape my reply, but the words didn't come. Instead, with a despairing groan, I felt my come jetting out of my dick. What didn't spatter Andrej's fist landed on the ground at my feet. Andrej let go of my cock, presenting his spunk-covered fingers to my lips.

'Lick them clean, dirty boy,' he ordered me as I sagged against him.

Obediently, I did as he said, my come bitter against my

tastebuds. When I'd lapped up every drop, he let go of me. I staggered and hauled myself upright.

'And now we say goodnight.' He gestured to my clothes. 'Put them on and go.'

'Yes, sir.' Now I'd come, all I wanted to do was curl up on the stable straw and go to sleep. Picking up my underwear, aware of Andrej's eyes on my wilting cock I dressed as quickly as I could.

I was at the stable door when Andrej called to me. 'I see you here again in two nights. Don't be late.'

'No, sir.'

My last view of him, before I closed the door behind me and made my weary way back to the hostel, was of his face buried in Smoke's mane as he murmured words of reassurance to the horse. Andrej was an enigma, unlike any other man I'd met. So cruel and forceful one moment, so tender the next. At times his treatment of me verged on contempt, yet beneath it I knew there was a kind heart. I'd never expected to find myself acquiring a dominant master, but now the idea had been planted in my mind, I couldn't think of anyone else I wanted to fill that rôle. And my education had only just begun, in so many ways. I could only imagine what my next lesson from Andrej might involve.

Chapter Three

WHEN I RETURNED TO the stables two nights later, I felt sure I could cope with whatever Andrej had in store for me. I'd managed to sneak back into my room undetected after my visit to the stables, even though it was a real effort to climb the fire escape after everything I'd put my thighs through over the previous hour or so. As Andrej had instructed, I took a bath before crawling into bed, the hot water leaching some of the stiffness from my limbs. My senses still thrilled to the memory of his strong hand gripping and manipulating my cock, coaxing such a powerful orgasm from me. I replayed the scene in my mind as I drifted off, dreaming of all the dark, deviant things he might require me to do before my education at his hands was over.

His instructions were burnt into my brain. Pausing on the threshold of the main stable block, I quickly stripped out of my clothes. Again, there were no lights on in the building. I had no idea whether Iréna had living quarters at the stables; if she did, there was no sign of her. It was just as well. I had no idea how I would explain to her why I was standing in the stable yard, naked and sporting the beginnings of an erection.

Leaving my clothes in a neat pile by the wall, I pushed the stable door open. 'Andrej?' I called, stepping inside. 'Sir?'

'So, you came, boy.' Andrej stepped out of the shadows, a halo of light from the lamp he carried throwing his chiselled features into stark relief. 'But I never doubted you would. When you find the man who is destined to be your master, it is hard to keep away from him.'

There were so many questions I wanted to ask. How had Andrej come by what seemed to be an innate sense of dominance, and what had he seen in me to suggest I would respond to it so readily? Why did it feel as though he knew things about me I didn't even know about myself?

I had more sense than to ask any of them. Instead, I said, 'I'm ready for my lesson, sir.'

'Good. Today you learn to ride at the trot. More difficult than walking your horse, but you have the best teacher.' Andrej smiled as he led me over to where Smoke was tethered, the mounting block already in position by his side.

With growing confidence, I climbed on to his back, patting his neck affectionately. Already he was starting to feel like my horse, trained to respond to my commands.

Andrej untied him, fastening a long rein to Smoke's bridle. 'For this, we go outside and I will lead you on the lunge rein.' He must have sensed my apprehension at being on horseback in the open air naked, middle of the night or not. 'Don't worry, boy. No one will see you.'

I clung on to the reins as Andrej walked Smoke out into the field behind the stables. My eyes slowly grew accustomed to the gloom, the darkness broken by the light from Andrej's hurricane lamp.

'OK,' Andrej began. 'For a novice rider – especially one who has not earned the privilege of wearing clothes – it can be very uncomfortable to ride a trotting horse. So I teach you how to post the trot. This means to move with the bumping motion, not against it.'

He encouraged me to raise my backside up slightly from Smoke's back, using the muscles of my upper leg to tense against the horse.

'Is actually easier for you to do this bareback,' Andrej informed me. 'There is no temptation for you to put all your weight in the stirrups.' Urging Smoke to walk forward, he continued. 'When you are ready, give him a little tap with your heels and make him trot.'

That's what I'd done the first time I'd tried to ride him, and I remembered how badly that had gone. This time, I had Andrej to prevent Smoke from bolting. Taking a deep breath, I used my heels to encourage the stallion to increase his pace, feeling myself bumping painfully against his back as he trotted along, my cock in danger of being trapped beneath me as it bobbed and bounced.

'Follow his rhythm,' Andrej told me. 'Count for me. One-two, one-two.'

I did as he asked, counting in time to the rhythm of Smoke's gait. There was something almost hypnotic about the motion.

'Now rise on one and down on two. Move with him, not against him. And relax, boy ...'

It took me a little while to grasp the necessary technique. My first instinct was to grip Smoke's sides tight with my knees, still afraid I would be sent tumbling at any moment, but under Andrej's patient tuition, I relaxed and my ride became smoother. I wasn't sure I would be able to post the trot if Andrej wasn't there to keep the horse steady. But in terms of what would be required from me on set over the next few days, where Smoke would be equipped with a saddle and stirrups and we would only be moving in short bursts, the lesson I'd had tonight would help me appear a more accomplished rider than I was.

I had no idea how much time had passed when Andrej told me to bring Smoke to a halt, only that my thighs were cramping and I craved a glass of water. 'That is enough for tonight,' he said. 'You've done well, boy. You work hard and you listen to me. You must want what I have to offer very much ...'

Why was there always a double meaning to his words? 'Yes, sir.'

Andrej led Smoke back into the stable, allowing me to dismount. He tethered Smoke, praising him and feeding him a generous handful of horse pellets he took from the pocket of his tight-fitting cream breeches. I stood watching, hands behind my back, awaiting my next instruction. Somehow, I didn't think Andrej would simply allow me to dress and go back to the hostel.

'Very good,' he said, giving Smoke one last loving pat before returning to me. 'You are beginning to show me the proper respect. What do you have to say to me, boy?'

Thanking him was the correct response, but those weren't

the first words that came to my parched lips. 'Please, sir, may I have some water?'

He didn't acknowledge my mistake. Instead, his lips quirked in a cruel smile. 'You want water? Come with me.' Grasping me firmly by the elbow, he marched me out into the yard to where a horse trough stood. 'Drink,' he ordered, pushing me down to my knees and gripping a hank of my hair, lowering my head towards the trough.

I didn't even think to argue, even though this was probably the most demeaning thing I'd ever had to do. I simply put my lips to the surface of the water and drank it down in long, noisy gulps. When Andrej raised my face again, I did what I should have done moments ago. 'Thank you, sir,' I murmured.

'Get up,' he ordered me. 'And tell me, did you enjoy being forced to do that?'

'No, sir,' I replied honestly.

'Then tell me, why is your cock hard?'

I didn't need to glance down to know it was true. Though I didn't fully understand why, this was my body's natural reaction whenever Andrej made me submit to him.

'I – I don't know, sir.'

'I should dunk you in the trough till that thing goes down, but we both know that would only make it harder. So I take you inside and show you what happens when you get an erection without my permission.'

That hadn't been in the rules he'd given me. How could I not fail to get aroused around Andrej? The way he looked, the way he smelt – a musky mixture of sweat and horse, along with a trace of spicy cologne – was too much for me to resist.

Andrej led me into the small, wooden-walled tack room, pleasantly warm after the chill of the stable yard. Reins and bridles hung from racks on three of the four walls, along with a selection of whips and crops which made me shudder just to look at them. They were common enough pieces of equipment in riding stables, but I couldn't help thinking back to Andrej's comment about punishing me whenever he felt I deserved it. In the middle of the room stood a polished wooden trestle with a saddle slung over it. I was ordered to stand by it, hands on my head.

Andrej made a slow circuit, looking at my naked body from every angle. Under his scrutiny, my cock surged up harder than ever, despite my attempts to think about anything that might make my erection subside.

'Has anyone ever beaten you, boy?'

'No, sir.' I'd grown up in a house where my parents enforced discipline by grounding me or taking away privileges, and corporal punishment was a distant memory by the time I reached comprehensive school. The idea of being spanked or strapped was completely alien to me. I had no idea how different my experience was from Andrej's, but one thing was certain: before tonight ended, I would know what it felt like to have my arse thrashed.

'Then I will go easy on you. But only this time.' He pulled the saddle off the trestle. 'Bend over this.'

Despite my dread of what might be about to happen, I did as I was told, draping myself over the thing. It wasn't as broad as Smoke's back, but it still supported my body comfortably. Andrej was bustling around in the corner, looking for something. As he returned to me, I saw he was carrying a number of lengths of rope. Almost before I knew what he was doing, he'd taken hold of my wrist, tying it to one of the legs of the trestle. Working with a speed that suggested he'd done this before, he secured my remaining limbs in turn, leaving me splayed out and ready for my punishment. Wriggling in my bonds, I discovered there was a little give, but not enough to give me any chance of freeing myself without Andrej's help.

'Remember what I told you before,' Andrej said. 'At the end, you thank me. And as I beat you, you will think on what you have done and try to make sure you do not make the same mistake in future.'

He took one of the riding crops down from its rack, coming to stand in my eye line so I could get a good look at it. The implement had been designed for use on the sturdy flanks of a horse and I shivered, wondering how much it would hurt when Andrej whipped my more sensitive skin with it.

But the crop wasn't the only thing to attract my gaze. As

Andrej held the whip in front of his crotch, I could see his bulge, cradled in the soft breeches. Having me bound and helpless, waiting for my punishment, turned him on, and my own cock stiffened in response.

'Relax, boy. Breathe deeply and go with the rhythm,' he crooned, repeating the instructions he'd given me when I was learning how to trot, but this time in a more intimate tone. Moving behind me, he ran his hand over my bare backside. 'Oh, Jamie, if only you could see the way you look at this moment. Such a beautiful virgin arse, waiting for the kiss of my crop.'

His caress dipped lower, brushing the crack between my cheeks and the pouch of my balls. I moaned.

'Oh, don't worry, boy, I have no intention of beating you there. I only want to discipline you, not cause you damage. But you need to know that this is all mine – this cock, these balls ...'

'Yes, sir.' The thought of being owned by Andrej, body and soul, even on a temporary basis, made my cock throb against the smooth wood. I was frustrated and in need of release, but that would only happen when – or if – my master decided I had earned it.

Abruptly, the hand was withdrawn from my private places. 'This will hurt, boy,' Andrej warned me, 'but you will learn to welcome the pain. It will remind you of how you have displeased me, and remind you never to do it again.'

Somehow, I reckoned, I would always find some way of displeasing Andrej, whether I was aware I'd done it or not. Otherwise, he'd have no excuse to discipline me.

The crop was almost soundless as it sliced through the air. I certainly felt the impact of the blow, pain exploding like a firework in my left cheek.

My yell was anguished, and I tugged at the ropes holding me in position.

'Steady, boy,' Andrej murmured, just as he soothed his fractious horses. 'Ride out the pain.'

Easier said than done, I wanted to tell him as the crop fell again, cracking against my right cheek this time. 'Oh, sweet Jesus!' My arse was on fire, and I'd only taken two strokes.

How much more did Andrej have in store for me?

Thankfully, he decided six was quite enough, but he spaced the remaining four cuts evenly, two on the lower curve of my cheeks and two on the backs of my thighs. Those last two had me jigging and dancing, fighting to ride out the fierce burning sensation, and as I did, I started to feel it changing. Endorphins raced through my body. I'd expected my cock to wilt in reaction to my cropping, but it was still hard and straining.

My master came to stand in front of me once more, presenting the crop to my lips. Without being asked, I kissed it, silently expressing gratitude for my punishment.

'Good, but you only thanked the instrument that whipped you. You must also thank me.'

Andrej laid the crop aside. He made short work of unbuttoning the fly of his breeches. Now it was his cock awaiting the feel of my lips. I studied it for a moment. Unlike me he was circumcised. Big as he was, I still beat him in the length department, but the smooth shaft and domed head almost cried out to be worshipped with my mouth.

When my lips closed round him, he muttered something in his native tongue. The implication was clear enough, as was the way his eyelids fluttered closed in bliss. I couldn't use my hands to pleasure him, and my restricted position meant Andrej had to push more of his length into my mouth, rather than me shifting to take him in, but I quickly established a rhythm, sucking him with vigour. His salty precome leaked out, and I relished the taste as I lapped it up.

'Oh, so good,' he muttered, running his hands through his hair, wrapped up in his own pleasure. 'You are the best, my only boy ...' Again his speech reverted to Czech, his sentences more strung out as I played my tongue over the sensitive place just below his head, and the scar where his foreskin had been removed. That pushed him over the edge. He thrust himself as deep into my mouth as he could, letting out a string of what I'd realised, from the way they peppered the conversations between the Czech members of the film crew, were swear words. Come shot down my throat, gone before I could taste it, then he pulled out, leaving me gasping like a landed fish.

Without ceremony, he zipped himself up before unfastening the ropes tethering me to the trestle. My cock still stood at full mast, aching for attention. Andrej looked at it and smiled.

'You really need to come, don't you, boy?'

'Yes, sir.' I hoped he'd do what he did last time, wanking me in that swift, sensual fashion of his.

'Well, bring yourself off. Show me how you do it when you're on your own.'

If I was on my own, I wanted to tell him, I'd have soft sheets to lie against, a plentiful supply of baby oil for lubrication and one of my well-thumbed gay porn mags to hand. The lack of home comforts didn't matter, I realised as soon as my fingers closed round my length. Everything I'd done to please Andrej tonight, from stripping naked in the stable yard to swallowing his seed, had been acting as a slow, sure aphrodisiac. The pain of my cropping had turned to pleasure somewhere in the process, and any lingering shame I felt at tugging my cock under Andrej's amused gaze simply added to the mix. I was hornier than I'd ever been, and as my hand made its steady ascent of my shaft, adding a twisting motion at the top, I knew I'd be coming within moments.

Strokes speeding up, I cupped and rolled my tight balls with my other hand. I thought I heard Andrej say, 'Oh, yes, so fucking hot,' but it seemed as though his voice was coming from miles away. The blood sang in my ears, heart pounding as I succumbed to the inevitable. Gouts of spunk shot from the end of my cock, puddling on the floor of the tack room.

When the orgasmic shudders passed, it was as though a spell had been broken. My watch was in the back pocket of my jeans, but I didn't need to look at it to know how late it was. I had another early call in the morning, yet I'd let Andrej keep me here till the small hours without complaint.

'Should I go, sir?'

He nodded. 'But well done, boy. I am proud of you – for everything tonight.'

I turned to leave. He caught me by the arm.

'Wait.' Our faces were inches apart, his eyes so dark with desire they were almost black. His mouth came down on mine in a bruising kiss that I returned with a passion I'd barely known I possessed. That kiss was the sweeter for all the calculated cruelty which had come before.

When we broke apart, we were panting, giddy with desire.

'Now go,' Andrej said, 'before I am tempted to ask you to stay with me.'

Scrambling into my clothes out in the yard, I found myself wondering which of the darkened rooms in the main buildings was Andrej's. It would be so much nicer if I could simply crawl into bed with him, safe and loved in his arms. I shook my head. Enticing as that image was, it wasn't wise to start thinking about him in those terms. Not when this could never be anything more than an on-set hook-up, to be filed away as a beautiful memory once I was back in England.

I set off down the deserted road back to the hostel without a backward glance.

Chapter Four

'JAMIE, JAMIE!'

I was trying to sleep, but someone insisted on pounding their fists against the door of my room.

'Come on, Jamie, get your lazy arse in gear!'

I buried my head under the pillow, hoping they'd give up, but they were persistent. 'OK, OK, I'm up!' I yelled back.

'Well, get a move on. The minibus is leaving in a couple of minutes.'

The clothes I'd worn last night were scattered on the floor. It felt like only moments since I'd peeled them off and crawled into bed. I tugged on my jeans, a thick sweatshirt and boots. I didn't bother with underwear, partly because I didn't think I could bear the feel of tight cotton against my still-tender skin and partly because I knew I wouldn't be needing it today. Ravenous after my exertions in the stables, I could do with some breakfast, but there wasn't time for that. At least Viv and Lyn in the catering wagon could be relied on to provide me with a strong, sweet cup of coffee and a hot bacon roll once we were on set.

Taking the stairs two at a time on the way in my hurry to reach the lobby, I was greeted by a sarcastic round of applause.

'Mr Desmond, how kind of you to grace us with our presence,' Marc Brannigan said. 'Now, stop holding us up and get in the bus.'

Today more than any day previously, I felt every bump in the road, wincing as I landed on my sore arse time and again.

'You all right, mate?' Jack Forrester, my co-star in this morning's scene, asked, spotting the discomfort etched on my face.

'Yeah. Just didn't get the greatest night's sleep, that's all.'

'I know what you mean.' Jack grinned. 'I don't think I've ever slept on a thinner mattress.'

I'd have been happy to pass the rest of the journey in silence, but Jack seemed eager to talk. There was a nervous edge to his chatter, but that was understandable. He was about to take part in his first ever nude scene, after all.

We were filming a pivotal scene in the film. In it, Jack, who played King Arthur, and I had been riding for days. Tired and battle-weary, we came across a mountain pool and took the welcome opportunity to bathe. In this remote location, Arthur poured his heart out to me about his fears for his realm. His knights had become obsessed with their search for the Holy Grail, and in his absence, his incestuous son, Mordred, was plotting to usurp the throne. But he still remained confident in the love and loyalty of his queen, Guinevere, his most trusted knight, Lancelot du Lac, and the wider support of the Grail Fellowship. This impassioned speech was going to be intercut with footage of Lancelot fucking Guinevere in her marriage bed, making Arthur a cuckold in his absence, and Lucan, Tom Stratford's character and previously one of Arthur's closest allies among the knights, plotting in secret with Mordred to bring about the ultimate ruin of Camelot.

Jack was clearly anxious about having to strip for the camera, even though we would be spending most of the scene in the pool. I didn't get the chance to allay his fears, because all too soon the bus was pulling up at the day's filming location.

My chance to grab some breakfast was thwarted as I was hustled off to make-up. Fortunately, Kyle, the production's runner, was on hand to fetch me something from the catering wagon.

'Here you go,' he said, handing me a paper bag containing a bacon roll, thickly smeared with ketchup. 'Viv did the bacon extra crispy, the way you like it. She said she's thinking of popping along to watch when you get your knob out. She's heard it's worth it ...'

I couldn't prevent a blush rising to my cheeks. Gail, the make-up girl, was grinning from ear to ear as she carefully applied a gruesome fake scar to my hip bone, the remnant of a wound Bedivere had sustained in an earlier battle. I wore nothing but a towelling robe, and she'd managed to get a good peek at my crown jewels as she adjusted it to apply the scar.

Mind you, I mused, as Kyle disappeared from the make-up trailer, if Andrej was here, he'd make me sit naked for the whole process, my cock on display to anyone who cared to come in and look. It gave an involuntary twitch at the thought. I hoped Gail wouldn't notice and start speculating about the cause. I didn't make a big thing out of my sexuality, but I certainly wasn't in the closet, which surprised quite a few people on first meeting me. Perhaps it had something to do with the rôles I played, perhaps because I didn't come across as in any way effeminate, but the general assumption among people who didn't know me was that I was straight. Not that any of it mattered; up on screen I could be anyone the viewing public wanted me to be.

Marc Brannigan popped his head in the door, bringing me back to awareness of where I was. 'How's it going, guys?'

'Just about done,' Gail replied. 'I'll be sending Jamie off to costume very shortly.'

'Great.' The director turned his attention to me. 'Now, Jamie, just to let you know there's been a slight change to the way I need you to play this scene. It's freezing out there today, and if you and Jack stand in that water for more than a couple minutes, you'll more than likely end up suffering from hypothermia. And none of us wants that, right? So instead I just want you to crouch by the side of the pool and splash water over yourselves, OK? Play it right, you'll come across as even more pissed off with life.'

'Sure.' I nodded, as Marc disappeared back to where the cameras and lights were being set up, ready for filming.

Gail eased me up from the make-up chair. I took a moment to admire the scar in the mirror. Whoever had constructed it had done a beautiful job. With its puckered edging and angry red tones, it really did look as though at some stage I'd been sliced open by a vicious blade.

Then it was on to costume, where I was helped into my

lightweight armour and the thin shirt and hose I wore beneath it, all of which would be coming off again soon enough.

Out by the pool, Jack was already waiting, deep in conversation with Marc about the scene. Catching the end of what they were saying, I managed to establish that Jack had a clause in his contract meaning, unlike me, he only had to show a back view to the camera. One of the perks of having the higher profile that came from appearing in a long-running TV series, I supposed. Still, I knew Fin would be more than pleased Jack was finally going to be revealing the arse he'd admired so much. With a start, I realised this was the first time I'd thought about Fin since filming had begun. When I'd first flown out here, I'd been looking forward to sharing all my gossip with him on my return to England. Now, though I could easily see Fin and I downing pints in Tubby McNulty's, enjoying the *craic* just as we'd always done, I could no longer picture the evening ending in bed. Being with Andrej had changed everything.

'Jamie! Looking good,' Marc said. 'Let's get on with this. The light's just about perfect.'

Directors talk about "the golden hour", the time when the light takes on a special quality as the sun rises or sets. The reason for our pre-dawn start today was to make the most of this magical light.

We rehearsed the walk down to the pool so markers could be placed, giving us our starting positions should we have to re-take the scene. I was sure Jack hoped, as I did, we wouldn't have to do this more than once unless there was a major mistake. As Marc had pointed out, it was cold in these woods, and neither of us wanted to spend more time undressing and walking round naked than we had to.

At least we didn't have to worry about the horses for once, a hasty rewrite to the script having established that they were down in a camp Arthur had established on the other side of the hill. After everything that had happened over the last few nights, I was much more confident around Smoke, but Marc was worried the animals might get restless and cause an unnecessary interruption to filming.

'I'm still not sure I can do this,' Jack whispered to me. I

knew he was referring to the act of baring all.

'You'll be fine, mate,' I assured him. 'The secret is to just blank everyone out. And it's not like you're having to simulate sex. That's much more awkward, believe me.'

Once Marc was satisfied with our positions, he called action, and Jack and I strolled down to the pool together. I didn't have many lines in the scene, but my reactions to what my king had to say were important. While, unbeknown to him, all around him was crumbling, the treachery of those he believed he could trust leading to his final, fatal encounter with Mordred, I remained his rock, his sounding board.

'I grow tired of all this, Bedivere,' he sighed. 'Sometimes I wish it was someone other than I who had been chosen to rule. Someone else who bore this burden.'

'You cannot think like that, my liege. Come, this cool water will clear your head ...' Following Marc's instructions, I dropped my helmet to the ground and began to remove the rest of my armour. Jack glanced round, as though worried his enemies might come upon us when we were relaxed and vulnerable, then shrugged and followed my lead.

There was something strangely liberating about stripping off in these ancient woods, even with a film crew in close attendance. Jack had carefully angled his body so the camera would only focus on his back. My gaze moved down from the sculpted planes of his shoulder blades to his arse, firm and muscular. He was very nicely put together, and I found myself trying to get a sneaky glimpse of his cock, wondering if it was as impressive as the rest of him. However, he'd already crouched down at the water's edge, leaving me the focus of the camera's attention.

I peeled down my hose, baring myself from the waist down. It was hard to pretend there wasn't a lens capturing every detail of my nakedness, lingering just long enough on my limp cock for the audience to ascertain what a big boy I was before moving away.

I thought I heard a couple of gasps as I stepped out of my hose, and wondered whether Viv had, as she'd suggested to Kyle the runner, stepped away from the catering wagon for a few minutes to watch me strip. For all I knew, it could equally have been a reaction to the sight of the scar bisecting my hip. The noise didn't break my concentration. Fully immersed in my rôle, I joined Jack at the water's edge, scooping handfuls of icy water from the pool and pouring them over my face and chest.

We played the scene out without mishap, Jack displaying a passion and range of emotion he'd never really tapped into during his *Holby City* days. When someone you're acting with hits that kind of pitch, it goads you into responding, raising your own performance, and I almost wanted to whoop with delight when Marc called, 'Cut!', knowing we'd nailed it first time.

Marc wanted to take parts of it again from a different angle, capturing the emotions on my face as Arthur unburdened himself of his hopes and fears, but I was in the zone now. It no longer mattered that I was naked in a freezing wood in the Czech Republic, cameras trained on my naked body and, I was sure, recording the occasional flash of my cock as I moved. In my head, for these few moments, I really was Sir Bedivere, knight of the Round Table, prepared to follow my king to the ends of the Earth and beyond.

Those shots completed, Jack and I were handed our robes and told to go and warm up.

'I don't know about you, mate,' I said as we headed to the catering wagon, ready to brave any saucy comments from the girls as they poured us coffee, 'but I thought that went really well. And women are just going to cream themselves over you when they see your body.'

Jack looked sheepish. 'I just did what you said. Made myself believe we were the only two people there. It wasn't easy, but ... Can I ask you something?'

'Sure,' I replied, expecting Jack to quiz me further on the etiquette of nude scenes.

'Those bruises and stuff on your arse and thighs. What have you been doing to yourself?'

So that explained the gasps when I took off my hose. I should have known the beating I'd received from Andrej would leave marks, but in my sleep-deprived state I'd completely forgotten to check. Thinking fast, I came up with an excuse bearing elements of the truth. 'Oh, I hadn't been on a horse for a while, and I knew I was really rusty, so I've been getting a couple of riding lessons in with Andrej. And – well, I've fallen off and landed on my backside a few times. You're not going to tell Marc, are you?'

'No way. What you do off-set is no business of mine.'

We joined the small queue at the wagon, my mouth watering at the cooking smells wafting from it. 'If the bruises look so obvious, I'm surprised no one said anything.'

'They probably thought the same as I did,' Jack replied. 'It just made you look even more like someone had given you a good pasting.'

If only you knew how close that was to the truth, mate, I thought. *If only you knew.*

Much as I wanted to see Andrej again, to suffer under his lash and submit to his desires, the filming schedule contrived to keep us apart. Brannigan had managed to secure the services of one of the best fight arrangers in the business, Max Wade, to choreograph the battle sequences. However, he would only be with us for four days before flying back to Hollywood, where he was committed to working on a big-budget vampire action movie. This meant long days rehearsing and filming the fight scenes, at the end of which all I could do was crawl into bed and fall asleep as soon as my head hit the pillow.

Not that it wasn't enjoyable work. As soon as I had my sword in my hand, and was running through my moves with Max, I felt the adrenaline pumping. Using the cross-trainer, which I did three times a week when I wasn't working, helped keep me in shape but was boring. Sword fighting offered an equally intense workout, but I couldn't see my gym adding it to their list of exercise classes any time soon.

The scenes were being filmed using hand-held cameras, as Marc wanted the action to have the shaky, disorientating feel of actually being in a pitched battle, but it was as easy to blank their presence out as it had been when I was crouching naked by the mountain pool with Jack Forrester.

Although my riding skills had improved tenfold since I'd

started paying my midnight visits to the stables, only the most experienced horsemen would be on their mounts in these fights, which was great news as far as I was concerned. The thinking was that this would cut down on the risk of accidental falls. With such a tight schedule, the production couldn't afford to have actors or stuntmen out of commission due to injury.

After three days of filming, all the other fight sequences were in the can and all that was left was the final battle between what remained of Arthur's Round Table of knights and the ragtag band of traitors and mercenaries led by Mordred. This was the most complex of all the scenes Max had choreographed. The script called for Arthur and Mordred to pit themselves against each other in a fight to the death, the rest of the action almost incidental to this duel. As recorded in the legends on which the script was based, Arthur ran Mordred through with a spear, but in the process his son struck him a mortal blow with his sword. Loyal to the last, I carried Arthur from the battlefield, but my efforts to save him were in vain and he died a slow, squalid death, raving and plagued by visions of all those who had betrayed him. At last, his body would be ferried away to Avalon, while my duty was to take Excalibur, his now blunt and bloodied sword, and throw it into the water, to be claimed by the Lady of the Lake. Reading the script when Keira sent it to me, I'd had tears in my eyes, and I really hoped my acting in that final scene would do justice to the writer's vision.

Of more immediate concern was my part in the fight. I was pitched against the traitorous Lucan, and Tom Stratford and I were given thorough instruction from Max on what he wanted us to do. Tom, who gave every impression that he'd been born on horseback, would bear down on me, spear in hand. I would be too quick for him, though, and my sword would slice through his arm. We rehearsed the scene a number of times, first with Tom having removed his prosthetic limb so I could practise my swing unimpeded, then with an arm specially constructed for him by the props department. When we filmed the fight for real, the prop limb would be filled with bags of fake blood, designed to spurt out and make it appear I really had chopped Tom's arm off.

Breaking for lunch, Tom and I wandered over to the catering wagon. We hadn't had much time to chat over previous days, and Tom decided to rectify that as he sat down at the long wooden table with his plate of vegetable chilli and rice.

'So, what do you think of Max?' he asked.

'I'm impressed,' I replied, tucking into my own meal and relishing the bite of the spices. If there was a better on-set catering company than Viv's, I had yet to be fed by it. 'I know Brannigan said he's a slave driver, but I really feel like we've got a lot done these past few days, you know?'

'Yeah, it was a real coup for Brannigan to get him, from what I understand, but I think they go way back.'

'But I'm learning from everyone here. Not just Max, Andrej, too ...' Why had I said that, even if it was true? It was a good job Tom had no idea of my true relationship with the riding instructor, otherwise I'd have sounded like a teenager with a crush, compelled to drop the name of the person I fancied into every single conversation.

I was spared having to elaborate as Jean-Paul, the actor playing Lancelot, slid on to the bench next to me. '*Ça va*, guys?' He glanced at the heaped mound of chilli. 'Jamie, I see Viv is giving you a big portion again, *non*?'

'Hi, Jean-Paul.' The French might not have had much of a reputation for humour, but Jean-Paul loved his *Carry On ...* films and never failed to make me laugh with his acute grasp of double entendres. The three of us settled into easy banter, laughing and discussing the hard work lying ahead of us between now and the end of the shoot, and my craving to be with Andrej again faded to a low ache.

There was a message waiting for me when we returned to the hostel that evening. The receptionist handed it to me with a cheery smile. 'I took a call for you earlier, Mr Desmond.'

'Thanks,' I said, glancing at the piece of paper as I crossed the lobby to the stairs. It read, *Come to the stables tonight. Andrej.*

I might have been worn out from the exertions of the day's filming, but those words made my aches and pains melt away.

Max had suggested those of us who'd been involved in the battle scenes have a drink with him in the bar before he left to catch his flight, but I reckoned I'd be able to sneak away after a glass or two without anyone noticing.

Away from the set, where he was the model of professionalism, Max was good, raucous company. I could have stayed and listened to the scurrilous stories about the famous names he'd coached all night, but Andrej was waiting for me, and I knew the likely penalty for being late. When Max launched into a story that involved him breaking up a fistfight between two very well-known stars in the bar of an Amsterdam hotel, that seemed as good a time as any for me to make my move. All eyes were on him as I crept out of the bar, setting off for the stables at a jog.

As before, I stripped naked in the stable yard, but when I walked into the area where Smoke was usually kept, there was no sign of the grey stallion.

'Hello?' I called. 'Anyone at home?'

'Boy!' Andrej's voice came from somewhere ahead of me. 'Come this way.'

I walked in his direction, wondering what was happening. Was he expecting me to practise my riding tonight, or had he brought me here for other reasons?

My question was answered when I found him standing in an empty stall at the far end of the stable building. As always, he looked impeccable in his cream breeches, black roll-neck sweater and shiny black boots, and my heart lurched at the sight of him. He flexed a riding crop, the same one he'd used on me the last time I was here.

'Where's Smoke?' I asked, hastily adding, 'Sir?'

Andrej walked towards me, pulling on his leather riding gloves. 'There is no riding lesson tonight. You are here so I can teach you more about the application of the crop. You have only begun to sample the pain it is capable of inflicting – and the pleasure that follows.'

'Whatever you want, sir.' He could beat me black and blue if he wished; like almost all films, *Grail* was being shot out of sequence, and tomorrow was one of the rare days when I wasn't required on set.

'But first, I require you to perform another service for me. My boots have become dusty on the way over from my quarters. I want you to clean them till they shine.'

'Of course, sir. Where will I find a cloth?'

'Cloth?' Andrej laughed. 'Use your tongue, boy.'

Knowing I had no choice but to obey, I dropped onto all fours, feeling the straw on the stable floor pricking at my bare skin. In truth, Andrej's boots were far from dirty, but what he really wanted me to do was show him deference. Snaking out my tongue, I lapped at the supple leather, tasting a faint trace of polish, but nothing more unpleasant than that. I'd just finished working on his right boot and was about to start on the left, when I heard Andrej call, 'Hey, what are you doing there?'

I looked up to see a familiar figure silhouetted in the entrance to the stall. Tom, the expression on his face somewhere between shock and appreciation of the scene.

'I – I'm sorry. I saw Jamie slip out of the hostel, and I was just curious to see where he was going at this time of night, so I followed.'

'Come closer.' Andrej beckoned him with the crop. 'It's Tom, isn't it? I recognise you now. Brave, and a strong rider ... So, tell me more.'

'Well, when we got to the stables, I suddenly realised why Jamie looks like he knows how to ride a horse now. He's been coming here for lessons. Or that's what I thought, until I saw him strip off – then I didn't know what to think.'

'You're partly right. The boy has been coming here for lessons. But he needed to be taught about more than just how to ride. But maybe you know this? Maybe you and he are lovers?'

Tom shook his head. 'No, I'm not into men.'

'But you see your friend here, naked, licking my boots, and maybe it excites you just a little. Enough to stay and watch, I think ...'

Glancing over at Tom, I wondered whether it was just my imagination that had his faded jeans straining at the crotch.

'Maybe you can help me too,' Andrej continued. 'Come over here and hold my boy while I find something to secure him.'

Tom almost ran to join us. Without being instructed, he grabbed both my wrists in his strong left hand, pinioning them to the wall over my head. While Andrej disappeared in the direction of the tack room, Tom asked, 'Are you OK with all of this?'

'What? You being here, or–?' I gave him a reassuring smile. 'Honestly, Tom, I'm fine. I want this. I need this. I never realised till I met Andrej, but there's a big part of me that thrives on being punished and humiliated.'

'And watched?'

My laugh echoed round the empty stall. 'I'm an ac-tor, darling. I live to be watched.'

'You care to share the joke, boy?' I hadn't heard Andrej return, but now he strode towards us, holding what looked like the remains of a couple of lunge reins. With Tom's help, he stretched my arms out wide, tying them to rings attached to the wall. Again, he made sure the knots weren't so tight as to be painful, but while I could tug at my leather restraints, I couldn't escape from them.

Once my wrists were secured, Andrej fastened my legs in place, spreading them wide apart. As he worked, he took the opportunity to brush the insides of my thighs, never quite rising as high as my cock, which was already fully erect. Satisfied with his handiwork, he stepped back a pace.

'Perfect,' he murmured. 'Hard and ready for me.'

He took something from his back pocket. It was a whip, with about a dozen foot-long suede tails. Definitely not the sort of item you'd use to discipline a horse. It must have come from his own private toy box.

'First, we warm you up with this ...' Andrej lashed the whip across my right flank. I let out a hiss as it landed, but the breath had hardly left my throat before another stroke followed on the left side. It wasn't as painful as the crop had been, but my pale skin gradually reddened under the skilful placement of the whip. Over and over, the tails struck my thighs, my chest and even my nipples. Several times, they came dangerously close to stinging my cock, but Andrej always spared me that torment.

Looking over to where Tom stood, transfixed, I saw him

rubbing his cock through his jeans. In his position, I was sure I'd be doing the same. I must have been a really horny sight, naked, bound and enduring this erotic punishment at Andrej's hand.

At last, my master let the whip drop. He gave me a couple of moments to recover from my beating, stroking my face and throat with his gloved fingers.

'You took that very well, boy,' he said, pressing his lips to mine and kissing me hard. I strained towards him in my bonds, wanting more of his caresses. 'But this will test you, I think.'

Picking up the crop, he trailed it up one thigh and down the other. My eyes were drawn to the movement of the flat leather keeper as he brought it ever closer to my cock. As the implement hovered over my crown, I realised I was holding my breath. The silence in the stall was broken only by the harsh rasp of a zip being undone. I knew if I looked at Tom again, he'd have his dick out.

Andrej tapped my cock with the crop, lightly at first, then just a little harder. I moaned, trusting him not to push me past my limits. He finished off by casting the crop aside and slapping the head of my cock with his leather-clad hand.

'Oh, please,' I groaned, not knowing whether I wanted him to stop or do it all again.

He peeled off his gloves. 'That is enough for now.'

Sagging in my bonds, I watched him undress. I hadn't seen him naked before now, but he was a vision to behold, muscles honed by all the hours spent riding and training his horses. When he removed his briefs, his cock bobbed up, just as beautiful as I remembered it. My mouth watered at the thought of sucking it again, but Andrej had other ideas.

Beckoning to Tom to help him, he started to unfasten the reins holding me in place. Tom trotted over, hard cock sticking out of his fly. My fingers itched to play with his fat veined length, but as far as I was concerned he was off limits.

Between the two of them, they untied me and arranged me over a bale of straw.

'Are you ready to be fucked, boy?' Andrej asked, running his hand over my arse.

'Yes, sir,' I replied, thrilling to the prospect.

I heard him spit, wondering if that would be enough in the way of lubrication, then felt him rub his wet fingers over my arsehole. It took very little effort for him to push one up inside me.

'Oh, that feels good.' I sighed, as he thrust the finger in and out, opening me up enough that he could push a second one in alongside the first.

The digits withdrew, and the head of Andrej's cock replaced them. Inch by inch, he eased his way inside me, until my rear passage was crammed with hot thick cock. Now I was the one who was being ridden bareback, and nothing had ever felt better.

'Fuck, that's horny,' Tom exclaimed, and I looked over to see his jeans round his ankles and his fist shuttling up and down his length. He might have claimed it had taken a while for him to learn how to wank with his left hand, but as far as I could see, he'd more than mastered the technique. The sight of him, lost in his own bliss, spurred Andrej to really pound into me, pushing me hard on to the straw with every thrust.

For long minutes we moved together, to the accompaniment of Tom's hand slapping rhythmically against his cock. Then Tom groaned in despair. I turned my head just in time to see his come oozing out over his fingers.

Andrej reached underneath me, never ceasing in his thrusts as he grabbed my cock and jerked it. I came as he filled me with his spunk, two bodies reaching the height of ecstasy together, then slowly drifting back down to earth.

'*Děkuji*, boy.' Andrej kissed the nape of my neck as he thanked me. 'And thank you, too, Tom, for being such an ... interested audience.'

'Come on, mate,' Tom said, as I nestled sleepily into the straw beneath me, 'we'd better get back. I don't think anyone else noticed us leaving, but you never know.'

Reluctantly, I disentangled myself from Andrej's embrace. 'Thank you, sir. For my punishment. And for everything.' The words "I love you" hovered at my lips, but I couldn't say them, not in front of Tom. I didn't realise then how soon I would come to regret that reticence.

Chapter Five

I'D THOUGHT IT MIGHT be awkward, sitting with Tom at the breakfast table the next morning, but he didn't even mention what had happened in the stables. For him, I suspected, it was just a spicy memory to take away from his time on set. It didn't change our friendship in the slightest. For me, it was yet another way Andrej had chosen to exert his dominance over me. Would he treat it as a one-off, or would he invite others to come and watch me being whipped and fucked?

I didn't get the chance to find out. That evening, the receptionist took another message for me. I scanned its contents with growing unhappiness. Andrej's father was gravely ill, and he'd had to return to his home town of Roztoky to be with him. He hoped to be back before the end of filming, but in the meantime Iréna would be taking over his on-set duties. *I'm sorry it has to end this way,* he added.

Stuffing the note into my pocket, I trudged up to my room, feeling as though I'd been punched in the stomach. I'd never been under any illusions that my relationship with Andrej was anything other than temporary; I just hadn't expected to have my master taken away from me so suddenly, without the chance to bid him a proper goodbye. There was so much I wanted to say to him, and now I'd never be able to. Less than a week remained before *Grail*'s cast and first unit packed up and returned to England, leaving the second unit to film the establishing shots, views of the forest landscape and the castle doubling as Camelot's exterior that would stitch the storyline together. Whatever happened to Andrej's father – and reading between the lines I gathered the man was dying – I'd be gone before Andrej returned to Ledeč nad Sázavou. Iréna would make a decent enough replacement for him in terms of looking after the horses, and I was pretty sure she could pull off the rôle of the strict riding instructor without too much difficulty, but I wasn't looking to grovel at the feet of a dominant mistress. I wanted Andrej.

Brannigan had also received the news about Andrej's sudden departure, and broke it to the rest of the cast as we sat round the dinner table. Tom gave me a secret, anxious glance. Grateful for his concern, I smiled weakly, doing my best to convince him I was all right.

That night, and the nights following, I slept in fits and starts, waking from dreams where Andrej kissed the stripes his crop had left on my arse, telling me between kisses how much he loved me. Why hadn't I told him how I felt? It wouldn't have persuaded him to stay, not given the reason for his departure, but it might have encouraged him to give me some way of keeping in contact with him until his return.

I didn't have the luxury of moping in my room, as I would have done had I been in London; I had one last vital scene to film and people I couldn't afford to let down by sulking and being difficult. So I summoned up all the hurt, all the loss I felt, and channelled it into the speech I gave as I tossed Excalibur into the waves, mourning the passing of Arthur and his court. It wasn't scripted for me to start crying, but I couldn't prevent the tears flowing, and I choked on my words a couple of times. As I strode away from the water's edge, wrapping my tattered cloak around me, it was to a thunderous round of applause from Brannigan and the crew.

'Jamie, that was incredible.' Brannigan clapped an avuncular arm round me. 'I don't know where that came from, but ... Wow!'

'Thanks,' I replied. He was one of those directors who was quicker to criticise than praise, and I knew his words were heartfelt. But I didn't want to talk about the catalyst for my performance; I just wanted to get coffee from the catering wagon and warm up. I'd had enough of the Czech cold; London wouldn't be much more welcoming, but at least it was home.

* * *

The answerphone light was blinking as I stepped into the flat, clutching the pile of post that had built up in my absence. For one crazy moment I thought one of those messages might be from Andrej, then I reminded myself we hadn't shared details like phone numbers, and anyway, he had other things to worry about at the moment.

Fin had called, which was no surprise. 'How's it going, Jamie? Met any hot guys I should know about? Give me a ring when you're back and let's go for a drink, OK?'

More importantly, there were a couple of messages from Keira, letting me know about auditions she'd lined up for me in my absence. Within the week, I'd landed the title rôle in a touring production of *Entertaining Mr Sloane*. I'd be on the road for the best part of three months, playing theatres everywhere from Plymouth to Darlington. It was exactly what I needed to help me forget about Andrej and move on with my life, and I threw myself into rehearsals with single-minded determination.

Caught up in the crazy touring schedule, and the inevitable search for more work once the engagement was over, I lost track of *Grail*'s release date. So it came as a surprise to find my invitation to the official Leicester Square première falling through the letterbox. Checking a couple of the most respected movie blogs, it became obvious the film was generating a serious buzz among those who'd already seen test screenings. They always say you should never read reviews of your work, and if you do, you shouldn't believe them, but my name cropped up with regularity, and all the comments were positive. 'An outstanding break-out performance from Jamie Desmond,' read one. 'He literally lays himself bare as the film progresses.'

'OMG! This is the Bedivere you want to bed!' squealed one of the more excitable celebrity bloggers, drooling over how well-endowed I was. I reckoned there was going to be plenty more where that came from once the film was in cinemas.

I wasn't used to these glitzy, high-profile occasions. Fin had joked in the past that most of the films I'd appeared in weren't released, they escaped. The fact the studio deemed *Grail* worthy of all this fanfare was a sure indication they reckoned they had a hit on their hands, but everything felt slightly unreal as my taxi pulled up at the bottom of Irving Street and I stepped out into the gently falling rain. Heads turned as I dashed up the pedestrianised street towards the cinema, but I didn't think anyone recognised me. They just seemed intrigued by the sight of a harassed-looking man in a tuxedo picking his way through the dawdling tourists.

The paved area in front of the cinema was a scene of organised chaos. Hundreds of people stood cordoned off behind crash barriers as the stars of *Grail* and a number of invited celebrities made their way along a freshly laid section of red carpet. I looked round for Tom, keen to catch up with him again, but failed to spot him. Jack Forrester was posing with a couple of teenage girls while their friend snapped away on her cameraphone. Katie McGivern, who played Queen Guinevere, was talking to an interviewer from Radio Five Live, sheltering under a golf umbrella to keep her Vera Wang dress dry.

'Oh, and here's Jamie Desmond.' A microphone was thrust under my nose and I found myself face to face with the perky blonde presenter of a late-night ITV 2 entertainment show. 'Jamie, tell us who you play in the film.'

'Um, I'm Bedivere. I'm one of King Arthur's knights.'

'Great. And I understand you do all your own stunts. How hard was that? I mean, you had to ride a horse, sword fight ...'

Of all the questions she could have asked. I took a breath. 'Well, I had some really great teachers. And I think when people see the film they'll realise how much work we put in to make everything look authentic.'

'And what about your nude scenes?'

Somehow, I had the feeling I was going to be discussing that topic more than any other in the weeks to come. 'Oh, that wasn't hard at all.'

She blushed. 'Well, thanks for that, Jamie.'

With that, I was able to disappear into the cinema foyer, handing my invitation to one of the uniformed ushers. Climbing the stairs to the main auditorium, I heard a familiar voice behind me. 'Jamie, is that you?'

My heart missed a beat. I turned, and saw Andrej,

resplendent in an elegant evening suit, bow tie neat around his neck. 'Andrej ... What are you doing here?'

He smiled. 'I come to watch the film, same as you. You seem surprised.'

'It's just ... It's been a while. How are you?'

'Well. For a while after my father died, things were not so good, but I am better now.' It was the first admission of vulnerability he'd given. In my eyes, it only made him stronger. 'I got the invite to the première, and I have a few days free, so I thought I would come over here, to see you all again.'

People were trying to get past us. Andrej took me by the elbow and led me up the stairs, coming to a halt by the men's toilets. 'I did not realise till I saw you just how much I have missed you, boy.'

That one word brought so many emotions flooding back. I fought the urge to drop to my knees and kiss Andrej's feet.

'I've missed you, too, sir. I've really tried hard not to, but–' I lowered my voice, conscious of Jack Forrester passing by. He knew I'd had riding lessons from Andrej, but nothing more, and I didn't want to alert him to the truth of our relationship. 'When you find your master, it's really difficult for anyone else to compare with them.'

I didn't mention I hadn't even looked for someone else to take Andrej's place. I'd met up with Fin a couple of times since I'd returned from the Czech Republic, unsure how I'd react if he tried to persuade me to go back to his place. However, while I was away he'd met a woman he was crazy about, and for once in his life he was experimenting with monogamy. Much to his amazement, he was enjoying it.

'So I am your master, hey?' Andrej sounded amused. 'If that is the case, you will come with me now, into the bathroom, and you will worship my cock.'

It was an outrageous suggestion. The film would be starting in a few minutes. We should be taking our seats in the auditorium. But I didn't hesitate. I pushed open the door to the gents' and went in.

The door to the cubicle closest to the far wall was ajar. Andrej dragged me inside, slotting home the bolt. Arms holding each other tight, we kissed with a ferocity summing up the depths of our emotions. Regret at how we'd parted, and the time we'd spent never knowing if we'd meet again, mingled with delight at being reunited. But above all, pure desire. Our tongues probed and tangled as I properly explored Andrej's mouth for the first time.

His hands moved lower, grabbing my arse cheeks and pulling me on to his crotch so I could feel the stiffness of him, pressing at me through layers of fabric. I was just as hard, wanting him as much as he wanted me. From time to time we broke the kiss to gaze at each other with smiling eyes, almost unable to believe circumstances had brought us back together, until Andrej seemed to recall the other reason why he'd brought me in here.

Unzipping his fly, he pulled his hard cock out for me to admire all over again. Without being told, I crouched down so my head was level with his crotch. It wasn't the most comfortable position I'd ever adopted, but I didn't fancy kneeling on the toilet floor, however clean it might be.

As soon as I slipped Andrej's helm between my lips, I knew I wouldn't be crouching there too long. For a man who'd exhibited such iron self-control when I'd sucked him off before, he was already losing the battle not to come. I kept the pace slow, gripping the base of his shaft to prevent him pushing deeper into my mouth and coming before I'd had my fill of him. I breathed in his delicious masculine scent, detectable even though he'd obviously showered before changing into his finery. Glancing upwards, I saw his eyes were closed and he was gripping tight on to the paper dispenser, fighting the urge to thrust.

The sound of water running intruded from somewhere close by, followed by a quick, harsh blast of the hand drier. I held my breath for a second, till whoever was outside pushed the door open and left, then I returned to what I'd been doing. My tongue swirled over Andrej's cockhead, lapping up the precome pooling in the slit. He grunted, past the point of giving any coherent instructions, master utterly in thrall to his servant. As I drew figures of eight over the smooth flesh, weaving wicked patterns with my tongue, it all became too much for him. Doing his best to stifle his moans, not wanting to draw attention to our illicit activity, he shot his load into my waiting mouth.

Hauling me to my feet, he kissed me again, not caring that he could taste himself on my lips. We held tight for a moment, then he readjusted his flies and we hurried out, conscious the film had begun.

The auditorium was packed, but we found a couple of spare seats right at the back, and settled in. Until now, I'd only seen snatches of the film when Brannigan showed us the daily rushes; this was the first opportunity I'd had to watch the finished version.

The audience were following the action with rapt attention, which was a good sign. Andrej said nothing till it came to my nude scene with Jack. It's always disconcerting to see yourself blown up to twice your normal size, even more so when the focus is on your bare arse. As Jack had pointed out at the time, my skin was battered and bruised. Only Andrej and I knew those marks had been left by his riding crop, just the night before. I remembered the feel of that crop, slicing into my backside as I writhed against the wooden trestle, and my cock stirred in my boxers.

On screen, I stood up and stretched, the camera lingering on my dick. Audible murmurs of appreciation came from around us, mostly female.

Andrej's hand settled on the growing bulge in my evening trousers. 'They all want your cock, boy,' he growled in my ear, 'but you know it's mine, don't you?'

'Yes, sir.' I shifted in my seat, anxious for him to pull down my zip and slip his hand inside my fly.

'I know you have not come yet, and I know how badly you want to, but you must be patient. My hotel is just on the other side of the square. When the film is over, we will go there, and you will spend the night with me.'

I'd never wanted anything more. The prospect of falling asleep in Andrej's arms, and waking to see his beautiful face, was thrilling. Yet I hesitated. This man could offer me everything the likes of Fin never had – stability, honesty, love –

if only he didn't have to return to the Czech Republic.

'I'd love to, Andrej. But I know that in the morning, you're going to walk out of my life again.'

'Not this time. Yes, I have to go home, but only to sort out a few things then I'll be back. You see, I have a job with a stable in Hertfordshire, starting in two weeks' time.'

'That's fantastic news!' Excitement caused my voice to rise, earning me a stern look from the man sitting next to me.

'We will be together, and I will be able to give you all the instruction you need. If that is what you want.'

'It is, sir. With all my heart.'

Andrej smiled, dark eyes full of adoration, and took my hand in his. '*Miluji tě*, Jamie. That means I love you.'

'And I love you.' Though I felt confident in expressing my emotions, I didn't attempt the Czech pronunciation. That was one of the many things Andrej would teach me over the months and possibly years to come, and I was determined to prove myself a willing pupil.

People say there's no such thing as a good lie. But if I hadn't claimed to be able to ride, I'd never have won the part in *Grail*. As the credits rolled and the audience rose in a standing ovation, I had the feeling this film was going to propel my career to heights I'd only dreamed of. More importantly, without that lie, I'd never have met my gorgeous master. He really hadn't punished me properly for telling it, but I knew now he had all the time in the world to put that right, and I couldn't wait for him to begin.

STUD TO GO

Chapter One

THE BLOKE CYCLING PAST my table had a fantastic arse. Faded blue denims outlined taut cheeks that flexed as he stamped down hard on the pedals of his rickety, black-framed bike. He wove at speed through the knots of tourists meandering, oblivious to his presence, in the middle of the road. As quickly as he'd appeared, he vanished round the corner into the narrow cobbled street running alongside the café, but the sight of him took my mind off my problems for a moment.

Turning my head sharply, I did my best to avoid making eye contact with the cheery blonde waitress who'd served me. I didn't want her to realise quite how long I'd been sitting here, nursing my stone-cold *koffie verkeerde*. With so little change in my pocket, my choice was between having another drink or leaving her a tip for this one. I knew what she'd prefer.

Amsterdam's a great city – when you have the money to enjoy it properly. But I was broke, and my prospects of improving my financial situation any time soon were pretty dire. So here I was, making my coffee last as long as I possibly could while enjoying the free show presented by pedestrians passing along this busy expanse of the Kloveniersburgwal – and the occasional cute cyclist.

It had all been so different when I'd first moved over to Holland. I'd landed myself a great job, working as the webmaster for an up and coming design agency, based in a small, vibrant office on the Herengracht, one of the main canals that holds in the centre of Amsterdam like a girdle. My work colleagues, mostly media-savvy 20-somethings, were a friendly enough bunch. They knew all the hippest clubs, the newest restaurants, the latest places to see and be seen, and they welcomed me as part of their social crowd. Friday nights would find me in one of the gay bars on the fringe of the red light district, waiting for that special guy to make his presence felt in my life. Even though I hadn't spotted him after the best part of four months, I was determined to keep looking, feeling more at home here than I ever had back in Leeds, the city of my birth.

Then I walked into the office one Wednesday morning to see Trea, the receptionist, in tears as items of computer equipment were being boxed up, ready to be taken away. People stood round wearing dazed expressions as they watched desks and chairs being carried out to a waiting removal lorry.

I caught the arm of the company's CEO, Jaap, as he passed me grim-faced, a pile of manila files under his arm. 'What's happening? Where are they taking everything?'

'Sorry, Ben, the company's gone bust. What can I tell you? It's been on the cards for a while, but I only found out this morning the bank has pulled the plug.'

'But the expansion plans, the office in London?'

He shook his head. 'They weren't prepared to loan us the money, based on our future growth projections. Said given the current economic climate we're too much of a risk. They called in what I already owed and – well, here we are.'

Jaap was still expressing his regrets as I salvaged my personal possessions from the IT room, bundling them into a cardboard box. There would be nothing in the way of severance, just our pay for the days we'd worked that month. From the way he spoke, I gathered we were lucky to receive even that.

I honestly had no idea the company was in such dire straits when I accepted the contract. If I'd known, maybe I'd have thought twice about moving over here, giving up my flat and leaving a job that might have been as boring as hell, but was pretty much secure. All I knew now was I needed to do whatever it took to stay in Amsterdam, the city I'd so thoroughly fallen in love with, and that meant finding fresh employment as soon as possible.

I spent the rest of the morning in an Internet café, printing out copies of my résumé to leave with all the multilingual recruitment agencies in the city. But I had to do something to bring in money in the meantime. Unfortunately, knowing almost nothing in the way of Dutch apart from, 'Hello,' and, 'Thank you,' all the casual work I'd have been able to take at home, like waiting tables or tending bars, was closed off to me. There might have been openings at one of the Irish theme pubs on the main tourist drag, but the thought of serving beered-up stag parties looking to line their stomach with a full English breakfast before heading off to get stoned in a coffee shop just didn't appeal.

My former colleagues were no help. I'd hoped one of them might be able to put in a word for me somewhere, but I quickly lost contact with them, our friendships too fragile to survive outside the bubble of office life.

Which left me sitting outside this café, staring into the middle distance and wondering what I'd do if I wasn't able to pay the rent on my apartment at the end of the month. No closer to coming up with a solution, I'd finally drained the last of my coffee and was fishing enough euros out of my shorts pocket to pay for it when a voice at my elbow said, 'Can I get you another?'

I turned to see a man in his late 30s, dirty-blond hair held back from falling into his eyes by a pair of designer sunglasses. He smiled, and I wondered whether he was coming on to me. Not my type, I quickly decided. Too smooth, too over-familiar. I waved his offer away. 'Thanks, but I've places to be getting to.'

'Like where? You were sitting in this same spot when I walked by an hour ago. Doesn't strike me as though you're a man in a hurry. More like a man who'd be interested in a business proposal, maybe?'

Without giving me time to refuse, he settled in the seat beside mine, catching the waitress's eye with no effort. Speaking in rapid Dutch, he ordered drinks for both of us.

'Let me introduce myself. Edwin De Boer.' He held out a hand for me to shake, his grip firm.

'Ben Donovan.' My tone was guarded, not sure where this was going.

'Nice to meet you, Ben. I'm right in thinking you were in Homme last Friday night?'

Homme was my favourite club, where the music was loud, the drinks cheap and no one minded the odd curious straight couple or group of girls coming inside to join the party. Given my current situation it also helped that, apart from Saturday nights, entry was free.

'I thought of talking to you there, but it's not really the place for a serious discussion.' He broke off as the waitress placed our drinks in front of us; midnight-black espresso for Edwin, another milky coffee for me. Popping a piece of the spiced *speculaas* biscuit that accompanied his coffee in his mouth, Edwin munched thoughtfully for a moment before continuing, 'You see, I'm looking to take on people for my agency, and you're very much the type I need.'

He pulled a business card from his wallet, pushing it across the table towards me. Expecting the details of an agency recruiting for the IT sector, I was startled to be confronted instead by a photograph of a blond male model, his shirt unbuttoned to show his bare chest and tanned, toned six-pack. Above his image were the words, "Stud To Go". Below it, "Amsterdam's premier male escorts".

'An escort agency? Are you kidding me?' I turned the card over to see Edwin's name and an address on the Singel canal. The business at least appeared to be genuine, even though his offer struck me as anything but.

'What, you think this is just some kind of elaborate pick-up line?' He shook his head, smiling at my naiveté. 'I've been with the same man for four years now; I don't need anyone else. But I run a quality escort service, the best in the city, and I definitely have a vacancy on my books for a young, black-haired, blue-eyed guy who's as cute as you, Ben. It's not a combination I see so often on my travels.'

My grandfather was to thank for that. He'd moved to England from Dublin in search of work, back in the 30s. Maybe there was a touch of the nomad in the Donovan genes, along with our distinctive colouring, to explain why I too felt compelled to seek my fortune in a foreign land. But I didn't explain any of that to Edwin. Flattering as his comments were, I was still trying to wrap my head round the concept of becoming an escort, selling my body to make ends meet. 'So ... say I was interested in your proposal. What would it involve, exactly?'

'Well, we offer a service visiting homes and hotel rooms, naturally.'

Visiting strangers, having sex with them. Could I really do that? Was I prepared to fuck and be fucked by men I didn't necessarily find attractive, men I might not even like?

'But where we differ from the other agencies in the city,' Edwin continued, 'is that we also provide escorts for men looking for someone to accompany them to dinner or some social function. There are more wealthy men in this city who are willing to pay for company than you might expect.'

Upmarket arm candy for the single and successful. That sounded much more like it. Though the longer Edwin and I sat talking, discussing the workings of his business, the more my mind wandered to a scene where I found myself in some anonymous hotel room off the Damrak, undressing while a faceless man counted out my fee up front. Slowly, I stripped out of my clothes as he watched, stroking his cock with increasing eagerness as more of my body was revealed to him. When I was down to nothing but tight briefs that clung to the thick swell of my erection, I climbed on to the bed, crawling up to take his helmet in my mouth. Sucking while he gave instructions, I relished the salty, recently showered taste of his flesh. Swallowing more of him down, I knew the momentum was building to the point where I would peel down my underwear and offer him my receptive arse ...

Realising Edwin was speaking, I snapped out of my erotic reverie with some difficulty. My cock had hardened in response to the fantasy, chafing against the seam of my jeans, and I was uncomfortably aware just how long it was since I'd last had a decent fuck. Unorthodox as Edwin's job offer was, it couldn't fail to end the dry spell I'd been going through.

'So what do you think?' he asked.

It wasn't something I'd ever imagined myself doing when I moved over here, but realistically it was either this or getting hold of a joke shop mask and a cloak and joining the ranks of the itinerants who posed as living statues in Dam Square. And what kind of masochist really wants to spend all day, rain or shine, standing on an upturned beer crate between Freddy Krueger and the Grim Reaper? Especially when he could be spending quality time in the company of charming, intelligent, successful men.

'I can't really believe I'm saying this,' I admitted, 'but, yeah, I'm willing to give it a go.'

'Good man.' Edwin beamed, genuinely delighted I'd said yes. 'Come over to the office with me, we'll fill out the paperwork. And I'll need to take a couple of photos of you for the website.'

'Just one thing.' I rose from my chair, waiting as Edwin settled the bill, including the cost of my original coffee, I was pleased to see. 'I don't want to sound rude, but how did you decide on the name of the business? I mean, Stud To Go. It sounds more like you're offering takeaway pizza than male company.'

'Blame my old partner, the one who founded the agency. He wanted something people would remember. And believe me, Ben, they certainly do.'

Edwin's office was a brisk ten-minute walk from the café, on a stretch of the Singel just beyond the floating flower market, where tourists gawped at the mountains of tulip bulbs and exotic blooms in rainbow shades, or giggled over the tacky "grow-your-own cannabis" kits and the shop that sold Christmas decorations all year round.

Entering through a plain black wooden door, we climbed three thigh-achingly steep flights of stairs. Following Edwin into the agency, I was greeted by the sight of a woman in her early 40s, face studded with piercings and hair dyed a pink so vivid it must glow in the dark, deep in conversation on the phone.

'So he'll be at your hotel within the next hour, OK?' Her voice had a low, husky rasp. I imagined she could make a fortune working on sex chat lines. 'And I promise you won't be disappointed. Robin is a real cutie, and he's very willing to please ...'

Spotting my surprise that the woman was speaking in English, Edwin said, 'A lot of our clients are English or American. You know what it's like, alone in a strange city. For sure, there's always porn available on the hotel TV channels, but sometimes you just want the real thing ...'

'OK, Mr Peterson. Thanks for using Stud To Go.' She put down the receiver. Before she could pick it up again to let the escort know all the details of his booking, Edwin stopped her.

'Hey, Marliese, I'd like you to meet Ben. He's going to be working for us. We've just come to sort out his details.'

'Sure. Hi there, Ben.' Her eyes twinkled with amusement as she sized me up. 'So you're the cute English student Edwin was looking for, hey?'

I wanted to tell her I wasn't a student, and hadn't been for a good four years now, but it seemed I was keeping her from her business. Edwin led me through into his office, opening a drawer and pulling out a one-page form.

'OK, so I just need a few details from you, Ben. Full name, address, cell phone number, height, weight ...'

Once I'd given him the necessary information, he reached under his desk for an expensive-looking digital SLR camera. 'Right. Give me a big smile ...' Edwin fired off a couple of shots before continuing, 'And now one of you without the shirt, please.'

I didn't object, simply peeled my T-shirt off over my head, grateful for the fact my enforced leisure time had given me the opportunity to wander out to the Westerpark for a spot of sunbathing that had tanned my skin a light shade of honey. Though I wasn't in bad shape, if – and this thought had my cock stiffening again – I was going to be stripping off in front of strangers on a regular basis, I should maybe start doing a few exercises to really tone up my biceps and abs.

Edwin simply murmured, 'Nice,' as he lined up his shot. I struck a pose that I hoped was relaxed but enticing. He seemed satisfied with the results, nodding with approval as he checked the image on the back of the camera.

'Great. We'll have you listed on the site by tomorrow, then the bookings will start flooding in, for sure.'

The process of signing up had all been painless enough, but one thing still nagged at me. 'Why did Marliese call me a student just now?' I asked, pulling my T-shirt back on.

'Oh, we put all the guys who work for us into categories, mostly for the ease of clients browsing on our website for a home call. Twinks, jocks, black guys, exotic – and students, of course. It's all part of the fantasy. Now, there are a couple of important things you have to know if you're going to be working for us – we have a no tolerance policy on recreational drugs, and no penetration without a condom, even if the guy offers you more for bareback sex.'

I didn't think I'd have a problem sticking to either of those rules. I said my goodbyes to Marliese as Edwin led me back out through the main office. He shook my hand, his grip firm and purposeful. 'Thanks again for joining us, Ben. You won't regret this, I promise.'

As I made my way back down to street level, I could only hope he was right.

Chapter Two

I WOULD HAVE THOUGHT my encounter with Edwin had all been some kind of dream, fuelled by my desperate search for work, if I hadn't checked the Stud To Go website the following afternoon and seen myself listed, as promised, in the "student boys" section. Scrolling down the page, I decided I didn't look out of place among the other escorts on offer, most of whom radiated a definite boy next door vibe. Robin, the guy who Marliese had been in the process of sending to a client when we'd walked into the office, had floppy blond hair, a silver barbell through his left nipple and an expression that suggested he liked nothing more than to be over some older man's knee, pants pulled down for a bare-bottomed spanking. Gijs had a typically sharp-featured Dutch face and an appealing twinkle in his big brown eyes. Darryl, billed as an "Aussie surfer boy", was all abs and attitude, and I was convinced he'd once come on to me on a Friday night in Homme, which appeared to be one of Edwin's prime recruiting spots.

Clicking on the somewhat fractured English translation of my own listing, I was amused to see how they'd billed me. 'Ben is from England, loving to be in our beautiful city, and likes to play as hard as he studies. Good company in and out of the bed, with a nice, tight arse, a night with Ben is one to be remembered.' So no pressure there, I thought, wandering to the kitchenette of my small apartment to grab myself what turned out to be the last remaining beer from the fridge. Maybe I should think about cutting back on the booze for a while, as well as getting started on my new exercise regime. After all, I never knew when Marliese might call with details of my first booking.

The evening still carried a pleasant warmth, and I took my beer out on to the balcony to enjoy it. When I'd been looking for somewhere to live, I'd viewed a couple of larger places that were available for much the same rent, but the balcony had swayed it for me. In a city where almost no one had a garden, you took whatever access to outside space you could grab. It also helped that this apartment was on one of the quieter canals, dominated by squat modern tenement buildings rather than the thin, elegant gabled canal-side residences more familiar to tourists. Houseboats lined the canal – some former cargo barges, others simple box-like wooden structures attached to a fixed mooring – and I'd often look out of my window to see their residents pottering about, watering plants or, like me, having a relaxing drink in the sun. The brown-painted, weathered wooden boat directly beneath my apartment was owned by a big-breasted blonde who liked nothing better on fine days than to lounge on her deck in a tiny bikini – much to the delight, I was sure, of any straight male passers-by.

She was nowhere to be seen tonight, and instead my eye was drawn to a guy in the block opposite mine. His windows were thrown open, and he wandered around his bedroom in nothing but a pair of trunk-style underwear, their stark whiteness in delicious contrast to his mocha skin. I'd never noticed him before, but he was a real hunk, broad-chested and muscular, his hair twisted in chin-length braids that swayed as he moved. Fiddling with the controls of a portable CD player, he set music playing, too low to be heard from this distance. Then, to my utter shock and delight, he eased down his trunks in nonchalant fashion, kicking them across the room. Feeling guilty for staring, but unable to take my eyes off his thick cock where it swung between his legs, already beginning to rise, I took another gulp of my beer.

Did this man realise he was putting on a show for his neighbours, as he went over to the bed and lay down among a litter of throw pillows? Were his slow, deliberate movements intentional as he reached for a bottle on the nightstand, squeezing out some kind of lotion into his palm? All I knew, as he started to stroke his cock almost absent-mindedly, was that my jeans were suddenly far too tight, and I needed to be free of their confines before they strangled the life out of my hard-on. Slipping back into my bedroom, I stripped down to my own underwear, my eyes never leaving the stranger as his hand moved with more purpose along his length. His cock was at full hardness now, and I itched to pleasure it with my own fingers – or, better yet, my tongue.

Almost without realising what I was doing, I gripped my cock through my shorts, savouring the feel of it, hot and eager, in my hand. Already, a drop of wetness was soaking the cotton, and I couldn't have been much less excited than the guy I was watching. If only I could be down on my knees between his spread thighs, mouth crammed full of his meaty black dick, worshipping it with my lips and tongue. Though I scarcely wanted to admit it to myself, since the moment I'd first received Edwin's bizarre business proposal, I'd been unable to think of anything but sex. It's a common enough problem when you're not getting any, but now the need to come was so urgent, so all-consuming I had to do something about it.

Dropping my shorts to the floor, not caring that if the guy across the canal was visible to me, I might just as easily have an audience, I started to wank myself. Easing my foreskin slowly back and forth, I revelled in the sweetness of the sensation. No one knows the perfect way to bring you off better than you do, and my fingers moved in the fast, jerking rhythm that never fails to have me coming in moments. In other circumstances, I might have taken my time, put on a measured performance like the one I'd initially been watching, but I was just too eager. When I'd lost my job, my libido had taken a severe nosedive. I had plenty of time to spend pleasuring myself, but I lacked the desire. Now, I was hornier than I'd been in ages, driven by nothing more than base, frantic lust. A voyeuristic streak I'd never known I'd possessed had kicked in hard, and with the help of the spectacular show taking place in the apartment opposite, I knew it wouldn't be long before I lost my load.

As I continued to watch, a second man entered the bedroom, tall, lean and strawberry blond. The towel wrapped round his waist suggested he'd just emerged from the shower. Climbing on to the bed, he whipped away the towel to reveal one of the biggest cocks I'd ever seen, even in its limp state. Groaning, experiencing a sharp pang of envy as the black guy took hold of his lover's dick with his free hand, I tugged myself even more frantically. They kissed, the overwhelming passion they felt for each other obvious on their faces, and as their bodies twined together, I surrendered all control and shot my lot, jets of creamy come spurting out to spatter against the full-length window.

Weak in the knees from the strength of my climax, I slumped to the carpet. The half-drunk bottle of beer still stood on the balcony table. I was about to slip back into my shorts and retrieve it when I heard a sharp jangling noise coming from somewhere in the apartment. Head still fuddled with bliss, it took me a moment to realise it was my mobile phone. I followed the sound through to the kitchen, where the phone lay charging on the counter. Answering it, I croaked, 'Hello?'

'Ben, it's Marliese. You sound out of breath. Did I interrupt you in the middle of something?' She chuckled, low and throaty.

Only spying on two of the hottest guys I've seen in ages making out, I wanted to tell her. I suspected the idea would excite her just as much as it had me. 'No, I was just out on my balcony and I ran inside when I heard the phone ringing.'

'Well, I have good news for you. You've been booked for tomorrow night.'

'Great.' Immediately I knew it couldn't be a hotel call. Those only came from men seeking an escort on the spur of the moment. 'What does it involve?'

'You'll be accompanying Jeroen Storm to a charity fundraising dinner. You've heard of him?'

'Sorry, should I have?'

'He's a pretty well known photographer, in Amsterdam at least. His gallery's on the Leliegracht, and that's where you'll be meeting him at seven tomorrow. The dinner is at the Hotel Van Rijn. It's a formal occasion, so you need to dress appropriately.'

'OK, that shouldn't be a problem,' I lied, wondering where I was going to find a suitable outfit between now and tomorrow night. The most formal thing I had in my wardrobe was the suit I'd worn to my interview. I hadn't needed to wear it since, the design company having a strictly casual, "dress down" policy, and I knew it wouldn't cut the mustard at a black tie event.

'Right. You're booked from seven till ten. If Storm decides he wants you for longer –' Marliese paused just long enough for the implication to sink in '– then you can negotiate that between you, but be sure to let us know what's happening, so we can amend the fee.'

When I'd joined the agency, Edwin had explained that all my earnings would go through the books, and I'd be taxed just like an employee in any other profession. There were guys who worked on a self-employed basis, setting their own fees and arranging their own meetings, but he didn't feel that was as safe, either for the client or the escort. This way, I wouldn't get stiffed on the price, everything would be legal and above board and someone would know where I was at all times.

'Do you need me to do anything else?' I asked.

'Just keep your phone on – and have a good time.'

With that, Marliese wished me luck and hung up. More in need of a drink than ever, I found my discarded shorts, pulled them on and rescued the bottle from outside. The inch of beer left in the bottom was warm and flat, but that didn't matter. I was celebrating the start of my new life as a male escort, and whatever adventures it might bring.

Chapter Three

JUST BEFORE SEVEN THE following night, I strolled along the Leliegracht, enjoying the stillness of the summer night. In my hastily bought evening suit, I looked more confident than I felt. In search of a suitable outfit on my limited budget, I'd found myself browsing the stalls of the flea market on the Waterlooplein, more in hope than expectation. Lurking on a rail at the back of one stall, I'd discovered a vintage tuxedo and matching trousers in my size for the bargain price of twenty euros. Convinced it was a sign things were destined to work out tonight, I took it home and set about preparing myself to meet Jeroen.

Edwin employed a number of drivers, whose job was mostly to take escorts from one side of the city to the other on late-night calls, but that wasn't necessary in this case. Jeroen lived in the Jordaan district, home to any number of artists and quirky specialist retailers and a scant 15-minute walk from my apartment.

His gallery was situated between a shop selling crystal-heavy designer jewellery and a bookstore specialising in science-fiction and fantasy titles. As I passed, the bookstore's owner was closing for the night, hauling into the shop's interior a wooden advertising mannequin in the shape of a barely-clad female pirate.

Checking my reflection in the gallery window, I straightened my bow tie, feeling nervous butterflies fluttering in my stomach once more. With plenty of time to think about what I was about to do on the way over, it hadn't taken long for anxiety to kick in. What if I didn't like Jeroen? I'd Googled his website, hoping to find a photo of him so I'd know what I was letting myself in for, but the only shot I could find was a deliberately arty black-and-white one with half his face obscured by his camera. It gave me no clue to the way he looked, or even his age. And for all I knew, his personality might stink. But never mind that. What if, once he saw me in the flesh, he didn't like me, and chose to send me away?

Glancing in the window a second time, I couldn't help noticing the photos hanging on the walls all featured young men in various states of undress. My eye was drawn to one shot of a blond guy wearing nothing but a pair of jeans. The fly button was open, and he'd been caught in the act of sliding his hand down inside them, fingers disappearing into the dark haven where his cock lurked. The erotic charge of the pose sent an unexpected shudder of lust through me.

Composing myself, I rang the buzzer with Jeroen's name next to it. A moment's pause, then a voice answered, 'Hello?'

'Hi, it's Ben.' How should I describe myself? *Your escort? Your companion? Your stud to go?*

Jeroen saved me the bother by saying, 'OK, come up to the first floor,' and pressing the door release.

I pushed the door and went inside. He must have been doing well for himself, if he could afford two floors of this building, even if he only rented them. Real estate in this part of the city wasn't cheap, as I knew from my apartment-hunting experiences.

My date for the evening waited at the top of the stairs for me. Whatever I'd been expecting, it wasn't the stunning man of around 40 who smiled broadly in greeting. Thick, tousled blond hair framed cheekbones so sharp you could cut yourself on them, and a strong jawline balanced out a face that might otherwise have been almost too handsome to be taken seriously. Where my outfit was second-hand, his beautifully tailored tuxedo had been made to measure, cut to fit the contours of his six foot plus frame.

As Jeroen sized me up in return, I prayed he wouldn't find me wanting. To my relief, he stuck out a hand for me to shake, welcoming me to his home. Sparks seemed to crackle in the air at the contact, and the hairs on the back of my neck stood up. I couldn't remember the last time I'd felt such a strong reaction; a classic case of lust at first touch.

'Shall we go?' he asked, letting go of my hand a little regretfully, I thought. 'The invitation said seven for seven-thirty, and the hotel's only round the corner, but even so ...'

'Sure. After you.'

Once we were outside, Jeroen made sure the front door was securely locked before taking a left turn in the direction of the Herengracht. 'So, Ben, tell me about yourself,' he said, striding along at a fast, confident pace. Unlike me, he seemed to have no fear that when he stepped off the pavement, he might be walking straight into the path of an oncoming bike.

'There's not much to tell, really,' I replied. 'I've been living here for a few months, and like my listing says, I love this city.'

'So are you studying at the university, or –?'

I shook my head. 'I was working for a design company, but it went out of business. Being an escort is just a way of paying the bills till I get another job.'

'And how are you finding it?'

Our arrival at the hotel spared me having to tell him he was my first client. The Van Rijn, I'd learned in the course of my online research that afternoon, had been built in the 18th century, and had recently undergone an extensive renovation, making it one of Amsterdam's finest hotels. Tonight's dinner was being hosted by Thijs van Veen, the hotel's owner and the man behind its restoration, with the aim of raising money for a local children's charity.

We stepped through its doors into an atmosphere of understated luxury, with subdued lighting and thick pile carpets muffling our tread. Jeroen presented his invitation, and I wondered again what kind of man would pay in advance for two places at an event like this when he didn't have a companion lined up for the evening. Or maybe he originally had, only for something to go wrong ...

The white-jacketed waiter offering me a glass of Champagne distracted me from my musings. I took one, noticing that it bore a discreet "Van Rijn" logo. This world of attentive waiting staff and specially branded glassware was alien to me, though

Amsterdam's great and good seemed perfectly at home with the level of service, and I hoped I wouldn't do anything to let Jeroen down.

An announcement, first in Dutch, then English, asked us all to take our seats in the dining room. Jeroen and I found ourselves sharing a table with two other couples: making the usual polite social chit-chat, we learned they were Don, an American investment banker, and his wife, Janet, and the arts editor of one of the city's newspapers and his partner, who was visibly pregnant beneath her chic black dress.

'You, Jeroen, I recognise, of course,' Paul, the journalist, said. 'It's such a pleasure to meet you at last.'

'And this is Ben,' Jeroen replied, deliberately leaving the relationship between us vague as he introduced me.

'Hi, Ben.' Paul's partner, Natasja, was effusive in her greeting. 'What do you do?'

'Oh, I'm in web design, all very technical,' I replied breezily. From past experience, I knew my answer would deter her from pursuing the matter further. If I ever tried explaining the details of what my work involved, people's eyes glazed over or they dismissed me as some kind of Internet geek. Anyway, I reasoned, our dining companions would be far more interested in what Jeroen did for a living.

As the evening progressed, despite all my misgivings, the six of us had a riotous time. Dispelling the boring image associated with bankers, Don revealed he'd been a reservist in the US Army before he'd started working on Wall Street, and he had some fascinating stories about his time on active duty in Iraq. Paul, meanwhile, was swapping scurrilous tales with Jerome about prominent figures on the Amsterdam arts scene, several of whom were sitting on nearby tables. I chipped into the conversation when I could, even though I didn't know any of the people they were talking about. From time to time, Jeroen would catch my gaze. It wasn't simply my imagination that registered a lustful sparkle in his hazel eyes. He'd felt the same connection when we'd touched, I was sure of it.

'How did you enjoy the food?' Jeroen asked me, as coffee was being served.

'Delicious.' All the courses had been modern takes on Dutch classics, from a starter of white asparagus with air-dried ham, to meltingly tender venison stew with artichoke purée and sweet local strawberries marinated in fruit liqueur and served with vanilla cream. Several cuts above my usual diet of cheese toasties and microwaved TV dinners.

'Good.' His hand stroked over my upturned palm where it rested on the table, the kind of small, intimate gesture that would help to convince casual onlookers we were more than just acquaintances. He seemed pleased we were getting on so well. Maybe he'd been as nervous about this arrangement as I had.

Our attention was claimed by the event's organiser, letting everyone know the evening's centrepiece, the charity auction, was about to begin. The items on offer included a romantic weekend getaway in Paris, Argentine tango dance lessons, a private guided tour of the Van Gogh museum, a lesson in chocolate making from the city's finest chocolatier and the opportunity to have your portrait taken by Jeroen. He sat back, blushing, as the bids for his prize rose and rose. Even from the brief glimpse I'd had of his work, I realised he was a serious talent, and the money guests were willing to stake for the chance to be photographed by him reflected that.

By the time all the items were auctioned off, nearly fifty thousand euros had been raised for the chosen charity.

'This is where everyone sits round and basks in the warm glow of their altruism,' Jeroen whispered in my ear. 'I think maybe we should make our excuses and go.'

Glancing at my watch, I was surprised to see it was almost ten o'clock. Time for me to be slipping away, in any case.

Jeroen rose to his feet. 'Very nice to meet you all,' he said, 'but we really must be leaving. I have an early start in the morning.'

A brief exchange of business cards and promises to keep in touch, and we were on our way. Outside on the pavement, Jeroen lit a cigarette, inhaling the smoke deeply. 'Ben, this has been a really nice evening, and I don't want it to end just yet. Come back to my apartment so we can talk properly.'

'I'd love to,' I told him. 'I just need to clear it with the agency.'

He nodded. 'Tell them I'd like you for another couple of hours.'

Bringing their number up on speed dial, I only waited three rings before it was answered by a woman whose voice I didn't recognise. '*Goedeavond*, Stud To Go.'

'Hello, this is Ben, one of your escorts. I'm out on – er – a date with Jeroen Storm.'

A moment's wait, presumably while the information was brought up on the computer, then the woman said, 'Oh, yes. How's it going, Ben?'

'Very well. Jeroen's booking me for two more hours, and I'm going back to his place, if that's OK?'

'Of course. The extra will be charged to his card. Thanks for letting me know.' With a cheery, '*Doei*!', the Dutch phrase I'd come to realise was a casual way of saying goodbye, she put the phone down.

'All sorted,' I said.

Jeroen nodded, stubbing out his cigarette. We walked in companionable silence back to the Leliegracht. Even though it was still relatively early, few people were out and about. Ten o'clock on a Thursday night in Leeds, the party would just be starting. Here, even at weekends, once you moved away from the main squares where most of the clubs and restaurants were congregated, the streets were always quiet.

'Take a seat,' Jeroen said, letting me into his apartment. 'I'll make coffee for both of us.'

This was very much the home of a single man, I decided, looking around the big living room. A flat-screen TV hung on one wall, but the others were decorated with photos and paintings, evidence of Jeroen's artistic eye. A thick drape at the far end of the room could be pulled across, offering privacy to what were obviously the bedroom and bathroom beyond.

I made myself comfortable on a brown leather chesterfield, just big enough for two people. Expecting Jeroen to take the seat opposite on his return with the coffee, instead he surprised me by sitting beside me. Alongside the cafetière on the tray he'd brought with him was a small bottle of the strong, oily Dutch gin known as jenever. He poured coffee into two white china cups, then pulled the stopper out of the jenever bottle.

'Would you like a dash?' he asked. He'd taken the opportunity to undo his top shirt button and loosen his bow tie, the free ends dangling down, lending him a rakish air.

I wasn't sure coffee and gin were the best combination, but I nodded anyway. With Jeroen so close to me, his thigh touching mine as he reached forward to fuss with our drinks, I was in sudden need of a shot of courage.

Did he really just want to talk? And why would I be so disappointed if that turned out to be the case?

Leaving me to add cream and sugar to my liking, Jeroen drank deeply of his own coffee.

'Thank you once again for a very pleasant evening, Ben,' he said, setting down his mug. 'I really have enjoyed your company.'

'Well, thanks for choosing me.' I took a cautious sip of my drink. It tasted a lot better than I'd expected, the gin warming me all the way down to my belly. 'Can I ask you, out of interest, why did you choose me?'

'You have a certain look.' His words echoed the ones Edwin had used when he'd first approached me to work for him. 'I looked at some of those other boys and I knew I'd never be able to hold any kind of conversation with them. But you – well, you've obviously had plenty of practice at this type of thing.'

I laughed so hard I almost snorted coffee out of my nose. 'Can I tell you the truth, Jeroen? Tonight was my first night. I only joined the agency two days ago. I've never done anything like this before, I promise you.'

'Then we're a good match. I've never taken a paid companion to a gala event before.'

I sensed there was more he wanted to add, but he rose abruptly from the couch, and went over to his PC, standing on a table beneath the window. With a couple of clicks of his mouse, soft jazz floated from the free-standing speakers.

'But despite what I said earlier, I didn't bring you back here simply to talk.' Jeroen came to sit back beside me, even closer than before. 'I've been wanting to do this all night –'

Putting a hand round the back of my neck, he pulled my face to his and kissed me. When I'd ticked it on Edwin's form as something I was agreeable to – some escorts apparently considering it too intimate an act in a paid sexual encounter – I'd never expected to be kissed quite like this. Jeroen's lips were soft against mine at first, but as his passion increased, his tongue pressed hard into my mouth, seeking to possess it. Eagerly, I responded to his advances, my cock swelling in the confines of my tight-fitting trousers.

Breaking the kiss, I murmured, 'Need to be out of this penguin suit.' Aware Jeroen was looking at me oddly, I explained. 'It's an English expression for evening dress. You know, because it's black and white.'

'Yeah, I get it.' He unfastened my bow tie, before kissing me again. 'Let me help you ...'

Jeroen undressed me with authority, making short work of my shirt buttons and fly fastenings. I kicked off my shoes, letting them lay where they fell. Caught up in the urgency of the moment, I didn't have time to make a neat pile of my clothing. I wanted to be naked, and I wanted Jeroen to be naked too.

Grappling with the shoulders of his jacket, I stripped it off him. He paused for a moment to unfasten his fancy silver knot cufflinks and lay them down on the coffee table. I took the opportunity to stroke my cock through my white cotton briefs, worn because Edwin had told me there wasn't a client alive who didn't love the sight of a young man in nothing but tight white underwear.

The effect wasn't lost on Jeroen. 'Oh, yeah, keep doing that,' he told me, as he undressed himself down to his own paisley-patterned trunks. 'Get that big cock nice and ready for me.'

'Why don't we go through to the bedroom?' I suggested. 'I don't think there's going to be room on this couch for both of us to get really comfortable.'

'Sure,' he said. 'Follow me.'

Before I did, I fished in my jacket pocket for the condoms and sachets of lube I'd stashed there, remembering Edwin's rule about making sure to use protection. Not that I'd have done otherwise, if I'd met Jeroen under more usual circumstances. Hot as he was, I'd no idea how many lovers there'd been before me, and that meant playing safe.

Jeroen's sleeping area was small and cosy, dominated by a bed easily big enough for three. As he watched, I sprawled out on the covers, taking up where I'd left off in the slow stroking of my dick through my underwear.

'Take them off,' Jeroen growled. 'Show me what you've got.'

Without hesitation, I eased down my briefs. Free of the clinging cotton, my cock unfurled to its full length, rising up tight to my body.

'Very nice.' Jeroen climbed on to the bed beside me, a hungry glint in his eye.

'What about you?' I asked, keen for him to remove his underwear and give me my first look at what had to be a pretty impressive cock, if the bulge beneath the paisley was any indication.

'All in good time,' he replied.

Time was the one thing we didn't have, I wanted to tell him. I'd made sure to keep my watch on, so I'd know when the extra two hours Jeroen had booked me for were over. Until then, though, I was bound to follow his instructions.

He lay back, propped up against the pillows, so masculine and desirable. Wanting to explore every inch of him, I planted a slow trail of kisses down his chest and stomach, moving ever closer to his groin. When I reached the waistband of his trunks, I tugged them down, baring him to my greedy gaze. As big and virile as I'd hoped, his dick was neatly circumcised and topped with a smooth head, almost crying out for me to take it into my mouth.

Unable to resist such an inviting treat, I bent my head and slurped my tongue along his length, from base to tip. A slight waft of the lemon cologne he favoured came to my nostrils, mingled with the musk of his crotch, and I suspected he'd dabbed a little on his balls before dressing tonight.

Keen to taste more of him, I swallowed his cockhead, tasting the sharp saltiness of his precome. Growing bolder, trying not to think about how long it had been since I'd last had the pleasure of sucking a hot, hard cock, I took as much of him as I could down my throat. Jeroen groaned and muttered something in Dutch; I couldn't understand it, but it sounded very much like "good". If his words confounded me, his facial expression didn't. His eyes were closed and his mouth twisted in a grimace of pure enjoyment.

Spurred on by his reaction, I sucked with more vigour, pumping the base of his cock with my fist as I did. All he could do was push his hips up at me, wanting more, no longer able to shape the words to tell me what he needed and letting his body's reactions speak for him. In the past, I'd been with guys who hated sucking cock. They claimed they found it too demeaning, too submissive. I'd never shared that opinion. To me, bringing a man to the point where I had Jeroen now, writhing against the sheets, one more clutching swallow of my throat away from climax, was an art. His tool was his camera. Mine was my slurping, darting tongue, and I wielded it with exquisite skill.

'Fuck me.' Jeroen's words were faint, choked by lust. He cleared his throat and repeated the request more forcefully.

What the gentleman wanted, the gentleman got. Relinquishing my hold on his cock, I unwrapped a condom and skinned it on in matter-of-fact fashion. 'Roll over,' I ordered Jeroen, before tearing a lube sachet open with my teeth and smearing the stuff over my fingers.

Rump raised, head in the pillows as he waited for my approach, Jeroen had my cock surging upwards more strongly than ever. He'd offered his arse to me so willingly, and I ached to sink my cock into its depths, but he had to be prepared first. When Jeroen felt the cold goo being applied to his dark pucker, he groaned with blatant need.

A moment of resistance as my lube-slippery finger pushed at his entrance, then the muscle relaxed and I was inside him. 'More,' he begged.

'Are you sure?' I asked, pulling out so I could tease his hole with the tip of my finger.

'Yes, *verdomme*! Yes!'

The second finger entered him as easily as the first. I couldn't wait any longer; I had to know what it felt like to have my cock buried in that tight passage.

One firm thrust and I was home; a couple more and I was buried snug and deep. Jeroen grunted, welcoming the penetration.

My hand smoothed over the muscled contours of his back. How was it? I wondered, I felt closer to him at this moment – a man I barely knew and who was paying me for the privilege of fucking him – than I had to any of my boyfriends back home? *Stop thinking and start fucking,* a voice deep in my head ordered me.

Moving in a rhythm older than time, I thrust deep and hard, breathing in Jeroen's scent, breaking off to lick up the sweat that beaded on his shoulder blades. I needed to imprint on my memory the way his hair clung in damp tendrils to the nape of his neck, the soft slithering noises as he rubbed his cock against the covers, the ragged overtones of his breathing as he fought in vain against the urge to shoot his load. If I could squirrel all these details away, I'd have memories to sustain me on those cold winter nights when my escorting days were over.

Jeroen burbled in the universal language of a man about to come. Reaching underneath him, I wrapped my fingers round his cock just in time to feel his thick spunk oozing out, staining the sheet below us. Caught up in the sight and sound of his climax, his arse clenching hard around my shaft, I surrendered to my own orgasm.

When it was over, I slumped against Jeroen's back, satisfied and deliciously sleepy. Except, much as I wanted to, I couldn't doze off. According to my watch, midnight was less than ten minutes away.

Disentangling myself from Jeroen with some reluctance, I went to dispose of the condom. He pulled the covers around himself, watching as I went to find the clothes I'd left scattered across his living room floor.

As I dressed, I finally voiced the question I'd been wanting to ask all evening. 'So, Jeroen, why does a man like you need to hire an escort? I mean, you're handsome, successful – you could probably have any man you wanted. Surely you don't need to pay for sex?'

'It's complicated, Ben. I'd probably have to book you for another hour to explain it all properly.' Jeroen tried to smile, but his attempt at levity fell flat. 'But to make a long story short, I was with my last partner for six years. I never loved anyone as much as I did Ton, and I truly believed he felt the same way about me. Hell, we were even planning to get married. Then I went away for a couple of days, working on a photo shoot for the US edition of *Vogue* in the Greek islands. It was such a prestigious assignment, but one of the most difficult shoots I'd ever been on. I was so looking forward to getting home and seeing Ton, just to forget about all the madness and the tantrums ...'

Jeroen fell silent. When I glanced at him, I saw he was having difficulty continuing with his story, clearly caught up in reliving the painful emotions associated with it. He took a deep breath and managed to carry on.

'Anyway, when the taxi dropped me off at the apartment, I went racing inside, calling out his name, only to find him in the kitchen with some young Thai guy on his knees before him, sucking his cock. I went berserk. I threw a saucepan at this guy, telling him to get out of my home. He went scuttling off, pulling his pants up as he ran. And that left Ton. Oh, he told me everything I wanted to hear. That it was just a one-time thing, that it didn't mean anything, that it was me he loved. He said the guy just came round to deliver a meal for the two of us, to save Ton cooking when I got home, and he was tempted ...'

It sounded like a set-up from a bad porn DVD, only that would have resulted in Jeroen joining in, turning the scene into a juicy three-way. Real life has no such improbable endings, and Jeroen had instead found himself plunged into the misery of betrayal.

'Ton swore nothing like it would ever happen again, but how could I believe him? Once the trust is gone, you can never get it back.' Jeroen sighed. 'That was nearly a year ago, and I still can't face dating anyone on a serious basis. What's the point, after all? They only lie, they only let you down. So every now and again, when I really need sex, I pay for it. But like I told you, this is the first time I ever hired a man to accompany me in public. I'd have gone to the dinner tonight on my own, but that wouldn't have felt right. So –'

He didn't need to finish the sentence. 'Well, I hope you had a good time,' I said.

'I had a fantastic time. Thank you, Ben – for everything.'

'Well, if you ever feel like having another fantastic time, you know where I am.'

If this had been a normal date, I was convinced we'd have exchanged phone numbers at this point, but we were escort and client, and a different etiquette applied here.

Only bothering to pull on his shirt over his naked body, Jeroen let me out of the apartment. One last wave at the door, and I was on my way. A fine drizzle had started to fall, and I turned the collar of my jacket up against it, eager to be home.

Jeroen Storm had destroyed all my preconceptions about the kind of man who used an escort service. Honest and straightforward, he'd been thoroughly professional in his dealings with me. So why did I find myself wishing I could see him once more, in a situation that wasn't purely a business arrangement?

Chapter Four

I DON'T KNOW HOW long I'd have slept the following morning if I hadn't been woken by the banging and clattering of the refuse collectors emptying the bins from outside the apartment into the back of their lorry. Reaching for my watch, I was surprised to see it was gone ten o'clock. I hauled myself into a sitting position, my muscles carrying the faint ache that follows good sex. When I'd got home the night before, I'd been too tired to do anything other than crawl into bed. Now, I intended to enjoy a long, hot shower before breakfast.

Padding to the bathroom, I turned the shower on and let the water reach full heat before stepping beneath the spray. Catching sight of my reflection in the mirror as I did, I could hardly wipe the grin from my face. Scenes from the previous evening flashed back to me: Jeroen as I'd first seen him, cool and confident in his evening wear; the moment our lips had first met, accompanied by the faint taste of coffee and gin; the words he'd cried out as he'd come, telling me how much he loved the feel of my big cock in his arse.

I spent a long time lathering myself with spearmint-scented gel, enjoying the tingling sensation it created on my scalp and skin. At last, I dragged myself out of the shower, towelled off and went to make myself something to eat. The kitchen cupboards were almost bare, but I found the heel of a loaf of wholemeal bread, and a couple of eggs lurked at the back of the fridge. Putting the eggs on to boil, I poured the last of the orange juice into a glass. A supermarket run was definitely in order.

In the end, it was early afternoon before I finally reached the supermarket. Spending time in Jeroen's pristine apartment, lying in his crisply laundered sheets, had convinced me it was time I gave my own living space a spring clean. By the time I'd finished vacuuming the floor, washing the bed linen and cleaning the accumulated grime off the cooker hob, I was feeling distinctly virtuous.

My phone rang as I stood by the delicatessen counter, debating whether to choose ham or sliced chicken breast for my sandwiches. Almost without thinking, I answered it on the second ring.

'*Hoi*, Ben, how's it going?'

I recognised Marliese's husky tones immediately. Stepping away from the counter into a quiet corner of the store – a basic piece of etiquette I'd have carried out even if I wasn't taking a call from the receptionist of an escort agency – I replied, 'Great, thanks. Are you OK?'

'Yes, I'm good. But how was everything last night? Laura told me the booking was extended.'

Laura. That must have been the woman I'd spoken to last night. 'Couldn't have been better. Jeroen's a really nice guy.'

Marliese prevented me from reeling off a list of Jeroen's good points by saying, 'Pleased to hear it. And I hope you're in the mood to meet another nice guy, because I have someone who's dying to spend some time with you.'

'What? Now?'

'Don't sound so surprised, Ben. You know how it is when you feel an itch and it just has to be scratched ...'

I didn't, not really, not when it came to sex. I'd always tried never to let my cock rule my head; I knew the havoc that could cause. But the clients of Stud To Go worked to their own timetables, and if someone wanted to see me straight away, then I had to answer that call.

'OK, who and where?'

'His name's Greg Parsons, he's American and he's staying in Room 104 of the Hotel Grand Plaza. He wants you for an hour. I've told him you'll be there within the next 45 minutes.'

That was pushing it, given I still had to pay for my shopping and drop it off at the apartment, but Marliese didn't need to know all the details of my domestic life. 'Fine by me. I'm on my way.'

'Great. He hasn't asked for any toys, any special requests, so I'm guessing he just wants a straightforward suck and fuck. Have fun, Ben.'

'Oh, I will.'

Sticking my phone back in my pocket, I headed for the checkout, mind flashing to thoughts of this horny stranger, waiting in his hotel room for me to arrive. Forget food, I thought, watching the assistant scan my purchases; sex was on the menu, and I suddenly had a raging appetite.

Despite my fears that I wouldn't be on time, 41 minutes later I walked into the lobby of the Grand Plaza, trying my best not to look out of place in its plush surroundings. I'd dashed back to the apartment from the supermarket, and quickly stowed my shopping in the kitchen cupboards before sprucing myself up with a clean T-shirt and a spritz of cologne. Hopping on to the tram at Marnixstraat, I'd pressed my pay-as-you-go travel card against the reader, realising I needed to top up the balance if I was going to be making many more of these unplanned journeys. The rush hour hadn't kicked in yet – not that the traffic in the city centre ever found itself seriously backed up, even at the busiest times of day – and within five minutes I was at my destination, Dam Square.

The hotel stood on the far side of the square, an oasis of quiet luxury in one of Amsterdam's busiest tourist spots. A grey-liveried doorman held the door open for me, nodding as I passed. I doubted his smile would be quite so broad if he knew why I was there.

A striking blond receptionist, hair pulled into a ponytail so tight it was acting as a makeshift facelift, greeted me with studied politeness as I approached the front desk.

'I'm here to see Greg Parsons in Room 104,' I told her, hardly daring to raise my voice above a whisper.

'He's expecting you?'

'Yes. I'm Ben, a student friend of his.' She gave me an appraising look. I hoped my stripy T-shirt and the backpack slung in casual fashion over my shoulder would convince her I was who I claimed to be.

She reached for the phone, dialling Parsons's room. 'Mr Parsons? I have your friend, Ben, in the lobby ... Yes, I'll send him up.' Putting the receiver down, she said, 'His room is on the first floor, to your left.'

'Thanks very much.'

I took the stairs two at a time, not wanting to keep the man waiting any longer than I had to. When I knocked on the door of his room, a gruff voice answered, 'Just a moment.'

After some banging and rustling, he opened the door to me, ushering me inside. We gave each other a quick once-over as we shook hands. Parsons was in his late 40s, at a guess, heavily built and running slightly to seed, with curly hair and a dark growth of beard. His voice had the kind of thick Texan drawl that made me think of oil wells and cattle ranches. All he wore was a hotel towel, knotted around his waist. Not my usual type, by a long chalk, but hardly a guy to run screaming from, either.

'So,' I said, deciding we didn't need much in the way of small talk, 'how do you want to do this?'

'The woman from the agency said you're a great cocksucker.'

Did she now? I'd have words with Marliese the next time I spoke to her. 'I like to think I try my best.'

'Modest as well as cute,' he drawled. 'I knew I'd made a good choice. But why don't you take your clothes off, boy. Let me see just what I'm paying for.'

Parsons made himself comfortable on the bed as I undressed. He had a glass of whisky on the nightstand, a miniature bottle from the room's mini-bar standing empty beside it. Taking a mouthful, he studied me with intent. I couldn't fail to notice how his hard-on was pushing at the towel, eager to be free.

There's a way to undress in front of someone for the first time that makes you look sensual and in control. Footwear comes off first, so there's no hopping round, trying to get your trousers off over your shoes. Then your T-shirt, peeled off slowly so your lover gets a good look at your bare chest. Give him time to imagine what it would be like to run his tongue down your abs, following the thin trail of hair that disappears into your waistband. Trousers next, eased down and stepped out of, leaving you standing in just your underwear. By now, your cock should be good and hard, just as mine was, straining up and anxious to be unleashed.

'Turn round,' Parsons ordered me. He'd unfastened the towel and was stroking his circumcised cock with slow, measured strokes. 'I want to see your butt as those tighty-whities come down.'

It was an odd request, but I complied, presenting him with the sight of my taut arse cheeks as I removed my briefs.

'Very nice,' he murmured, voice thick with lust.

I heard the chinking of ice cubes. When I turned round, he was setting down his empty whisky glass. The sight of the half-melted cubes remaining in the bottom of the glass gave me an idea.

Going to join him on the bed, cock bobbing as I crawled into position between his legs, I reached for the glass. Popping one of the ice cubes into my mouth earned me a quizzical look from Parsons. I let it melt down to nothing, then bent to wrap my lips round the head of his dick. I'd once had the same thing done to me by an of ex of mine, drunkenly fooling around together after some university block party, and I hoped it would have the same effect on Parsons as it had on me.

It did. His eyes widened as he registered the feel of my cool mouth around his hot shaft. 'Oh, my God, they were right. I've never known anything like this. Oh, Ben, don't stop ...'

Dipping my head lower, I tongued all the way down to his balls, then back to the tip. My actions were accompanied by a soundtrack of moans and groans from Parsons. I'd never been with a man who'd been quite so vocal about his gratification, and I hoped he didn't get too loud when he came. I didn't want anyone in the neighbouring room to alert reception to the noise. Still, maybe they'd just think he was watching porn on his TV – if a hotel this swanky had a porn channel available for its guests.

'Oh, yeah, keep doing that.'

Glancing up, I saw Parsons pinching one of his fat pink nipples, grimacing with pleasure. Changing tack, I moved in closer, so I could lick along the thick seam that divided his balls, before taking each of the fuzzy, wrinkled sacs between my lips in turn. He liked that, enjoying it even more when I broke off to suck on the last of the ice in his glass, chilling my mouth again.

He'd obviously showered before our rendezvous, the bland scent of aloe vera soap lingering faintly on his balls, so I had no qualms about running my tongue over his arsehole. Parsons spread his thighs wider, wanting more. Part of me couldn't help wondering how I'd taken this path, leading me to rim a complete stranger in a five-star hotel bedroom, but there was no use pretending I wasn't enjoying myself. It seemed working as an escort was enabling me to experiment in a way I'd never done in any of my relationships. Perhaps it was due to the freedom of knowing I'd never see this guy again, never have to be nice to him over breakfast or make any of the inevitable compromises that come from living with a partner. Not that I didn't want the opportunity to experience those things again, if the right person came along – and contemplating such a situation caused Jeroen Storm's face to swim into my vision.

That wasn't good, thinking about another man when my sole focus was supposed to be the man whose crotch my face was buried in. Banishing all thoughts of the sexy photographer to the back of my mind, I worked harder on Parsons' arsehole, reaming it with the point of my tongue. He writhed against the towel, begging for more.

'Roll over,' I asked him. He complied, presenting his plump arse cheeks to me. I spread them with my fingers, able in that position to lap at the whole length of his crack before concentrating on his brown pucker. Parsons' enthusiastic cries were muffled by the heap of pillows, which was no bad thing. The way he was humping the bed, I reckoned it wouldn't be long before he came. But he'd paid for an hour, and I wanted to string the moment of his orgasm out just a little longer so, slightly to his reluctance, I got him to turn over once more.

Any disappointment on his part faded when I swallowed his helmet again, tasting thin, salty juice leaking from its slit. Grasping his shaft at the base, I gave him a long, luxurious blowjob, swirling my tongue over and around his cockhead with sensual strokes. Every time he tried to jab himself deeper into my mouth, I held him steady, letting him know I was in charge here, and he would only come when I judged he was ready. That had the effect of revving up his excitement even more, and although I did my best to keep him on the boil for as long as I could, well before our hour together was up, his gluey spunk oozed its way down my throat.

I thought he might want me to fuck him. God knows I was in need of some relief by now, my cock rigid and in need of attention, but I hadn't even thought to touch myself while I sucked Parsons off, and he hadn't given me any instructions to that effect.

'That was fantastic, Ben. I've never had a blowjob like it. I'm going to sleep like a baby, I just know it.'

He must be talking about tonight, I thought, but he quickly put me right by adding, 'You can go now. And thanks for everything.'

Parsons watched as I dressed, with none of the finesse I'd given to my earlier striptease. Stuffing my swollen dick back into my jeans was almost impossible, but I managed it. The Texan, towel securely in place once more, escorted me to the door. He patted me fondly on the arse as I left.

'Next time I'm in Amsterdam, I'll be sure to ask for you again. Have a nice day, Ben.'

The door clicked shut behind me, leaving me standing in the corridor with a raging hard-on. Of all the things I'd imagined happening to me while working for Stud To Go, not getting to come in the company of a client hadn't been one of them. I took the stairs down to the lobby slowly, hoping I could somehow wish away my erection with thoughts of all the chores I still needed to do around my apartment, but it didn't work. Parsons' throaty cries of ecstasy had formed themselves into a persistent ear worm, like one of those tunes you just can't get out of your head, and when I ran a tongue over my lips I could still pick up the bitter taste of his come.

Salvation appeared ahead of me in the shape of the men's room, just to the right of the hotel bar. I slipped inside.

Fortunately, all three cubicles were empty. I locked myself into one, dropped my jeans and underwear and took myself in hand. I was so horny, it only took a dozen swift strokes of my fist before my spunk arced out into the pristine porcelain toilet bowl. No one but me would ever know every one of those strokes was performed to the image of Jeroen Storm's clutching arse being plundered by my cock.

I flushed away the traces of my furious self-pleasuring, cleaned myself off, zipped my fly and went to splash cold water on my face. Staring at my flushed reflection I realised I'd got it bad for a man I'd probably never even see again. It didn't have to be a problem. As long as I kept my lust for Jeroen to the realms of fantasy I was sure I'd be able to cope. I only hoped that wouldn't prove as hard as I thought it might.

Chapter Five

GRADUALLY, MY LIFE FELL into the closest I'd had to a routine since I'd lost my job with the design company. If I'd been with a client the night before, I liked to sleep late, before having breakfast at a little café a couple of minutes' walk from my apartment. Otherwise, I went jogging, taking a route up my own canal, the Lijnbaansgracht, and round the fringes of the Jordaan, pounding the pavements with my headphones in, listening to rock music with a driving, motivating beat. A determination to get in the best shape of my life fuelled my efforts, knowing the fitter I was, the more stamina I'd have between the sheets. In the afternoons, I continued to apply for jobs that required my IT skills, though the search for full-time employment didn't seem quite so urgent now I had money in my pocket once more.

That money came in useful when I had to go on a little shopping expedition. Edwin liked all his escorts to have a supply of sex toys to hand, along with plenty of condoms and lube, in case a client made any special requests. Until now, everyone I'd visited had been looking for a simple fuck and suck, but I knew I needed to be prepared.

One afternoon, I made a trip to Jonny's, an erotic boutique on the fringes of the red light district catering exclusively to gay men. Unlike English sex shops, which tended to have discreet items of lingerie in their window displays, assuming those windows weren't blacked out altogether, Jonny's made no such concessions to passers-by. Mannequins modelled harnesses and leather body adornments whose purpose I couldn't even begin to guess at, and at the heart of the display were some of the biggest dildos I'd ever seen in my life.

The young, shaven-headed guy behind the counter barely

raised an eyebrow when I walked in. Browsing the racks of toys, bondage equipment and fetish wear, I rapidly realised just how vanilla my sex life had been. Until now, it had never struck me that a kilt might be regarded as a kinky outfit, but a couple hung among the more traditional items of rubber and leather gear, as did extremely convincing-looking doctor's scrubs. Dozens of dildos stood in neat rows on shelves, most of them modelled on the cock of some porn star or other. If you liked your sex rough, there were any number of items to add pain to your pleasure, from horsewhips to nipple clamps to butt-plugs so wide they made my eyes water just thinking about having them inserted. I hurried past something billed as a "ball crusher" with a little shudder, thinking those games were just a step too far for me. The Stud To Go website listed me as prepared to be a bottom, as well as a top, but I knew I didn't have the experience – or the inclination – to get involved in the heavy-duty end of BDSM play.

At least my exploration of Jonny's had given me a pretty good idea of what my clients might want. I picked up a seven-inch dildo with thick veins running along its length and a neat, tapered head, a pair of padded leather handcuffs, a black butt-plug at the smaller end of the scale and, out of sheer curiosity, a cock ring. Adding a couple of packets of condoms and a box of water-based lube sachets, I took my basket of goodies to the counter.

There was still no reaction from the assistant. Obviously I didn't have "sex shop virgin" branded across my forehead. He rang up the items on the cash register in the same matter-of-fact fashion as if I was buying eggs and milk at the supermarket. When he handed me them in a plain black plastic bag, he murmured, 'Enjoy!', then returned to his viewing of the DVD playing on the TV screen behind the counter, some pirate-themed extravaganza from the brief glimpse I'd had.

I'd just returned home with my bag of purchases when the phone rang. Snatching it up, I found myself speaking to Marliese.

'Somebody likes you,' she giggled. For a straight women working among men who were almost all exclusively gay, she had the most flirtatious phone manner.

'Really? And who might that be?'

'Jeroen Storm. He wants you to accompany him to a cocktail party tomorrow, out in the Eastern docklands. You're free, I take it?'

For Jeroen, any time. 'Of course.'

'OK, you need to be there by half-past seven, so we'll be sending a driver to pick you up. Any questions?'

'No, that all seems straightforward enough. Cheers, Marliese.'

Grinning like a maniac, I put the phone down. Jeroen wanted to see me again. *As a client,* I told myself sternly. However good the sex had been, and however close I'd felt to him in the moments afterwards, ours was strictly a business arrangement. He didn't want a real boyfriend, just a pretend one. If I kept reminding myself of that, I'd be fine.

When the driver arrived to collect me the following evening, I was pacing the balcony in nervous anticipation. Frank was a big, bull-necked man who looked as though he'd been hired as much for his muscle as any driving ability. Dark glasses hid his eyes and his hair was shaven down to the scalp. Despite his forbidding appearance, he was in the mood to chat, telling me about my destination for the evening, KNSM Island.

An artificial island, built as the headquarters of the old Royal Dutch Steamboat Shipping company, its name was an acronym of the company's official, tongue-twisting title, which Frank pronounced effortlessly in his guttural tones. When the cargo shipping industry had gone into decline, the island had become a home to those on the margins of society, junkies and squatters, until they'd been moved on so the whole area could be redeveloped, much like London's Docklands. However, where London had seen the old docks turned into the financial and commercial district of Canary Wharf, Amsterdam's Eastern Docklands had been transformed into a thriving residential area.

According to Frank, it had something of a reputation as a "yuppie haven", with its pricey restaurants and shops selling designer home wares. 'But we get a lot of business from the guys out here, so what do I care?' he said with a grin. 'OK, here we are.'

I'd arranged to meet Jeroen at a little waterside café, close to where the party was being held. There was no sign of him, but the traffic had been light and Frank had got me to my destination with more than ten minutes to spare. I ordered a *koffie verkeerde* and settled down on a bench outside the café to wait.

Where the redevelopment schemes in the centre of Amsterdam, such as my own apartment block, were unimaginative and almost uniformly drab, the architects rebuilding the docklands had been given free rein to produce eye-catching buildings. Looking at the one dominating the skyline on the opposite side of the docks, designed so that chunks had been cut out from its long, column-like shape, I decided it resembled nothing more than a giant game of Jenga, abandoned halfway through.

'Hey, Ben!'

I'd been so engrossed in studying the man-made landscape, I hadn't heard Jeroen arrive. The rear lights of the taxi that had delivered him disappeared round the corner. I drained my coffee and we greeted each other with an embrace.

He looked just as good as I remembered, casually dressed in an olive green jacket over a white T-shirt and jeans. His appraising smile let me know he approved of my choice of outfit, a teal-blue shirt left untucked over black trousers.

'Nice to see you again,' he said. 'How've you been?'

'Oh, keeping busy.' *Fucking strange men in hotel rooms, buying butt-plugs in case I'm hired by a man who likes having his arse packed, the usual.* 'So, whose party are we going to?'

'You remember Paul Robijns? We met him at the charity dinner?'

I nodded, picturing the big, jovial newspaperman and his petite, pregnant wife. They'd been good company, and I'd liked them.

'Well, it's his 40th birthday. He's just having a modest celebration, but he invited me – well, he invited us – along. I could have come on my own, made some excuse about why you weren't with me, but to be honest, Ben, I had such a good time that night, I really wanted to see you again.'

Not knowing what to say in reply, feeling like a giddy teenager who's just had their secret crush reciprocated, I followed Jeroen a hundred yards or so along the dock, to one of the biggest boats moored there. A nameplate riveted to its prow read *Roosje*.

He stepped on to the wooden planking leading along the side of the ship. 'This is Paul's place. Come on.'

The boat's main door stood ajar. Jeroen knocked on it, calling out a greeting in Dutch before descending the spiral staircase down into the spacious living quarters. Natasja met us at the bottom of the stairs, giving each of us a quick hug in turn. I hung back a little, cautious of her swollen belly.

'It's OK, Ben. I'm not going to pop.' She laughed. 'So glad the two of you could make it.'

'Are we the first to arrive?' Jeroen asked, handing Natasja a bottle of red wine.

'Not quite. Some of Paul's friends are already here. They're out on deck with him, if you'd like to join them there.'

Jeroen led the way, through the living room cum kitchen, up a short flight of steps into the wheelhouse, which still had its steering wheel in place. Behind the wheelhouse was a small area of deck where Paul, martini glass in hand, was talking to a group of half-a-dozen men and women, their ages ranging from early 20s to late 50s. He broke off as we approached, coming over to shake our hands and make the introductions. The oldest man was Natasja's father, the other guests being friends who worked on the paper alongside him, or so I gathered. Despite myself, I only had eyes for Jeroen.

Paul poured us both a glass of wine. 'I've never met anyone who lived on a boat before,' I said, accepting my drink from him. 'It's really impressive.'

'We were lucky to get it,' he admitted. 'As soon as they come on the market, they're gone. And this was a working boat only twenty years ago. It's over a hundred years old, and it used to travel along the rivers here and in Germany, taking cargoes of raw materials, coal and iron, down the Rhine. But the conversion job was beautiful. We really haven't had to do anything to it since we bought it. Go take a look round if you like.'

'Thank you, I will.'

Jeroen saw me leave. I suspected he wanted to follow, but he'd been pounced on by Paul's friends, eager to talk to the celebrated photographer.

Natasja was on her way up to the deck as I passed through the wheelhouse, along with a sober-suited man in his 50s – another of Paul's friends, I assumed, or maybe his boss. 'I hope you don't mind me poking around, but Paul invited me to have a look at the living quarters,' I explained.

'No problem,' she replied. 'And there's more wine in the kitchen when you're ready for it.'

'Lovely, thank you.'

Leaving behind the sounds of laughter and conversation coming from the deck, I took my time admiring Paul and Natasja's home. The bulk of the *Roosje*'s hull was fitted out with a small but well appointed kitchen at one end and a living room at the other, with a long, L-shaped leather couch running along the walls, surrounding a wooden stove with a funnel-shaped chimney to take away the smoke. I imagined it was a cosy place to cuddle up on cold winter nights, listening to the water lap against the side of the boat. There was a sound system with discreet speakers no bigger than my clenched fist, and a wide-screen TV, with a DVD player and what looked like a digital satellite receiver stacked beneath it. A bookcase ran along the other wall, packed mostly with Dutch translations of books by English and American authors. Looking more closely, I realised the couple liked their crime thrillers, as well as owning all the books in the Harry Potter series.

Built into the prow was their bedroom. I poked my head round the door briefly, not wanting to intrude on their privacy too much. Next to it stood the bathroom. Filled with green trailing plants and half-burned candles in iron holders, it had a round tub easily big enough for two people. I could see why Paul and Natasja had fallen in love with the boat. The place was a regular little love nest.

Making my way down a steep wooden staircase, I came to a second bedroom, with two narrow bunks and a small wardrobe, ideal for overnight guests. A cot stood in pieces against the wall, waiting to be assembled, and I realised when the baby was born, this would become its room. Hearing voices somewhere above me, I glanced up towards a skylight in the roof. Visible through the frosted glass were the feet of the party guests. No one seemed to be missing me.

Exploring further, I discovered a little en suite bathroom, its floor tiled in marble, fitted with an enclosed shower. Popping my head out of the bathroom porthole, I found myself looking directly at a small floating platform belonging to the neighbouring boat. With no gardens available to the people who lived on the water, these platforms acted as an effective substitute, covered with pot plants and ornaments, and with more than enough room to set up a deckchair or two on sunny days. I was admiring the display of busy lizzies and geraniums, starting to think I should maybe go back upstairs and help myself to another glass of wine as Natasja had suggested, when I felt strong hands grasp me around the waist. I shot upright, almost cracking my head on the lip of the porthole.

'Hey, careful there.' Jeroen laughed.

'Sorry, you startled me. I didn't hear you come down the stairs.'

'That's OK. I wondered where you'd disappeared to, and Natasja told me you were exploring the boat, so I thought I'd come and find you. We weren't boring you up there, were we?'

I shook my head. 'Not at all. I just know that if I'm around, people have to make the effort to speak English to include me in the conversation, and I didn't want to impose on everyone like that. Besides, I really wanted to have a nose around. I've seen boats like this moored on the canals in the city centre, and I always wondered what they were like on the inside.'

'And is it like you thought it would be?' Jeroen stood close enough that I could breathe in his distinctive lemon-scented cologne. I longed to push his wind-blown hair back from his face. But I was here as his companion for the evening, nothing more.

'It's amazing,' I replied at length. 'But I expected to feel more as though I was on the water. You notice it when a boat goes past outside, but apart from that, you could almost be on dry land.'

'You'd feel it more on a smaller boat. But down here it's so quiet, so private. You could do anything you wanted to, and no one would ever know ...'

Jeroen took a pace closer to me. My back rested against the cool, wood-panelled wall. My cock was rising in my pants. I wanted this man with a passion that almost drove the breath from me, but still something made me pause as he reached for the top button of my shirt.

'I thought this was purely a social event tonight,' I said.

'It was – at first. But seeing you again, I realised I wanted more than just that. I need to see that gorgeous body of yours again, get my hands on that big, hard cock. And, after all, I am paying for it ...'

As he spoke, he undid my shirt buttons. He kissed me, reacquainting himself with the feel of my mouth. I grabbed the back of his head and drew him to me, crushing his lips against mine. His desire was as fierce as my own, his hand fumbling with the waistband of my trousers. Arching my pelvis towards him, I aided him to pull them and my underwear down in one slightly jerky movement. Happy to be free, my cock sprang up to meet him.

'Oh, yes. Just as beautiful as I remembered.' Jeroen slithered down my body, till his head was level with my crotch. Holding my shaft by the root, he rolled it over his face, painting his smooth cheeks with my precome. It was one of the filthiest things any of my lovers had ever done, and I knew I'd remember him for that moment, even if we never saw each other again. He was clearly delighting in having my cock to play with. Grinning like a small boy about to taste his favourite lollipop, he popped my cockhead into his mouth.

Arms above my head, palms flat against the wall, I gave in to his oral onslaught. He sucked my dick as though he couldn't get enough of it, tongue swirling in sloppy figures of eight over the tip before flicking hard against the spot just below the head that was the key to my pleasure. It wouldn't take much to make me come; already I could feel the spunk churning in my nuts, ready for release. But we didn't have much time, despite all Jeroen's assurances of privacy. One missing guest could be overlooked for a while. Two might provoke a search party.

'So good, so very good.' Planting kisses all the way down to my balls and back, Jeroen paused for a moment, letting me catch my breath, before swallowing more of my shaft than before. His throat surrounded me like a velvet-lined vice. He knew exactly what he was doing, how much suction to apply to have me rising on my toes, preparing to spill my load. Did he know the trick with the ice cubes? If not, would I ever have the opportunity to demonstrate it to him?

Why worry about things you can't influence? I told myself sharply. Why not just enjoy this for what it is, one of the hottest quickies of your life? Jeroen cupped my balls, tickling them with his long, artistic fingers, and all my concerns evaporated. There was no longer room in my head to think about anything but the pleasure rushing through me. I bit the back of my hand so I wouldn't cry out, my come spurting out on to Jeroen's tongue. Slumping back against the wall, drained by the force of my climax, I murmured my gratitude to him.

My urge was to return the favour, to give him the same erotic thrills he'd given me, but Natasja's voice came floating down the stairs, accompanied by approaching footsteps, creaking on the old wooden treads. 'Jeroen? Ben? Are you OK down there?'

'Sure,' Jeroen replied, as I hastily pulled my trousers back up. 'I was just admiring the plumbing down here.' He winked at me, and it was all I could do not to burst out laughing at the outrageous double meaning.

By the time Natasja put her head round the bathroom door, I was respectably dressed once more.

'I'm just about to serve up the hot food,' she told us. 'I wouldn't want you to miss out. I really want Ben to try the bare bottoms in the grass.'

I gawped at her, wondering if I'd heard her right, and Jeroen burst out laughing.

'Don't worry, Ben,' he said, 'it's a traditional dish from the Noord-Brabant region. It's made from sausage, French beans and mashed potatoes. Very hearty, very filling. And I'm sure you must have quite an appetite ...'

Snatching up my wine glass, I followed Natasja and Jeroen up the stairs. He was right. I did have an appetite. But not for Natasja's home cooking, however tasty it might be. I was hungry for more of Jeroen's kisses, for the feel of his mouth on my cock. But unless he chose to hire me again, that wasn't likely to happen. I had to deal with the possibility that our unorthodox relationship might have run its course tonight. Summoning up a smile, I went to rejoin the party.

Chapter Six

ROBIN WAITED FOR ME in the lobby of the Hotel Pelikaan, his floppy blond locks and pouty features familiar to me from his website profile. He sipped a Coke through a straw, the perfect picture of barely legal innocence, even though I reckoned he was a good few years older than he looked. Marliese had told me the two of us were here to visit a man who liked to take the dominant role; a pretty young sub like Robin must be his dream come true.

'Hey, you must be Ben, right?' Robin rose to his feet, extending a hand to bump his fist against mine.

'I hope I haven't kept you waiting,' I said, looking at his almost empty glass.

He shook his head, draining the last of his drink with a noisy slurp. 'No, it's fine. I only live round the corner. I come here for a drink sometimes. The bar manager is a friend of mine.' From the way he grinned as he said it, I got the impression they were more than just friends.

The Pelikaan was at the budget end of the hotel scale. Close to the Artis zoo, its exterior needed a coat of paint and the furnishings in its lobby were faded and moth-eaten. A far cry indeed from the luxurious ambience of the Grand Plaza, or even the type of bland chain hotel aimed at the business traveller where I made most of my outcalls.

'So what did Marliese tell you about this guy?' I asked Robin, as we approached the reception desk.

'Enough. He's called Markus, he's German and he's a professional poker player. Oh, and he likes his boys two at a time. You brought the things he asked for?'

I nodded. Marliese had told me I'd need handcuffs and a

butt-plug, but the rest of my toys were stashed in my back pack, just in case the client decided he needed something extra to spice up the fun. It wouldn't be the first time I'd been asked whether I had a dildo with me mid-fuck, and I liked to be prepared.

Robin spoke to the desk clerk, a bespectacled, middle-aged man nearly as shabby as his surroundings, in rapid Dutch. The man glanced at me and I smiled. I heard Robin use the words "Engels" and "student". I didn't understand any of the rest of the sentence, but his explanation seemed to satisfy the clerk.

'*Dank u wel.*' Robin nodded his thanks to the clerk. 'OK, Ben, he's up on the fourth floor.'

The lift was out of order, which gave us plenty of time to chat as we climbed the stairs to Markus's room. Needing to satisfy my curiosity about my fellow escort, I asked, 'So how long have you been doing this?'

'Escort work? Oh, nearly four years now. I was never any good at exams, but there's always work for a guy who's good with his mouth, you know what I mean?' He winked at me.

'And you still enjoy it?'

'Sure. I get to work my own hours, and there's no way I'd earn the same kind of money waiting tables or pedalling tourists round the Grachtengordel in a cycle rickshaw.'

'Ever had any bad experiences?' I gestured to the threadbare carpet, the picture frames thick with dust. 'I mean, places like this aren't exactly salubrious. Do you never worry about who might be hiring you?'

'I trust Marliese. She has a sixth sense for weeding out time-wasters, or those who might turn dangerous. And guys like this Markus, they have the money, they just like it nice and sleazy. That's why they book into hotels like this to fuck boys. It's all part of the game.' He came to a halt before the door of Room 413, where Markus waited for us. 'Now, let's go see what he wants, shall we?'

He rapped on the door. A moment later, it was opened by a tall man with thinning blond hair, dressed in a black roll-neck jumper and black jeans. Handsome in a pale, severe kind of way. Markus eyed the two of us up and down, nodding in approval.

We'd barely got through the door before he ordered us both to strip down to our underwear. No small talk, no offer of a drink. It seemed he was one of those clients for whom the scene started the second you were inside his room.

In moments, Robin and I stood before him, in matching white briefs. A quick glance down told me Robin was getting hard in his underwear, as was I. Before I'd started working for Stud To Go, I'd never considered I might get off on being told what to do, but it seemed part of me never failed to respond once the guy I was with started barking out orders.

Markus came up close to us, squeezing Robin's cock through his briefs. 'Mm. Hung, just like the website said ... Hands on your head.' His tones were clipped, precise. He looked over at me. 'You too.'

We did as we were told. I watched as Markus pulled down Robin's briefs just far enough that his cock flopped out, resting on the bunched-up white material. Then it was my turn. Markus felt me up, assessing my dimensions. My excited cock jerked under his touch. 'And you are well hung, just as was promised.' He yanked down my underwear, just as he'd done with Robin.

'Now I can see what you both have to offer, but I need to know you are as obedient as you claim to be. Take hold of each other's cocks, and play with them.'

I hadn't been expecting that, but I didn't object. Robin was already grasping my length, running his slender fingers slowly up and down it. In return, I grabbed his fat, uncut dick. He might not have been quite able to compete with me in terms of inches, but he was thick. If he was in your mouth, or your arsehole, you'd certainly feel him stretching you wide.

Under Markus's unblinking gaze, we wanked each other, putting on a show that couldn't fail to turn him on. It was hard to tell how it was affecting him, though. His jeans were baggy enough at the crotch that we couldn't see if he was erect, and like all the best poker players, he'd trained himself not to reveal his emotions. His lack of reaction only added to the aura of control he radiated.

Eventually, he snapped, 'Enough. You have proved you

know how to obey. So get out the items I asked you to bring.'

I rummaged around in my back pack, bringing out my toys. Robin did the same. I couldn't help noticing the butt-plug he'd brought was considerably bigger than mine. Pretty certain what Markus intended to do with them, I was glad I'd plumped for one that was a sensible size for novices.

'You have lube also?' Markus asked.

Robin was the first to reply, bringing out a generously sized bottle from the depths of his bag. 'Yes, sir.'

'Very good. Come here.'

Clutching the lube and his plug, Robin got down on his knees before Markus, bowing his head. That little show of deference seemed to impress our temporary master. No wonder Robin got so much business. More naturally submissive than I was, he also knew exactly how to push the buttons of his dominant clients.

Markus smeared lube all over the bulb of the plug, getting it good and slippery. 'Present your arse, boy,' he ordered.

Robin did as he was told, getting on to all fours so his rump stuck up in the air. For the first time, I noticed he had a tattoo inked on his left buttock, a little red devil clutching a pitchfork. Markus didn't comment, simply got on with the task of probing Robin's arsehole with his well lubricated fingers.

'How easily you open up,' he commented, pushing a couple of fingers deep into Robin's rear passage. 'Your arsehole simply devours my fingers, and still there is room for more. What kind of slut are you?'

'Your slut, sir.' Robin battled to keep the excitement out of his voice as Markus fingered his arse. My cock was rigid. I'd never been part of a threesome before, never experienced the thrill that came from watching another man being played with so brazenly only feet away from me.

Markus eased his fingers from Robin's arse with an audible squelch. Grasping the pointed end of the butt-plug, he guided the monster-sized toy into Robin's relaxed hole. It took much less effort than I'd expected, and though Robin cried out at the penetration, there was far more pleasure than pain in his exclamation.

Once Robin's arse was securely pegged, Markus reached for the handcuffs. Unlike mine, they were made of solid, heavy steel, designed for serious use. I wouldn't have been at all surprised if they turned out to be genuine police issue. Hauling Robin up on to his knees, he pulled the boy's wrists behind his back before cuffing them. Robin's cock stood at full mast, and he gave me a cheeky wink when Markus wasn't looking, letting me know how much he'd enjoyed being placed in restraints.

'And now you.' Markus turned to me. Without being told, I adopted the same position Robin had, palms and knees flat against the floor. It didn't look as though the cleaner had run a vacuum over the thin, floral-patterned carpet today – or the day before, for that matter.

Nothing happened at first. I assumed Markus was studying the vision I presented to him, arse exposed, underwear still bunched beneath my cock. Then cool, lube-slick fingers ran along my bum crack, making me shudder with lust and anticipation. Pressing at my arsehole, Markus murmured, 'You are tighter than I expected, but I like that. Have you taken many cocks there, boy?'

'A few, sir,' I admitted, as his finger slipped inside me. I tried not to whimper as it pushed deeper, finding the hidden gland that brought so much pleasure when rubbed in the right way. Feeling Markus touch me there, I knew I might come without much more provocation. But I didn't think that was what he wanted. If the little I knew about dominant men proved accurate, our sexual release would be entirely at his discretion.

He pulled out, easing the tension, but the relief was only temporary. Something pushed at my arse again, bigger and more substantial than a finger. Markus had greased up the butt-plug. When I'd bought it, I'd never dreamed the first person who'd be taking it inside them would be me, but there was no turning back now. Bearing down against the intrusion, I felt it breach the ring of muscle guarding my arsehole.

'And now to cuff you.'

I got up on my knees, placing my wrists in the small of my back. Markus crossed one wrist over the other before securing the leather handcuffs in place. They were tight, but comfortable, though I hoped I wouldn't be wearing them for too long. He'd booked us both for a couple of hours, and that gave him plenty of time to have all the fun he wanted.

Unzipping his jeans, Markus brought out his cock, long and pale, its foreskin neatly trimmed away. 'You will suck it, taking turns,' he ordered us. 'The one who fails to make me come will feel the lash of my belt.' A cruel smile played across his lips. 'Of course, the one who does make me come will also feel the lash of my belt ...'

Robin said nothing, but the gleam in his eyes told me he approved of the rules of this game. Never having been beaten by anyone, apart from the odd playful spank to my arse, I was more apprehensive.

Markus came close, but not close enough that we didn't have to shuffle on our knees a little way across the carpet to where he stood. He presented his cock to Robin first, demanding to be sucked. Robin didn't hesitate, making an O of his lips and wrapping it around Markus's tight, purplish helmet. He sucked hard for a few moments, his throat working convulsively, before Markus abruptly pulled out and ordered me to take over.

If Markus intended this to be a battle of competing techniques, it was one I was determined to win. Unable to use my hands to aid in giving my master pleasure, I settled instead for long, expansive licks along his length, nuzzling my nose in the crisp fair hair at his crotch and breathing his musky scent. Like Robin, however, I'd barely got into my stride before my turn was over.

We continued like this for some time, sucking and licking, rolling his balls in our mouths, using any little trick we thought would bring on Markus's climax. He'd been clever, though. Not only did he have remarkable willpower, making us chop and change so often meant his excitement never really built to fever pitch. But no man can hold his orgasm off forever. As Robin sucked away, almost all of that considerable length buried in his talented throat, the German gave a strangled groan. Pulling his mouth off Markus's cock, Robin made a great show of licking traces from his lips. He smiled at me in triumph. I'd lost the challenge, and we both knew what that meant.

Markus uncuffed my wrists before throwing me face down on to the bed. He eased the butt-plug from my back passage, as if deciding it had tormented me long enough, and pulled my briefs all the way off. Rubbing the life back into my wrists, I watched in apprehension as he unbuckled his belt. Pulling it free of his trousers, he folded it in half, clutching the two ends in his fist.

'It was a good try, boy, but not good enough,' he told me. 'For that, you must face the loser's punishment. Four lashes of the belt.'

It didn't sound too bad, but as the first blow landed, I yelled as though I'd been sliced in two. Pain sizzled across my buttocks and I reached my hands behind me, rubbing my punished flesh to try to soothe the ache.

'Move your hands, boy,' Markus said. 'I'd hate to catch your fingers. Just think how that would sting.'

Obeying meant he'd whip my arse again, but I had to do it. The belt came down hard for a second time, parallel to the first stripe. Howling out my agony, I consoled myself with the fact there were only two more lashes to come.

Markus decided to apply those to the tops of my thighs, taking the pain to a whole new level. My erection wilted almost to nothing. Tears formed in my eyes and I blinked them back, telling myself I'd survived my first proper beating. My punishment over, Markus, in a sudden show of tenderness, took a pot of salve from his nightstand, applying it to the welts his belt had left.

'Arnica. It will soothe the ache and lessen the bruising. I wouldn't be surprised if that little slut friend of yours –' he glanced over at Robin '– doesn't carry around his own supply.'

Leaving me lying on the bed, he went over to Robin and unlocked his cuffs. Robin's posture was tense, expectant, more than ready to feel Markus's belt striping his body.

'So, do you think you were a worthy winner, slut?' Markus asked him.

'I aim to please, sir,' Robin replied cheekily.

'So cocky, even after everything,' Markus said, though it was clear Robin was telling him exactly what he wanted to hear, giving him every excuse to increase his punishment. 'Let's see if you still have that swagger after eight lashes.'

Robin wasn't fazed in the slightest. He stepped out of his underwear and took up a position bending over the end of the bed, backside thrust out. I couldn't help wondering how many times he'd done the very same thing, how many men had gazed, as Markus did now, at his taut young arse, ripe and ready for a beating.

Just like me, Robin yelled and screamed after every blow. I couldn't help thinking his cries were more theatrical than mine, that he was laying on the agony for the benefit of his client. It had to be hurting him, but I reckoned he was simply more used to the pain than I was.

By the time Markus had finished with him, his arse cheeks and thighs were marked with raised, sore-looking welts. Markus took his time applying the arnica cream, and I couldn't help noticing that a couple of times, his fingers strayed into the crack of Robin's butt, where the end of the plug still jutted out from his hole. He toyed with the plug, causing Robin to whimper, but didn't remove it.

'So, we are almost finished,' Markus observed. He seemed to have a better idea of how much time had passed than we did. 'Just one last thing. You looked so cute playing with each other before that I want you to do it again. Only this time you are allowed to make each other come.'

We didn't have long, but it didn't take long. Much to my surprise, my cock had revived watching Robin take his whipping, and I was more than ready for him to wrap his fingers round it and begin to wank. In return, I did the same, and together we worked to bring each other to a swift, panting orgasm. Under Markus's watchful gaze, Robin gave my dick the last few jerks that had my spunk jetting out over his fist. Dizzy with pleasure, I just about had the presence of mind to keep on stroking Robin's cock. Seconds behind me, he reached his own climax, the sensations no doubt heightened by the big rubber plug still packing his arse.

'Well done,' Markus said. 'And that will be all.' Just like that, the scene was over, and Markus, no longer the imperious master, was just another tourist renting a cheap Amsterdam hotel room.

Washing in the tiny sink in the en suite bathroom, dressing, collecting our scattered sex toys, Robin and I barely said a word to each other, still coming down from our joint high. Only once we'd said our farewells to Markus and left the room did we feel able to discuss the experience.

'Well, that was intense, for sure, but I think we made him happy,' Robin said as we took the four flights of stairs back down to the lobby. 'And I don't know about you, but I need a drink. Join me for one?'

'Sure,' I replied, expecting him to go straight to the hotel bar. Instead, he led me out of the hotel and round the corner, to a small, cosy brown café, so called because of the colour of its walls, stained by centuries of ingrained tobacco smoke. The tables outside, bedecked with yellow and white parasols, were already occupied, but we found a spot inside without difficulty.

As my backside made contact with the hard wooden chair, pain reawakened in my nerve-endings. I winced, and Robin grinned. 'Don't worry, it will ease soon. You took your beating very well, I have to say.'

'Thanks. It didn't feel like it at the time.'

He picked up a menu, giving it the kind of cursory glance that suggested he was familiar with his contents. 'The food here's delicious, and cheap.' He grinned at me. 'I can always tell when the sex has been good, because I have a hell of an appetite afterwards.'

A waitress came over to take our order. I had the urge for a Belgian *kriek* beer, with its sharp cherry taste. Robin asked for a blond beer, and the daily special, which turned out to be pork schnitzel in a mustard cream sauce, served with hand-cut chips and vegetables. It sounded so appetising I ordered a plateful for myself.

The food, when it arrived, was every bit as good as Robin claimed, and we ate in silence for a few minutes. Eventually, Robin said, 'So, Ben, you know my story. Tell me yours.'

'There's very little to tell, really. I lost my job, Edwin offered me work. I've been with Stud To Go for just over a month now.'

'And you like it?'

'Oh, yes. I didn't really know what I was letting myself in for, but I'm enjoying it a lot more than I ever thought I would. Markus took me into some new territory today, but you could probably tell that. But I might just have been lucky with the guys I've met.' I took a long swallow of my beer before continuing, 'Have you had any clients that just made you want to get the hell out of the room the minute you saw them?'

'No, like I said, Marliese helps take care of that. But the people who've seen my profile on the site, they know I'm a bottom when they ask for me, so I suppose I'm catering to a more specialised clientele. Not that I have a problem with that.' His face took on a serious expression for a moment. 'The only ones you have to look out for, Ben, are the ones who fall in love with you.'

'Does that happen often?'

'Fortunately not. But about a year ago, I was visiting this guy in Amstelveen. A businessman by the name of Geert. One of the best clients I ever had. He asked for me once a fortnight, at least, and he loved to spank my arse. It was good, at first, but then he started buying me presents. Body jewellery, bottles of liqueur, things he knew I'd like, but I always felt uncomfortable accepting them. It's really against the agency's rules, you know.'

I didn't know, but I made a mental note in case such a situation arose.

'Then one night,' Robin continued, 'we were lying in bed after he'd punished me, and he gave me this big speech about how much he loved me, and how he wanted me to move in with him. That's when I knew I had to call an end to the arrangement. I told Marliese if he ever called to request my services again, she was to tell him I wasn't available. And I've never seen him from that day to this.' He fixed me with his piercing blue eyes. 'Oh, I know it sounds cruel, but it was the only choice I had. I mean, how can it be love if you're paying for it?'

'What would happen if it was the other way round?' I asked.

'If you fell in love with a client?'

'I don't see it happening,' he said, stabbing at a spear of baby corn with his fork. 'I have a boyfriend, and he accepts completely this is how I earn my living, because he knows for me this is purely business, nothing more. But if I did, I'd have the same choice – him, or the agency. And unless he was really special, someone I absolutely knew I wanted to spend the rest of my life with, the agency would win out every time.'

Robin had given me plenty to think about as I beckoned the waitress over to order another round of beers. I couldn't admit it to him, or anyone, but the feelings I had for Jeroen Storm whenever I was in his company went way beyond a pure business arrangement. Though I didn't see myself ever facing the dilemma Robin described. I hadn't seen Jeroen since the night on Paul Robijns' boat, and unless he chose to request me via the agency, I had no idea when – or if – I was going to see him again.

Chapter Seven

LIGHTNING SCISSORED ACROSS THE sky, bright white against the heavy grey thunderclouds. The rain was torrential, hitting the cobbled pavements with such force it bounced back with a hard splash. When I'd woken that morning, the weather had been fine, not a hint of the oppressive heat that usually preceded a summer storm in the heart of the city. I'd set off for my regular jog in just a light T-shirt and sweat pants, and already I was soaked to the skin. Barely halfway home, dashing blindly along the canalside, head down as I tried to work out the quickest way back to my apartment, I didn't hear the voice calling to me at first.

'Hey, Ben! Ben, is that you?'

This time the words registered. I turned to see a familiar figure waving to me from a doorway. Without being aware of it, my zig-zagging route home had taken me down the Leliegracht, past the Storm Gallery.

'Come in,' Jeroen urged me. 'Get out of the rain.'

'Thanks,' I said, following him inside, my training shoes squelching on the polished wooden floor of the gallery.

'*Verdomme!*' *Damn it!* His favourite curse word, the one uttered at the height of his passion, in the moment before his orgasm hit him. 'You look like a drowned rat. Maybe you should have checked the weather forecast before you set out.' His smile was wicked as he led me through to the back of the gallery, into a small photographic studio. 'You're lucky I was here. My assistant, Lena, should have been running the gallery today, but the shoot I was supposed to be going on has been cancelled. Maybe it's just as well. I've been in London, Milan, Cape Town ... I've barely spent a night in my own bed all month.'

Maybe that explained why I hadn't heard from him. His work was simply keeping him too busy to think about anything else. It gave me hope to cling to that he might actually want to book me in the future. Running into him in these circumstances was an unexpected treat, even though I didn't think he'd be too happy about the fact I was dripping water all over the place.

'If you go through there, you'll find the changing room my models use,' Jeroen told me, pointing to a door. 'You'll find plenty of towels. And I have a pot of coffee on the go, if you'd like some?'

'I'd love a cup, thank you.'

The changing room was compact, with a wooden bench running along one wall, a well-lit make-up mirror and a white-tiled area at one end, a shower nozzle protruding from the wall. Towels were piled up on a shelf, as Jeroen had promised, with a laundry hamper beneath them. As I stripped out of my wet things, drenched right through to my underwear, and towelled down my naked body, I heard Jeroen bustling about on the other side of the door. When I emerged from the room, a towel fastened round my waist, he took my clothes from me before handing me an orange china mug bearing the legend "Hup Holland Hup". It was the catchphrase of the Dutch national football team, and I wondered how Jeroen had come by the mug. He didn't strike me as much of a football fan – but, thinking about it, there was so much I didn't actually know about him.

'I'll go and put your clothes in the dryer upstairs,' he said. 'It shouldn't take too long. I was going to invite you up there, but then I had an idea. I'll explain when I come back down.'

He left me standing at the back of the gallery while he disappeared up the open stairs that led to his apartment above. It gave me a few minutes to take a better look at the pictures adorning the walls. When I'd first taken a look through the window, my eye had been drawn to the photograph of the blond reaching into his open jeans, but another portrait quickly became my favourite. Shot in some tropical paradise, it was a perfect back view of a naked, dark-skinned man walking through long, fronded ferns, the globes of his arse cheeks so round and tempting I longed to lick them.

'Having fun there?' Jeroen asked, descending the staircase.

'I was just wondering where this was taken,' I replied.

'Aruba, in the Caribbean. It's part of the kingdom of the Netherlands, did you know that?'

I shook my head. 'It looks very beautiful.'

'It is. I've been over there on holiday a couple of times. The guy in the shot, Clyde, he runs a bar in Oranjestad, the main town. We just got talking one night and he agreed to pose. It didn't take much persuading for him to strip off for me. But then none of the men you see here is a professional model. It gives the photos a freshness, an integrity, don't you think?'

'To be honest, I just thought he had a superb arse.' Blushing, I sipped my coffee. 'So what was the idea you wanted to talk to me about?'

Jeroen took a perch on the corner of his desk. 'I told you I was in London recently. Well, I was there to see a publisher, who's very interested in putting out a book of my work. Some of it will involve my fashion and landscape shots, but the majority of it will be the photos you see in this exhibition.' He grinned. 'Nothing sells quite as well as my boys. But I would like to feature some new portraits, ones that have never been seen before. And I wondered – would you consider posing for me?'

'Me? Are you serious?'

'Why not? You don't have to show your face, if that's what you're worried about.'

'Oh, that's not a problem,' I assured him. The more I thought about it, the more I liked the idea of being immortalised by Jeroen's lens. My daily jogging sessions were starting to have an effect; my chest and arms were more toned than they'd been in a long time, my stomach flat and tight. I might never look this good again. Why shouldn't I show off the results of all my hard work? And with my clothes still whirling round in the dryer upstairs, I knew I wouldn't be going anywhere else for a while.

I put my mug down on the desk. 'OK, let's do this. Where

do you want me?'

'I thought back in the changing room. That towel has possibilities ...'

Jeroen grabbed one of the lights from the studio, setting it up in one corner of the changing room. Once that was done, I was surprised to see him load a roll of film into his camera.

'I thought everyone had gone digital these days?'

'It depends. I'm looking for a grainy effect on these photos, and the old-fashioned way is the best. Low light and a high ISO film. I could do it all with Photoshop, but it's really not the same.'

He might as well have been speaking Dutch for all I understood of the technique he planned to use, but he was the expert in these matters and I trusted him. The evidence of his expertise was hanging on the gallery walls for all to see.

'OK, so what I'm going to do is have you sitting on the bench, with the towel between your legs so that it only just covers up the places people really want to see. Are you happy with that?'

I nodded. Just the thought of almost revealing all to him caused my cock to surge, and I put my hands in front of myself, not wanting him to see how turned on I was. Unknotting the towel, I adjusted it the way Jeroen had asked, and sat down, the slatted bench cool against my bare backside.

'That's good, Ben, but I want you to spread your legs just a little wider, and bring the towel in just a little more ... Great, now hold it there and look into the lens. Right into the lens. Give me your most sensual expression.'

I did as he asked, following the camera with my head as he moved round me. The shutter clicked again and again. Jeroen had gone into professional mode, concentrating on nothing but trying to get the perfect shot, but I was getting hornier by the moment. My rigid cock pushed at the fluffy towelling, and when Jeroen asked me to put one foot up on the bench, I did so gingerly, afraid of letting the towel slip and revealing my hard-on in all its glory.

He paused when the roll of film ran out. 'OK, I have to go and reload this. When I come back, I want you lying on the bench, the towel beneath you, arse in the air.'

On his return, I'd adopted the pose he wanted, feeling more exposed but even more turned on. My cock, trapped between my body and the bench, ached for relief. What would he have done, I wondered, if he'd walked back in to find me lying on my back, cock in hand? Would he have photographed that too?

That pose didn't seem to work for him as well as the previous one had done, and after a handful of shots, he asked me to get up and walk over to the shower. 'Don't worry,' he said, 'you've already got wet once today. I just want to shoot you with your palms against the wall, looking over your shoulder.'

It was a simple enough request, but I knew when I rose from the bench, he couldn't fail to see my erection. Sitting up quickly, I did my best to cover my excitement with my hands. It didn't work. Jeroen's eyes were immediately drawn to my crotch.

'Take your hands away,' he ordered. 'Let me see that beautiful thing.'

I did as he asked. After all, it was hardly the first time he'd seen me like this, naked and aroused. But the other times had been business. This was something entirely different.

'So, you're getting off on this, hey?'

'I'm sorry,' I said. 'I just couldn't help it.'

'There's nothing to apologise for, Ben. Seeing you with only that tiny strip of towel between your legs turned me on too. See.' He took my hand, pressing it to the front of his trousers. Beneath the fabric, his cock was a solid bar, aching for my touch.

'Should we be doing this?' I asked, remembering Robin's assertion there were lines you didn't cross. Punters didn't become lovers, that wasn't how it worked. Strong as the attraction between us was, Jeroen and I shouldn't be operating outside the confines of our relationship as escort and client.

'You want me to ring the agency, tell them I'm booking you?' he replied.

I shook my head. 'No. I know that's how it's supposed to work, but I want to know what it's like to fuck you when you're not paying for it.'

Jeroen laughed. 'Surely it'll be just the same? Your cock, my arse. My mouth, your cock. Whichever way you want it.'

He kissed me, so much pent-up desire in the action I couldn't fail to respond. Nothing felt as good as being in Jeroen's arms, my lips mashed against his, my hard cock rubbing against his trouser-clad crotch. If a line had been crossed, I no longer cared.

Picking up where we'd been forced to leave off on the night of Paul's birthday party, I asked Jeroen to sit on the bench. I didn't ask him to undress, and he didn't make any move to start removing his clothes. Somehow, being completely naked while Jeroen was fully dressed made me feel as though he was the one in control, just as it had when Markus had dominated me and Robin. It wasn't something I needed all the time – I wasn't a born submissive like Robin, and usually, I enjoyed taking the lead with my clients – but for now, it suited perfectly the dynamic that had been building between us from the moment I'd stepped into the gallery.

Waiting expectantly, he spread his thighs, as though he'd guessed what I wanted to do to him. Wadding the towel on the floor between his legs, I knelt on it, tearing at his fly buttons in my haste to get at his cock.

Bringing it out into the cool air of the changing room, I took a moment to admire the long, smooth length once more. My mouth watered at the thought of sucking it.

Jeroen sighed as I engulfed his helmet. Remembering what I'd seen Robin do, I did my best to relax my throat, letting him lodge snugly there. For a moment I kept my head still, getting used to the feel of him buried deeper than I'd thought possible. Moving slowly, breathing through my nose, I treated him to the most sensuous blowjob I could manage. His fingers curled in my hair as he fought the urge to thrust. Even so, my sucking was clearly having a profound effect on him.

'Keep doing that, Ben, and I'll come in no time,' he warned me.

Tempting as that sounded, I had something else in mind. When Jeroen had outlined the things we could do to each other, he hadn't mentioned the one I really wanted to experience. His cock, plunging into my receptive arsehole.

I pulled my mouth off his dick, a long string of sticky saliva stretching out before breaking as I raised my head. It looked like a scene from the X-rated films some of my clients liked to watch while they waited for me to arrive. Occasionally, they kept them on while we were fucking, so they could view some well-hung stud getting his arse reamed even as I was doing exactly the same thing to them. Until I'd started this job, I'd never realised quite how much gay porn was available to view in even the most respectable-seeming hotels.

'Let's get you out of these clothes,' I murmured, grabbing one of Jeroen's slip-on shoes and pulling it off. I tossed it over my shoulder, before doing the same to the second. His socks followed, while Jeroen shrugged out of his jacket. Standing up, he let his trousers fall to the floor. Beneath them, he wore trunk-style underwear, patterned in hot pink and with the name of its designer, a former Swedish tennis champion, stitched into the waistband. He lost those in record time, letting his cock spring free beneath the hem of his white T-shirt. As he made to take that off too, I stopped him, a thought occurring to me.

'Do you have condoms?' In my role as an escort, I never travelled without them, but today I'd come unprepared, never thinking sex would be on the agenda when I'd left for my jog.

Jeroen flipped his wallet out of his trouser pocket, and extracted a foil packet, which he tossed to me. 'There you go.'

I shook my head. 'You're the one who's going to be wearing it.' My voice was husky with need. 'Do it, Jeroen. Fuck me with your big, gorgeous cock.'

He didn't need any more in the way of invitation. Spreading a couple of towels out on the floor, he told me to lie down on my back. I hadn't expected that, but it made sense. Making love face to face was more personal, more intimate. None of my clients cared whether we could stare into each other's eyes as we fucked. By placing me in this position, Jeroen was subtly reminding me that, just this once, he wasn't my client, and the usual etiquette didn't apply.

That didn't extend as far as relaxing my strict "no glove, no love" rule, of course. Watching as Jeroen rolled the condom into place, I stroked my own cock, anticipating the moment when that latex-clad length would slide into me.

He spat into his hand, using the saliva to lubricate my arsehole as he pushed a finger inside it. When I groaned in response, he asked, 'You like that?'

'I love it,' I told him, wriggling my arse against the bench as the finger wormed deeper. 'Love the feel of you opening me up. Getting me ready for your cock ...'

Until I'd started working for the agency, I'd never been a great one for talking dirty during sex. But my clients liked it. They loved it when I told them how big they were, how hard, how well they sucked me, even if none of it was true. It was all part of the boyfriend experience the agency liked us to provide. With Jeroen, though, I meant every word, and he was responding, adding a second finger to the first as he probed my depths.

Deciding I was ready for him, he climbed over me. Putting my arms round his neck, I brought his face down to mine so we could kiss. Between kisses, I told him how much I wanted him, how I was longing to feel his cock sliding into me.

Unable to restrain himself any longer, he entered me, gradually inching deeper as my arsehole relaxed around the thick, fleshy pole. The fit was perfect, as though he belonged there. Gazing into my eyes, Jeroen started to thrust; long, steady strokes that hit the sweet spot every time. Sweat glistened on his chest, his thick mane of hair falling into his eyes with every forward movement. He looked wild and magnificent. The changing room echoed with the grunts and gasps that signalled our mounting pleasure, my exhortations for him to fuck me harder and the slapping of his body against mine. The air was thick with the musky aroma of sex and sweat.

'Can't hold back,' Jeroen panted. 'Got to come.'

With one last hard shove into my arse, he came, the veins on his neck standing out, face twisted with fierce, beautiful ecstasy. It was the last thing I saw before I closed my eyes and surrendered to my own orgasm, hand clutched tight around my cock.

When I opened them again, Jeroen was smiling down at me. 'I don't know about you, but I needed that.' Rising to his feet, he wandered over to the shower and fiddled with the controls. Water gushed out, pattering against the tiled floor. 'Join me?'

How could I refuse a request like that? Stepping under the spray with him, we lathered each other with the citrus-scented gel that stood on a frosted glass shelf built into the corner of the shower. I didn't make any attempts to reach for Jeroen's cock. Tempting as it would have been to get him ready for another bout of sex, I couldn't keep him away from his business in the gallery any longer.

Towelling myself dry afterwards, I asked, 'So do I get to see the photos?'

'Sure,' he replied. 'I'll have them developed in the next couple of days. Drop by the gallery next time you're passing and I'll show them to you.'

He didn't ask for my phone number, or offer his. It might have been an oversight on his part, but I didn't think so. By denying me an easy way to make contact, he was keeping his distance, preventing me from getting too close. Perhaps it was just as well; after all, he'd told me he wasn't looking for anything permanent, and I didn't need to get into a relationship that might force me to get out of the escorting business before I'd found alternative employment. But as I walked along the Leliegracht in my freshly dried running clothes, heading for home, I couldn't help wishing Jeroen would forget about the way his ex had betrayed him, open up his heart and let me in.

Chapter Eight

MY PHONE SAT ON the living room table, where I'd left it before going for my jog. Checking it, I noticed a voicemail message waiting for me. Had someone at the agency tried to get hold of me while I'd been at Jeroen's?

Playing it back, I heard a voice I didn't recognise. 'Hello, Ben. This is Maarten Van Der Vaart at Primacom. We've received your application, and we'd be very interested in talking to you about the position of front end developer. If you could contact me to schedule an interview, I'd be grateful.'

Racking my brain, I tried to remember who Primacom were. I'd emailed out so many job applications and copies of my résumé over the last couple of months, it was hard to keep track of them all. Then it came to me. They put together websites for a number of high-profile clients in the Netherlands and abroad. My job, assuming they took me on, would be to check for bugs in the system and ensure those websites were as user-friendly as possible for people who weren't particularly computer literate. Friends of mine back in England who worked in the IT industry referred to the job scathingly as "making sure things look nice". I didn't care. It was the first interview I'd been offered, and much as I enjoyed working for Stud To Go, I wasn't destined to be a career escort like Robin.

Dialling the number Van Der Vaart had left me, I found myself being invited along for an interview the following morning. I couldn't help thinking as I scribbled down their address details that if I found myself in ordinary, nine-to-five employment once more, it might take away the stumbling blocks to having the kind of relationship with Jeroen I craved.

Primacom's premises were out on KNSM Island, in one of the restored warehouses Frank the driver had mentioned when he'd been recounting the history of the area's development. Occupying a section of the ground floor, it had a plate-glass frontage allowing passers-by to see through to the open-plan office beyond. Half-a-dozen people sat at computer terminals, engrossed in their work. It was surprisingly easy to picture myself as one of them.

Taking a deep breath, clutching the portfolio containing samples of my design work a little tighter, I pushed open the door. The receptionist greeted me with a flawless smile, taking my name. 'Ah, yes, Ben. Maarten is ready for you, if you'd like to follow me through.'

I'd been expecting a formal interview, but Maarten Van Der Vaart lounged on a low-slung sofa, rather than waiting for me behind a desk. Casually dressed in a loose burnt orange shirt over dark jeans, looking more like a junior member of staff than the head of the company, he rose to greet me.

'Nice to meet you. Would you like coffee?' When I nodded, he asked the receptionist, 'Sofie, could you get Ben a coffee, please? Milk and sugar, Ben?'

'Just milk, please.' Despite the relaxed surroundings, I was more nervous than I'd expected. Maarten had printed out a copy of my résumé, and he read it through quickly. 'Well, you certainly seem to have the technical skills we're looking for. You've worked extensively with HTML, CSS, Javascript, all good ... May I take a look at your portfolio?'

The rest of the interview passed in a blur. I felt as though I had answers to all the questions Maarten posed, from why I'd left my last job to what I thought I could bring to the team at Primacom, and he appeared to be impressed with the work in my portfolio. He outlined the salary and benefits package I'd receive should I get the job, which compared favourably to what I'd been earning in my old job at the design agency, and made it clear he thought I'd fit into the team of designers and developers already with the company. The more he told me about the job, the more I was certain I'd be happy working there, but I couldn't get my hopes up. I wasn't the only person chasing this position, by any means.

'Just one last question,' he said. 'If you were to be offered the job, would you have to give notice to another employer?'

I shook my head. 'I'm working for someone on a temporary basis at the moment,' I told him, choosing my words carefully, 'but they know I'm looking for something permanent. I'd pretty much be able to start here straight away.'

'OK, that's good to know.' Maarten's expression was neutral, giving nothing away. 'Well, Ben, I have another couple of applicants to see before I make my final decision, but I'll be in touch with you one way or another by this time next week.'

I stood up, easing myself out of the sofa's squashy embrace. 'Thanks very much.' We shook hands at the door, and I flashed a smile to Sofie the receptionist on my way out. Crossing my fingers that the next time I returned to the island, it would be as an employee of Primacom, I set off in the direction of the tram that would take me back into the city centre. The number 10 line ran straight round to the stop at Elandsgracht, a couple of minutes' walk from my apartment; it couldn't have been more convenient – particularly if, as I hoped, I would be making this journey on a daily basis.

Lost in my thoughts, I was startled to look up and see a familiar, heavily pregnant figure walking in my direction. Natasja Robijns, on her way back from the supermarket with a couple of bags of shopping.

'Hey, Ben,' she said, smiling at my approach. 'This is a nice surprise. What brings you out to the island?'

'Oh, I've just had a job interview. A company called Primacom, on the Veemkade.' Recalling our conversation the night I'd first met her, at the charity dinner, I added, 'Boring Internet stuff, you know the kind of thing.'

'How did it go?'

'As well as they ever can. Now I'll just have to wait to hear from them one way or the other.' Gesturing to her shopping, I asked, 'Do you need a hand with that? I could carry it back to the boat for you, if you like.'

She seemed about to refuse my offer, not wanting to be made a fuss of, then changed her mind. 'Thank you, that would be nice.'

We walked over the road bridge that led to the dockside where the *Roosje* was moored. At this time of day there was hardly anything in the way of traffic; just the odd car and a man pedalling earnestly past us on an elderly bicycle, a wooden cart carrying two cute blond children fastened to its rear.

'So how's Jeroen?' Natasja asked.

Knowing that as far as she was concerned, the two of us were a couple, I replied, 'Busy, as always. Travelling here, there and everywhere. I haven't seen half as much of him as I'd like.' That at least wasn't a lie. 'He had some good news on his book project, though. A publisher in London's said yes to it.'

'Oh, that's great news. He was telling us at the party how much the book means to him. Say hello to him from me – and if you're free, we'd love to have the two of you over for dinner some time.'

'Thanks, I'll be sure to let him know.'

By now, we'd reached the boat. I set the shopping bags down on the narrow pavement while Natasja hunted in her bag for her keys.

'Would you like to come in for a drink?' she asked. 'We don't have any coffee, I'm afraid – just the smell of it makes me feel nauseous at the moment. That's how I knew for sure I was pregnant.' She glanced ruefully down at her prominent belly. 'But I have jasmine tea, and fresh mint.'

One thing I'd learned from my time in the city was how much the Dutch loved their mint tea. The sight of it being carried to tables was a common one in almost every café; boiling water poured over a generous handful of mint leaves, served in a clear glass mug. The offer was a kind one, but I hesitated, not wanting to find myself getting deeper into conversation about Jeroen. That could get very complicated.

The ringing of my phone saved me from having to lie to her. Checking the display, I saw Marliese was trying to get hold of me. 'I'm sorry, Natasja, I'd love to, but duty calls. Some other time, I promise.'

Waving her goodbye, I answered the phone, taking the details from Marliese of a hotel visit close to the Rijksmuseum.

No toys, no BDSM demands, just another lonely businessman curious to sample one of my famous blowjobs, she told me. Assuring her I'd be there within the half-hour, I set off for the nearby tram stop at a brisk trot.

Waiting to hear back from Maarten at Primacom was agony. How many other candidates for the job did he have to see? Were they better qualified than me? Would the fact I was English, rather than Dutch, count against me?

Escort work should have distracted me from worrying about a situation that was out of my hands, but for once the phone remained stubbornly silent. Then there was the small matter of the naked photos Jeroen had taken of me. I changed my daily jogging route so it took me past his gallery on the Leliegracht, hoping to see him, but every time I passed, the blonde who I took to be his assistant, Lena, was sitting at the desk. Perhaps he was away on another shoot. With no other way of getting in touch with him, there was nothing I could do but watch and wait.

On the Saturday morning, going stir crazy in my little apartment, I decided to wander out and take in some of the sights. Up on the Noordermarkt was a weekly farmer's market, selling everything from cheese to flowers to fresh herbs and spices. Weaving my way through the busy stalls heaped high with fresh produce, I treated myself to a punnet of ripe strawberries and a tub of organic Japanese rice crackers. If I ended up snacking in front of the TV, listening out for a phone that refused to ring, at least I'd have something healthy to munch on.

As I debated whether to go for a drink in the inviting-looking brown café I'd passed on my way to the marketplace, I almost collided with the last person I'd expected to see here. It was Jeroen, clutching a paper bag from which the end of a rustic loaf protruded. He looked stunned and pale.

He muttered some words of apology, as though he hadn't realised who I was, and made to walk past me.

I caught his arm. 'Jeroen, are you OK?'

He stopped short, seeing me properly for the first time. 'Ben,

I'm sorry. I was somewhere else.'

'Yeah, I can tell that.' A woman pushing a small, grizzling child in a buggy was trying to manoeuvre her way around us. Stepping to one side to allow her to pass, I continued, 'I was just about to grab a beer. Why don't you let me buy you one? You look like you could use it.'

He ran a hand through his hair in distracted fashion. 'Why not? Lena's in charge of the gallery today; I don't need to get back there for a while.'

The café was crowded, but we found a table in the old-fashioned back room, all red plush furnishings, with paintings of local views adorning the walls. Once our drinks – wheat beer for me, a glass of red wine for Jeroen – had been brought to us, I said, 'So come on, tell me what's wrong.'

At first, Jeroen seemed reluctant to discuss the problem. Then, with a heavy sigh, he launched into his story. 'I came out to the market, like I often do on a Saturday. They have a baker that does the best artisan bread, you know? Well, I was queuing at one of the stalls, and who should walk past me but Ton.'

The dreaded ex. The man who'd broken Jeroen's heart and left him wary of getting involved with anyone else. But we'd all bumped into a former lover long after we'd split up; it didn't have to leave us feeling shell-shocked. There was obviously more to this tale.

Jeroen gulped his wine. 'He didn't notice me: he only had eyes for the guy he was with. They were laughing at something, and the way they looked at each other, I knew they were in love. And it tore me up inside, to see him so happy, so oblivious to everything. I thought I was getting over him, but ...'

His voice trailed away to nothing. Tears shone in his eyes. I'd never seen him looking so wretched, the cool, controlled façade he usually presented to the world shattered into pieces. Reaching out, I took his hand in mine.

'Don't upset yourself over him, Jeroen. He's obviously moved on. You need to do the same.'

'That's easy for you to say. You're not the one whose heart he broke.' Realising he'd spoken so loudly he'd attracted the attention of a middle-aged couple sitting at the neighbouring table, he lowered his voice. 'I loved Ton, and he betrayed me.'

'But that doesn't mean every man you meet is going to do the same. You know that.'

He nodded. 'You're right, of course you are. But right now, it seems so hard to believe.'

I drained the last of my beer. 'Then let me help you believe it. Come on, Jeroen, let's get out of here.'

When we left the café, I didn't consciously intend to take Jeroen home. But somehow, driven by an impulse to console him I couldn't control, I found myself leading him away from the bustling market. Taking a well-trodden route down the Westerstraat, past my local supermarket, we crossed over the canal to stand before my apartment building.

There had to be rules about letting clients into your home, but at that moment I wasn't thinking of Jeroen as someone who'd paid me for sex. He was someone I had feelings for, and he was in distress. All I wanted to do was comfort him.

At least the place was tidy. I'd had plenty of time to catch up on my chores over the last couple of days. But the apartment, with its white-painted walls and flat-pack furniture, was a million miles away from the stylish comfort of Jeroen's home, and he had to notice that. He didn't comment, simply made himself comfortable on the sofa while I went to hunt out the bottle of decent Merlot I knew lurked somewhere in my cupboards. It had been a birthday present from the staff of the design agency, and I'd been saving it for a special occasion. This seemed as good a time as any to open it.

I poured a glass for each of us, took them through to the living room. Jeroen was standing at the window, looking down on the canal below. *If you time it right,* I wanted to tell him, *you can look across the way and see two of the hottest guys you'll ever set eyes on fucking each other's brains out.*

Handing him his wine, I put a hand on his shoulder. The stiffness in his muscles was all too apparent beneath his olive T-shirt.

'What you need,' I told him, 'is a back rub.'

He didn't make any objection as I set down my glass, kneading his shoulders with my fingers. Pressing my thumbs hard into the places where the tension lurked, I worried at the tight knots and, gradually, they loosened. Jeroen began to relax into my touch. 'Mmm, that's good,' he murmured, between sips of wine.

'I can make it better. There's massage oil in the bedroom.'

He needed very little persuasion to follow me, kicking off his shoes and removing his T-shirt before lying face down on the bed. The oil, cinnamon scented, was a recent addition to my escort's box of tricks, designed to help those clients who were stricken with pre-sex nerves. I warmed a little between my palms before massaging Jeroen's shoulders with slow, firm strokes.

'You have magic fingers, Ben.' He sighed in bliss as my hands moved downwards, finding another pocket of tension in his lower back and working to release it.

'OK,' I said eventually, judging I'd done as much as I could to ease his stress. 'You can sit up now.'

'That might be a bit of a problem.'

I didn't understand what Jeroen was driving at, until he rolled over and I noticed the prominent swelling at the crotch of his jeans.

'Maybe we should do something about that too ...'

Jeroen made no objection as I undid his fly. His cock, when I took hold of it, was rigid, primed for release. Between the two of us, we stripped him the rest of the way.

'Now you,' he urged. 'Get naked for me.'

I didn't bother with a slow, teasing strip. This wasn't about seduction, just the mutual satisfaction of a lust we couldn't deny. He kept his hand away from his erection as I shed my clothes, reserving the pleasure of stroking that delicious length for me.

Naked, I joined Jeroen on the bed. He lay back and let me go to work on him. My oily fingers closed round his cock, moving smoothly up and down. On every upstroke I gave a slow twist, my signature move whenever I wanked off a client. Subconsciously, I was trying to imprint myself on his mind, doing my best to make him forget about Ton – and every man who'd gone before him – if only for a little while.

It was working. Jeroen had recaptured some of his usual vitality, the fire in his eyes I found so exciting. Pushing me on to my side, he reached for my dick. Using two hands to wank me, he rolled my shaft gently between his fingers, like dough. I lost my grip on his shaft, overwhelmed by the sensations that shot through me at his touch. For all the tricks I had up my sleeve when it came to giving a good handjob, it seemed Jeroen could match them with one or two of his own. He kept on pumping me, the spunk churning in my balls, seeking release.

'If you keep doing that, I'm going to come,' I warned him.

'Then come for me, Ben. Because once you have, I'm going to roll you over and fuck your tight arse till you scream ...'

The twisting, teasing pressure of his fingers was impossible to fight against. Calling out his name, I jerked my hips hard as I came, come shooting out over Jeroen's two fists. With a smile of pure satisfaction, he guided me on to my belly. I lay, panting and expectant.

He must have picked up the bottle of lube from my bedside table, because the next thing I felt was cool, thick gel being squeezed into my butt crack. Jeroen smeared it into my hole, opening me with quick jabs of his fingers. I thrust my arse back at him, wanting to feel those fingers deeper inside me, hitting the secret seat of my pleasure. Even though I'd come so recently, I still hungered for more.

'Take me, Jeroen,' I begged, needing to be fucked with all the ferocity he'd promised. When he withdrew his fingers and nothing happened, I looked over my shoulder, about to berate him. Instead, I saw him fitting a condom over his cock, one of the ribbed ones I'd bought a couple of days ago with the intention of giving my clients extra stimulation when I penetrated them. As with my trusty butt-plug, I never thought the first person who'd sample one of those condoms in action would be me.

When Jeroen shoved into me, I knew I was in for the fucking of my life. All the hurt, all the anger he'd felt at seeing his ex so settled and happy was being channelled into the hard-driving strokes with which he pounded my arse. Being used in this way roused me to even greater heights of passion, and soon I was responding to every thrust with a cry of, 'Yes! Fuck, yes!' He couldn't fail to know how much I relished the feel of that big cock, sheathed in dimpled latex, possessing me completely.

His big body shunted mine along the mattress with every thrust. Somehow, I'd lost the power to form the words to urge him on, and now there were no sounds but our harsh grunts and gasps, coupled with the squeaking and rattling of the bedsprings. The headboard slammed against the wall, marking rhythmic time as we fucked. Jeroen slapped my arse cheek hard, the handprint he left in his wake branding me as his. It was his last coherent act before, sweating, heaving, letting loose all his inner demons, he came deep in my arse.

Rolling over so I was on top, I gazed into Jeroen's eyes, brushing his tangled hair away from his face. At that moment, I felt so close to him, so sure of his affections I couldn't prevent the words slipping out. 'God, Jeroen, I love you.'

Beneath me, he stiffened, pulling away from my embrace. 'Don't say that, Ben. Don't ever say that.'

I sat up, hugging my knees to my chest as I watched him pick his clothes up from the floor and begin to dress. What kind of mistake had I made by confessing my feelings for him? 'But you must feel it too. I've never made a connection to anyone like the one I have with you. Being with you – it just feels right, you know?'

'Well, maybe you should bury those feelings, because I don't think anything's going to work out between us. You're a great guy, Ben, and I really enjoy being around you. And the sex is superb ...' He pulled his T-shirt over his head. 'But you're an escort.'

'That doesn't seem to have caused you much of a problem until now.' Thinking of Robin, I added, 'And there are plenty of escorts who are in healthy relationships.'

'I don't think there's anything wrong with how you choose to earn your living, Ben.' He shrugged. 'What kind of hypocrite would I be if I did? But if I'm in a relationship, I want it to be an exclusive one. I wouldn't want to share you with anyone else. And how could that happen, when other men were paying you for sex?'

Fully dressed now, he made his way to the door. Slipping into a pair of jogging bottoms, I followed him.

'What if I had another job, working in IT, just like I used to?' I didn't mention my interview with Primacom, not wanting to jinx my chances of landing the post, but I had to know what my options were, whether there was any chance at all of our getting together.

'Then it might be different,' he admitted. 'But I know you enjoy what you do now, and I couldn't ask you to give it up for me.' He paused, hand on the doorknob. 'Maybe it's better if I don't book you again. We've had a great time, and I won't ever forget about you, but now I think it's over.'

'But Jeroen ...'

He shook his head sadly and left without another word, not looking back once as he headed for the stairs.

I fought the urge to run to the balcony and watch for him to emerge from the front door. He'd made his feelings clear, and shouting after him, begging him to come back, wouldn't change his mind. Slumping on the sofa, I wondered how I could have been so stupid. I'd found the special someone I'd been looking for since I first moved to Amsterdam, the man I wanted to give myself to heart and soul, and by uttering those three little words I'd blown any chance of making that happen.

Chapter Nine

THEY SAY THE BEST way to get over your last man is to get under the next one, and work offered me the opportunity to do just that. After several days when no one required my services, it seemed I was flavour of the month once more. A telecommunications trade show was being held at the RAI, the big exhibition and conference centre in the south of Amsterdam, and that type of event always provides rich pickings for escort agencies. Every night I found myself down on my knees in some hotel room or other, sucking the cock of a businessman with time on his hands and a desire to explore his bisexual side.

Trying not to think about Jeroen while I serviced my clients was difficult. I still couldn't believe I'd blurted out my feelings to him with no thought of the consequences, but love makes you do irrational things. I thought I'd broken through the barriers he'd placed round his heart, but he'd made his position perfectly clear, and nothing I could do would change his mind. Telling myself we were the right combination, we'd simply met at the wrong time, helped, but it didn't fully heal the pain I felt at watching him walk out of my life.

Laura couldn't understand why I stifled a laugh when she gave me the details of my next booking. We'd never developed the easy bantering relationship I shared with Marliese, partly because her English wasn't so fluent and she didn't get my jokes, but mostly because pink-haired, filthy-minded Marliese was a glorious one-off.

'Is there a problem, Ben?' Laura asked.

'Not at all. It's just that you're sending me to a client on the canal where I live, and I just wondered which of my neighbours is in the mood for sex.'

'So I can tell them to expect you within the next twenty minutes?'

'Absolutely. Thanks, Laura.'

The address I'd scribbled down proved to be closer to home than I thought. Crossing over the canal and following the street numbers, I realised I'd been booked by someone in the apartment block opposite my own. Now, this really was a bizarre coincidence.

I pressed the buzzer marked 5A. '*Hallo?*' a voice answered.

'Hi, is that Rick? It's Ben, from Stud To Go.' Even after all this time, I still felt as though I should be standing on the doorstep clutching a pizza in a flat cardboard box.

'Hey, Ben, come on up.'

The door release clicked open, and I climbed the stairs to the top floor. A faint smell of floor polish haunted the stairwell, and music and laughter came from behind a closed door, the sounds of someone kicking back and relaxing after a hard week at work. My destination was the apartment opposite. I knocked, and waited.

When the door opened, I tried to keep the surprise from my face. I knew this guy, with his dark skin and braided hair. Not too long ago – although it felt like another lifetime after everything that had happened since – I'd stood on my balcony and watched him strip out of trunks not unlike the pair he wore now, before treating himself to a slow handjob.

'That was quick,' he said. Clearly, he didn't recognise me. 'The agency said twenty minutes, so I thought that'll be half an hour at least …'

'Oh, I was in the area. But we do pride ourselves on a swift service.'

'Maybe not that swift, hey?' Rick grinned as he led me into the apartment. The sweetish reek lingering in the air indicated he'd been smoking a joint not too long before I arrived. Maybe that had put him in the mood for a fuck.

But where, I couldn't help wondering, was his lover? The strawberry blond with the enormous cock? Spying on them, I'd gained the impression the two were very much a couple.

Unless, of course, he was an escort too, skilled in offering the full boyfriend experience. Though if so, he wasn't among the guys on Stud To Go's books.

'So, would you like me in the bedroom, or –?'

'All in good time,' Rick replied, taking a seat on the arm of his sofa. 'First, I need to explain to you about the set-up.'

Set-up? Laura hadn't mentioned anything out of the ordinary when she'd given me the booking details. What had I missed? Fortunately, I had my toys with me, as always, but if Rick wanted anything unusual, I wasn't prepared.

'We've been discussing this for a while now,' he continued.

'We?' This situation grew stranger by the minute.

'My boyfriend, Piet, and me. This has been a fantasy of his for a long time, and tonight I decided I'd make it happen for him, seeing as it's our anniversary. He'd have come out to greet you, but he's a little – er – tied up at the moment.'

The grin Rick flashed me made the penny drop. At once, I knew what – or who – I'd find waiting for me in the bedroom.

'Well, why don't you take me to him? I'm sure he'll be more than ready for us by now.'

When we walked into the bedroom, I realised Rick had been busy while he waited for me to arrive. Piet, naked except for a pair of grey briefs that clung to his rapidly uncoiling dick, sat on a high-backed chair. His arms were bound behind him with a length of white rope. Similar ropes fastened each of his ankles to the legs of the chair. Horny and helpless, he was a delicious sight. Whatever his fantasy involved, I couldn't wait to fulfil it.

'See, I told you I'd find someone else,' Rick sneered at him, and I realised we'd moved straight into their pre-arranged scene. 'Someone who really knows how to fuck me. How's it going to feel, to watch me coming on another man's cock?'

Piet wriggled in his bonds, but the humiliating words appeared designed to turn him on. His cock pushed against his underwear, desperate to be free. Rick ignored him, pulling me into an embrace.

He kissed me, pushing his tongue into my mouth. His mouth tasted of breath mints, and the kisses were showy, for Piet's benefit, but I responded with passion. My fingers twined in

Rick's braids, pulling his face closer to mine, and my groin pressed against his, making him aware of my arousal. If this kinky couple wanted a performance from me, I was more than prepared to give them one.

Rick pushed me down to the bed, grabbing my belt. With almost indecent haste, he stripped me out of my trousers, while I kicked off my trainers.

His fingers traced the outline of my cock, all too visible in my white underwear. 'Look at that, Piet. Look how big and hard it is. That's going to feel so good sliding up into my arse ...'

He bent his head, mouthing my erection through the cotton. The groan I gave as his tongue flickered over my cockhead was echoed by Piet's, my lust mingling with his frustration. He had to know just how good it felt to be the focus of Rick's oral manipulation, and having to look without being able to join in, or enjoy his share of this sustained erotic attention, must be torment for him. Which, I guessed, was exactly the way he wanted it to be.

'Let's get you out of these.' Rick eased down my saturated briefs as I raised my hips from the bed to make his task simpler. Going over to Piet, he waved my underwear under his bound lover's nose. 'What do you think?' he asked. 'Should I gag you with these, so I don't have to listen to you moaning while I'm being fucked?'

'Please, no,' Piet replied, in a tone implying the exact opposite.

Rick just laughed, and tossed the wet garment into Piet's lap. Then he pulled down his trunks, letting both Piet and me feast on the mouth watering sight of his naked body, muscles hard and sculpted to perfection. Returning to me, he lay face down on the bed, presenting me with his gorgeous arse.

'I'm all yours,' he told me. 'Fuck me any way you want to.'

Aware of Piet's eyes following my every action, I covered Rick's taut black buttocks with soft kisses. 'Yeah, that's nice,' he murmured, as my kisses became licks, broad sweeps of my tongue that worked their way into the dark cleft between his cheeks. When I lapped at his furled arsehole, he begged for more.

'Do you like that?' I asked, breaking off from what I was doing. 'Does that turn you on?'

'Oh, yeah. Love having my arse licked. I only wish Piet would do it more often.'

From his tone, I realised that wasn't part of the scene, but a genuine request on Rick's behalf. Glancing over at Piet, I saw the words had hit home, and suspected from now on rimming would become a bigger part of the man's sexual repertoire.

My backpack lay on the floor. Delving into it, I brought out my dildo. Greasing it with lube, I pressed it at the entrance to Rick's arse. With a twist of my wrist, I pushed it home. His eyes widened at the feel of the thick, veined shaft slipping into him with surprising ease. I hadn't planned to use the toy on him, but sometimes spontaneous gestures are the best. Piet was enjoying the sight of his lover being fucked with the dildo, that much was certain.

'Oh, yes,' he crooned, 'give to him hard. Shaft his arse with that thing.'

Fixing him with my sternest look, I ordered him, 'Be quiet, or when it comes out of his arse, it goes in your mouth.'

Piet whimpered with pleasure at my show of dominance, and for a moment I thought he was going to come in his pants. Turning away from him, I continued to thrust the dildo in and out of Rick's hole. The planes of his back were sheened with sweat, and he ground himself against the mattress.

'Need you inside me,' he muttered. 'Toys are good, but the real thing's the best.'

Happy to oblige, I fitted myself with a condom, leaving the dildo lodged rudely in place. Rick raised himself on one hip, fisting his dick while he waited for me. When I was ready, I removed the toy, replacing it with the head of my cock. Buried deep in Rick's arse, I looked across to Piet, to see how he was reacting to his first glimpse of his fantasy coming true. Muscles straining with the effort, he was inching the chair closer to the bed, so he could get a better look at my cock plugging his lover's arse.

'Go on,' he urged me, 'give his arse a good pounding. He likes it rough.'

That was no lie. The harder I slammed my cock into Rick's clutching passage, the more vigorously he responded. Our bodies slapped together, the bed rocking beneath us. Driven to bring him to a climax neither he nor Piet would ever forget, I grabbed his cock, tugging it as the pace of my thrusts moved up a gear.

'God, Rick,' Piet murmured, 'if only you could have the view I do now. You look amazing on the end of his dick, baby ...'

His mouth was still moving, but I couldn't hear the words any more. The blood was singing in my ears, nerves growing taut in the build-up to my orgasm. I sensed Rick was close too, his breath coming in rasping grunts. Putting everything I had into the last few thrusts, I let loose with a flood of come, filling the condom. Rick howled out Piet's name, his arse gripping my shaft tight as he came.

Spent, I pulled free. Now I'd fucked Rick, was the scene over, or did he have more torment in mind for poor frustrated Piet?

Propping himself up on one elbow, Rick answered my unspoken question. 'That was great, Ben, everything we hoped it would be, but if you don't mind, I'd like to take things from here ...'

'Sure.' Dropping the used dildo into my back pack, I gathered my discarded clothes and went into the living room to dress. The last thing I saw was Rick snapping the elastic on Piet's underwear, tearing the skimpy briefs in two in his haste to get his hands on the monster cock I'd never had the opportunity to sample.

I couldn't help but envy their happiness. Would I ever find myself in a relationship like theirs, so secure in my love for my partner that I was able to help them fulfil their most cherished fantasies, even if they involved bringing another person into the bedroom?

Letting myself out of the apartment as quietly as possible, I trudged back home. Tempting as it would be to spy on Piet and Rick from my balcony, the two deserved to continue their anniversary celebrations in private. I needed a shower, my T-shirt sticking to my back with sweat. After that, all I wanted to do was fall asleep in front of the TV.

Barely had I let myself in through the door when my phone rang. If it was Laura ringing with another booking for me, I'd have to tell her I was sorry, but I couldn't manage it. Not tonight, not after all the effort I'd put into fucking Rick.

Instead, a man's voice said, 'Ben? How are you? I hope I haven't caught you at an inconvenient time. This is Maarten Van Der Vaart at Primacom.'

Chapter Ten

SO THIS WAS HOW my week was destined to end, with the news I hadn't got the job I'd so badly wanted. Why else would Maarten be calling me so late? He'd no doubt already rung to congratulate the successful applicant. Still, what else could I have expected?

Sitting down, bracing myself for the disappointment, I said, 'Hi, Maarten. What can I do for you?'

'I'm sorry for not getting in touch with you sooner, but I've been in meetings all day. I just wanted to welcome you as the newest member of the Primacom team. Congratulations, Ben.'

It took a moment for what he'd said to sink in. 'I got the job? Seriously? Thanks, that's fantastic news.'

'Well, it wasn't a difficult choice in the end. You were head and shoulders above the other candidates,' Maarten admitted. 'Now, I remember at the interview you saying something about not having to give much in the way of notice. We'd like to have you on board as soon as possible. Is there any chance at all of you being able to start next week?'

'I should be able to come in on Monday, if that's OK with you?' It would mean making a phone call to Edwin, but I wouldn't be able to do that straight away. It was Friday night, after all, and that meant he'd be at Homme, or one of the nearby clubs like Pleasure Parade, looking out for the next potential recruit to his stable of escorts. He wouldn't be happy that I was leaving the agency, but I knew he'd understand.

'That's perfect. We'll see you then.'

I could hardly keep the smile from my face. It was such a relief to learn all my pessimism had been misplaced. If only I could share my good fortune with Jeroen.

* * *

Edwin, when I finally spoke to him, was every bit as sympathetic as I'd hoped. At his request, I went over to the Stud To Go office to meet him, so he could carry out an exit interview – or so he claimed. If the look she gave me when I walked through the door was anything to go by, it was actually so Marliese could say goodbye to me.

'I'm sorry to see you go, Ben,' Edwin said, regarding me from the other side of his cluttered desk. 'You've been hard working, reliable and the girls have said how easy you are to deal with. It's a pity the real world beckons, but that's the way it goes, hey?'

I laughed. 'Well, I've really enjoyed it. More than I ever thought I would.' And I had so many memories to look back on, so many men whose desires I'd helped to fulfil. Dominant Markus, thrashing me with his belt while Robin looked on, awaiting his turn. Greg Parsons the Texan, lying back and letting me suck him off with a mouthful of ice cubes. Rick and Piet, a committed couple using my presence to act out their fantasies of frustration and voyeurism.

'And you know there's always a place for you here should you ever want to come back?'

'Of course. Thanks, Edwin.'

He came round to my side of the desk, and we shook hands. As much as I was looking forward to starting my new job and getting back into the sector for which I'd trained, part of me was going to miss my regular interaction with the team here.

Marliese rose from her seat as I emerged from Edwin's office. Normally such a tough old broad, tears glistened in her eyes and her voice cracked as she bid me farewell. 'Look after yourself, Ben. I'm going to miss you.'

'This doesn't have to be goodbye,' I assured her. 'Maybe when I've been settled into my job for a few weeks, we could go for a drink or something?'

'Sure, I'd like that.'

I pecked her on the lips, and she hugged me tight. The people I'd considered my friends at the design agency had melted away when the going had got tough, but I had the feeling Marliese would hold me to my promise to keep in contact.

Stepping out on to the pavement, busy with Saturday morning shoppers making their way to the flower market, I couldn't help feeling there was still one loose end to be tied up. Much as I'd tried, I couldn't stop thinking about Jeroen. We'd parted on such bad terms, and I longed to be able to put things right between us.

Turning back on my tracks, I walked along the Singel canal, in the direction of the Leliegracht. Not really holding out any hope of seeing Jeroen, my heart lurched when I stared through the gallery window and spotted him at his desk, in conversation with a smartly dressed red-haired woman.

He didn't glance up as the door chimes announced my entrance. As I neared the desk I heard him saying, 'And it will be an extra thirty euros to have it framed.'

Pretending to study the photos on his walls, even though he'd added nothing new to the display since the afternoon I'd posed for him, I waited till he'd finished his business with the redhead. Once she'd left the gallery, I approached the desk.

'Good morning, Jeroen.'

'Ben, what are you doing here?' His tone was chilly, guarded.

'Oh, I just happened to be passing, and it occurred to me I never saw those photos you took of me. I just wondered how they turned out.'

He appeared to be debating whether or not he should ask me to leave the gallery, and I started to think it might have been a mistake coming here. Then he said, 'Where are my manners? Of course you should see them. Just wait there a moment ...'

He went into the studio, emerging after a minute or so with a portfolio under his arm.

'Here you go.' He spread the photos out on the desk, letting me take a look. Pointing to one, he said, 'This is the one I'll be including in the book.'

It was one of the first batch of shots he'd taken, where I'd sat on the bench with the towel draped between my legs, only just covering the bulk of my cock. Only the two of us knew just how turned on I'd been as the camera clicked away. My eyes weren't drawn to my barely concealed crotch but my face. With half-lidded eyes and pouting lower lip, it was a study in desire. Desire for Jeroen.

'Wow, what can I say? This is amazing. I look like a model.'

Jeroen shook his head. 'No, Ben, you look like you. The camera holds a mirror to the truth, after all. How the viewer chooses to interpret that truth is up to them.' Putting the glossy black-and-white shots back in the portfolio, he asked, 'Was there anything else?'

No one had entered the gallery while we'd been talking. I wasn't taking his attention away from any potential customers, so I added, 'Yes. I got a new job. I start on Monday.'

'Really?' Despite the lingering frostiness, his smile was genuine. 'Congratulations. I know how much you wanted to get back into your old line of business.'

'The company is based on KNSM Island. Would you believe I bumped into Natasja Robijns when I went for the interview? She says hello, by the way, and she's delighted your book got accepted.'

'Thanks for passing that on.' A half-smile crossed Jeroen's face and I wondered if, just for a moment, he was thinking back to the party on the *Roosje*, the fun we'd had while Natasja and her husband entertained their other guests, little knowing that below decks I was half-naked, my cock in his mouth.

That smile gave me the courage to blurt out, 'Jeroen, I'm really sorry.'

'Sorry? For what?'

'The last time we were together, I know I came on way too strong. I shouldn't have, but I meant what I said. I love you.'

He paused in the act of zipping up the portfolio, posture stiffening. 'You seem pretty sure about that. I mean, you hardly know me.'

'But what I do know – Jeroen – is that I've never felt about anyone the way I do about you. You're handsome, talented, intelligent, and the only person who can't see how incredible you are is you.'

He was still staring at me, but his expression had softened

slightly. There had to be something I could say that would convince him I was sincere, and persuade him to lower his defences.

'The last time we were together,' I continued, 'you said you wanted an exclusive relationship. Well, now I'm going to be giving up the escort work, we can have that. And I know what happened with you and Ton, but if you keep letting that eat away at you, you could find yourself missing out on something really special.'

Jeroen put his hand on mine. 'You're really persuasive, you know that? But if – and I'm not guaranteeing anything here – we're going to have a future together, I need to take things slowly. I don't just fall in love at the drop of a hat, you know.'

'Slowly's fine by me,' I assured him, prepared to do whatever it took to make Jeroen part of my life, now and for as long as he wanted me.

'The truth is, Ben, I really like you. I have right from the start, more than I thought I ought to like someone whose company I was paying for, and that made me uncomfortable. But maybe you're right. Maybe I would be missing out if I let you walk out of my life.'

'Damn right you would ...' Tension was building between us, just as it always did when we were alone together. Tension that could only be shattered by my pressing my lips to his in a slow, melting kiss.

His tongue twined with mine as he cupped my face in his hands. Our breathing deepened, and my cock rose in my underwear, responding to the taste and scent of my gorgeous Jeroen.

He broke the kiss, panting and dishevelled. 'There's something I have to do before this goes any further.'

Wondering what he meant, I chuckled as he turned the sign on the gallery door to "GESLOTEN". *Closed.* Obviously some things were worth missing out on a sale for, I thought, as he rejoined me.

Pressing me up against the wall, kissing me with more fire, he tugged at my fly, beginning the process of stripping me. A process that started in the gallery and ended in his bedroom, leaving a trail of clothes strewn all the way up the stairs in his haste to see me naked. As he reached into my shorts, closing his hand around my rock-hard shaft, I knew that despite what I'd told him, I hadn't given up my escort duties entirely, even if I wouldn't be doing them for a living. From now on, I intended to devote myself to escorting Jeroen to bliss.

LAYOVER

Chapter One

THEY WERE MAKING OUT under the blanket. Oh, they were trying to be discreet about it, not wanting to draw attention to themselves, but Cal had been around long enough to know when a couple had got the hots for each other mid-flight. Give it enough time and they'd probably sneak off to the toilets to join the Mile High Club, but for now those subtle strokes under the blanket seemed to be keeping their desire on a steady simmer.

Every flight attendant had a story to tell about sex at thirty thousand feet, of muffled gasps and groans coming from behind a locked toilet door. Usually, the couple in question were travelling together, but it wasn't unknown for complete strangers to be overcome by a bout of transatlantic lust and feel the need to consummate it then and there. Even members of the crew weren't immune: Judy, currently serving refreshments to the passengers back in economy class, claimed she'd once enjoyed a mid-air fuck with a Swedish businessman on a flight from Heathrow to Stockholm.

Cal noticed the blond half of the couple bite the back of his hand, trying to stifle his cries as his excitement mounted. His lover's hand shifted back and forth beneath the blanket, tugging at what had to be a pretty big cock if the length of each stroke was a reliable guide. Praying none of the other passengers would call for his services in the next few minutes, Cal watched the erotic scene unfolding before him, his own dick stiffening in his uniform trousers.

He'd noticed these two when they took their seats, eyes wide, revelling in the novelty of turning right on boarding. They made a nice-looking couple, he couldn't help but note; one tall and blond, the other sturdily built, with a head of dark, shoulder-length curls. Serving them with a glass of bubbly each, Cal learned how they'd arrived at check-in only for the girl at the desk to notice traces of confetti clinging to their hair. They'd admitted they'd come straight from tying the knot, at a civil partnership ceremony held in a country house hotel on the outskirts of Cobham, and were about to set off for their honeymoon in Aruba. She'd given the pair an upgrade to first class, with the compliments of Celtic Air, and it seemed they were determined to take advantage of the seclusion travelling in these exclusive surroundings offered them. Lucky boys, Cal thought, jetting off to a tropical paradise to mark the start of their new life together. They could look forward to sun, sea, white sandy beaches – and plenty of sex, assuming they didn't wear each other out before the plane had even touched down.

Not that he should be too envious. For once, the work rota had been kind, giving him and the rest of the crew a 26-hour layover in Aruba before they had to return to Gatwick. Enough time to catch up on his sleep, preferably by the side of the resort pool. Or maybe he could join in the party Judy would no doubt be throwing in her room. She'd be pouring the tequila body shots and making plans to lure Jacques, the hot Parisian co-pilot, down to the beach for sex beneath the stars, if her previous exploits were any guide.

Cal loved to kick back and relax as much as any man, but unlike Judy, he didn't use layovers as an opportunity for a casual fuck. He'd never been the type to seek out a one-night stand, however cute a guy might be. Call him old-fashioned, but deep down he was looking for commitment, someone to share the ups and down of his life with. Exactly what the couple he was still spying on had been lucky enough to find.

With a smirk, the man who'd been wanking his partner slid down in his seat. Without even looking to see whether anyone might be watching, he darted his head beneath the blanket. Cal almost groaned aloud with envy, knowing the blond's cock was now engulfed in his lover's mouth. If he hadn't been on duty, he'd have been tempted to slip into the toilets and take himself in hand. But fate decreed at that moment the call light should flash on above a seat on the opposite side of the aisle. Thankful his jacket was long enough to hide the obvious bulge at his crotch, evidence of his sneaky peek at the two cute guys at play, he went to answer the call.

By the time he'd supplied the requested Bloody Mary and packet of pretzels, the couple were snuggled together, chatting in low voices as though nothing out of the ordinary had just happened. Cal flashed them his most professional smile as he passed along the aisle by their seats, on his way back to the galley to begin serving the in-flight meal. He'd keep his knowledge of their outrageous antics to himself, an image to return to as he lay in bed that night, hand wrapped round his own cock as he recalled the look of unbridled ecstasy on the blond's face. He only wished he'd been able to enjoy more of the show.

The Four Winds Resort Hotel stood on its own private stretch of beach, a couple of miles outside Aruba's capital city, Oranjestad. Designed as an intimate, couples-only retreat, it boasted a restaurant whose head chef had once worked at the Savoy in London, gym, spa and two swimming pools. It even had a hot tub out on the poolside deck, the perfect setting to sip a cocktail while gazing out over the ocean. All too often, Cal found himself spending his layovers in a hotel a stone's throw from the airport, looking out on nothing more inspiring than a stretch of car park, so the Four Winds' understated luxury and romantic ambience came as a very pleasant change.

As he waited at the front desk for his room key, the last member of the flight crew to be dealt with, the receptionist moved away to speak to a smart-suited man in his mid 30s who'd appeared behind the front desk. Cal couldn't see his name badge, but he had to be high up in the hotel's hierarchy, judging by the deferential way in which she addressed him. He was also one of the most handsome men Cal had seen in quite a while, with tufty dark hair, a long, straight nose and a sensual mouth framed by a neat beard. The kind of man Cal would have been keen to know better, in other circumstances.

'I'm sorry about that, sir,' the receptionist said to Cal, once she'd dealt with whatever the problem had been. 'Now, you're in Room 18 ...'

'Who was that?' Cal asked, intrigued despite himself by the man's air of calm authority.

'Oh, that's Justin Holford. He's the new resort manager. And he's a real improvement on the old one, I can tell you.'

Whether the receptionist based that assessment on management style or looks she didn't say, though Cal suspected it was the latter. She merely handed him the card key, pointed him in the direction of the stairs and wished him a pleasant stay.

Halfway along the first floor landing, Room 18 was more of a suite, with a spacious bedroom containing a comfortable-looking king-sized bed, and a small, airy living room whose French window let out on to a balcony overlooking the beach. Cal dropped his flight case on the bed and went to look out of the window, breathing in the sea air. Palm trees rustled gently in the breeze, and the sun had just begun to set, the sky suffused with a soft, pinkish-orange glow. The only thing that could improve the moment would be for Cal to have a cocktail in his hand – and the hot resort manager standing by his side.

His mind flashed to a vision of the man, naked but for a towel around his waist, walking out of his bathroom. In the fantasy, Cal lay on the bed, stroking his hard cock, waiting for Justin to join him. Discarding the towel to reveal his own rigid erection, Justin Holford would take charge of the situation; he knew it, grabbing Cal's wrists and pushing them together over his head. Justin's lips formed the words, 'Submit to me,' and Cal responded, letting Justin push the head of his dick deep into his mouth. Sucking hard, slurping his tongue over Justin's juicy cockhead, Cal would bring his lover to the point where he could do nothing but groan helplessly and shoot his tangy come down Cal's throat. And when he'd recovered, he would–

Get a grip, Cal chided himself. You're here to make the most of your free time, not spend it having filthy fantasies about some guy you haven't even spoken to.

A knock interrupted his musings. Judy popped her head round the door. She'd already changed out of her dowdy Celtic Air uniform, with its shapeless blue jacket and knee-length blue-and-red tartan skirt, into a black dress that revealed most of her long, slender legs and an eye-popping amount of cleavage. She might as well have had "AVAILABLE" branded across her forehead, but Cal would never dream of criticising Judy for her approach to sex. She was his best friend on the flight crew, and they'd each provided a shoulder for the other to cry on when a relationship didn't work out. Now, she seemed more interested in providing him with a stiff drink, if the bottle of tequila in her hand was any reliable indication.

'We're all meeting up in the bar downstairs,' she told him. 'Well, apart from Nicki and Graham. The "do not disturb" signs are up on their doors already, as always.'

It didn't matter where in the world they spent their layover, or whether the stop-off lasted hours or days. Nicki and Graham were the two attendants who could always be relied on to perform what was commonly known among flight crews as the "click-shut"; closing and locking their hotel room door the moment they were inside, making it clear they had no intention of socialising. Their idea of a good time appeared to involve tuning the TV to CNN, popping a couple of sleeping pills and nodding off, never mind if the party carried on all night in the room next door to theirs. And with Judy in the mood she appeared to be tonight, hunting out the tooth mugs from Cal's bathroom and pouring a generous amount of tequila for both of them, that was a definite possibility.

'Come on, Cal, hurry up and get changed,' Judy urged him, checking her reflection in the free-standing mirror and fluffing out her long, wavy blonde locks. 'We don't want to miss any of the fun.'

'Are you worried Jacques is going to get off with someone else if you're not around?' Cal teased, stripping off his uniform jacket and white shirt with the Celtic Air logo sewn over the left breast. He hunted in his case for his favourite peach-coloured T-shirt and baggy khaki shorts, more interested in feeling comfortable than dressing to impress, unlike Judy.

'Sweetie, I promise you when Jacques sees me in this, he won't notice anybody else.' Judy took a long sip of her tequila, wandering out on to the balcony. 'Wow, this view is amazing! Just look at that sunset ...'

Pausing in the act of taking off his trousers, Cal glanced out to where the sun disappeared into the ocean, sinking in a fiery red ball on the horizon. 'Yeah, that is something special.'

'The room they've given me looks out on the gardens,' Judy told him. 'They're beautiful in their own way, but they're nothing like this. Shame we only have the one day to make the most of this, isn't it?'

Cal stepped into his deck shoes before slipping his wallet and card key into his shorts pocket. 'Well, if you want to start making the most of it now, I'm ready to join the party.'

Judy tore herself away from her admiration of the Caribbean sunset and downed the last of her drink. For someone who stood barely five foot tall, she certainly had the ability to pack away the alcohol. In contrast, Cal had barely touched his own tequila. It might be a good idea to take it easy tonight, he thought. There'd be time to explore a little of the island tomorrow, before they had to check back in for the return flight, and he didn't want to ruin the day by waking with a killer hangover.

When they reached the bar, it was to discover Rob, the pilot, buying drinks for everyone on the crew. 'You have to try the cocktails,' he told them, gesturing to his own glass. 'This is their speciality, the Aruba.'

'Two of those then, please,' Judy said.

They watched as the bartender measured out gin, white Curaçao, lemon juice and something from a bottle Cal didn't recognise, before shaking them together. He strained the resulting mixture into two Martini glasses, handing one each to Cal and Judy.

'Mm, this is delicious,' Judy announced. 'But what's the secret ingredient?'

The bartender grinned. 'Orgeat syrup. It's made from almonds. You like it?'

'I love it,' she enthused.

She was right, Cal thought, tasting his own drink. It was delicious, and deceptively innocuous, given the amount of alcohol it contained. A couple of those would definitely be his limit, if he wanted to wake bright and refreshed the following morning.

Judy cast her eyes round the bar, looking for Jacques and failing to find him.

'Rob, honey,' she said, 'you don't have any idea where Jacques might be, do you?'

'He went out on to the terrace,' Rob replied. 'You'll probably find him on one of the loungers. He said something about wanting to watch the sun go down.'

'Well, you can't do that on your own, can you?' Judy replied with a giggle. 'Not if you really want to enjoy it. I'm off to join him.'

Cal stood making small talk with Rob for a few minutes. The easy-going Canadian was a recent addition to the Celtic Air team, having previously worked for a major airline in the American South-west. He gave the impression of being a little reserved on first meeting, but Cal knew from experience he could party as hard as anyone on his crew, while always managing to stay within the permitted alcohol limits. Times had changed since he'd first started flying, as he'd told Cal on more than one occasion, and these days it was a hell of a lot easier to be sacked for drinking on the job.

'Can I get you another one?' Rob asked, pointing to Cal's almost empty glass.

'Not right this moment,' Cal said, looking at his watch. Aruba was four hours behind the UK, and back home it would be 11 o'clock at night. Here, the evening was still young. 'I think I ought to pace myself. But I think Judy would probably like one – if she's not too caught up with Jacques, that is.'

As if speaking her name had invoked her presence, Judy sauntered back into the bar at that moment, hand in hand with Jacques. Cal couldn't help but notice the lipstick imprint on the Frenchman's cheek, and the tightness in the crotch of his jeans.

A pianist had taken up residence in one corner of the bar, playing jazzy versions of popular tunes. Still holding tightly to Jacques, a fresh cocktail in her free hand, Judy squealed, 'Come on, let's dance.'

Jacques seemed more content to watch her, as did every other straight man in the room, particularly once it became apparent that whenever she twirled her short skirt flared out, revealing a pair of pink thong panties that left most of her tanned arse cheeks bare. She must know that was the case, Cal thought, but she seemed not to care.

Her antics were the cue for the serious partying to start. Almost all the other guests had wandered away to eat dinner in the terrace restaurant, leaving the flight crew to dance and drink to their hearts' content.

Somewhere down her fourth or fifth cocktail, Judy took off her strappy heels, stood on the piano and asked, 'Who wants to see me do a strip tease?'

The response from male and female crew members alike was one of rowdy encouragement, whooping and cheering as Judy peeled out of her dress. Whirling the discarded garment above her head, she tossed it straight at Jacques, who caught it one-handed. Her strapless bra was the same shade of shell pink as her panties, and she was in the act of reaching behind herself to undo the catch and bare her breasts when an American-accented voice boomed, 'Ladies and gentlemen, please would you all stop what you're doing?'

Everyone turned at the sound. Even Judy obeyed the order, wobbling a little as she tried to maintain her balance on top of the piano. Standing in the doorway was Holford, the resort manager. Irritation flashed in his brown eyes at the scene before him.

'If you could think about calling it a night, it would be appreciated,' he continued. 'We've had a couple of complaints from guests in the rooms above about the noise, and it is getting late.'

Cal sneaked a look at his watch. Despite his resolve to get a reasonably early night, he was surprised to see it was already half-past ten. Not late by his usual standards, but the Four Winds catered to couples looking for peace and relaxation. Presumably it was Holford's job to make sure they found it.

The resort manager's stern presence served to kill the party atmosphere. People began to make their way upstairs to their rooms. Jacques helped Judy down from the piano. She didn't attempt to put her dress back on, simply wrapped it around her as Jacques led her out of the bar. Her triumphant little smirk made it clear to Cal she knew she wouldn't be sleeping alone tonight.

Placing his empty glass down on the bar, Cal followed the others, feeling slightly guilty. He loved to have a good time as much as anyone, but not when his enjoyment was causing other people a sleepless night. As he passed Holford, he murmured, 'I'm sorry if we've upset anyone. We didn't realise how much noise we were making.'

'Well, thank you. You're the only one out of your little party who's bothered to apologise for what's just happened, and I appreciate that.' Justin Holford looked Cal up and down, as though trying to place him. The scrutiny made Cal tingle, for reasons he found hard to explain. 'I saw you checking in this afternoon, didn't I? You're part of the flight crew, right?'

Cal nodded, sticking out a hand for Holford to shake. 'Callum Phillips. Cal.'

Justin's grip was firm, his appraisal of Cal so frank it was almost sexual. 'Justin Holford.'

'You have a beautiful hotel here,' Cal told him. He knew he should be heading upstairs, where that comfy king-sized bed with its big mound of pillows and 600 thread count Egyptian cotton sheets waited for him. But something compelled him to spend just a little longer in the presence of this broodingly gorgeous man.

'I'm pleased you like it. I've worked very hard since I arrived here to uphold its reputation as being among the finest hotels on the resort.' Like Cal, he seemed to have been bitten by the urge to continue their conversation. 'Is this your first time on Aruba?'

'No, but it's the first time I've been scheduled for a layover here. All these trips, and finally I get the chance to spend a night in paradise. It makes all the turbulence and being stuck in holding patterns over Heathrow worthwhile.'

Justin chuckled, revealing even white teeth. 'If you're looking for paradise, I could show it to you.'

'Now, that's an offer I can't refuse.' Cal told himself it was only his overheating imagination that saw an unmistakable sexual connotation in Justin's words. 'But aren't you on duty?'

'This time of night, the resort practically manages itself. If there happen to be any problems, Angel's on the front desk tonight. I can usually trust her to take care of everything. Come with me, Cal. If you haven't walked on Eagle Beach after dark, you haven't lived.'

'OK, lead the way.'

Cal followed Justin out of the bar and down the terrace steps, stepping out into the tropical night and whatever it might bring.

Chapter Two

HIS FEET SUNK INTO the soft white sand, and he pulled off his shoes so he could enjoy the feel of it between his bare toes as he walked. Justin showed more restraint, still dressed in his well-cut dark suit, but Cal supposed he'd been here long enough that the place no longer held any novelty for him. The beach was silent, apart from the soft hiss and drag of the waves. In less than 24 hours, Cal would be on his way back to England, and this moment would seem a lifetime away. Breathing deeply, inhaling the salt tang of the sea and the faint aroma of fragrant night-blooming flowers, he determined to etch it on his memory for ever.

Though it soon became apparent Justin intended to create his own lasting memories for Cal to take away. They walked for a while, steadily moving further away from the resort buildings along the deserted beach.

'So, your accent,' Justin said, 'it's Scottish, am I right?'

'Yeah, I'm originally from Glasgow,' Cal replied. So many Americans commented on what they called his cute accent, but very few recognised it for what it actually was.

'Interesting city,' Justin replied. 'I travelled all round Europe when I left college, back in the days when I didn't know what I wanted to do with my life, and Scotland's one of the most beautiful places I visited. I loved the wildness of the Highlands, you know, the feel of being so far away from the urban sprawl. Nature really speaks to me ...'

They were passing through a clump of dark, looming palms. Justin pressed Cal up against the rough trunk of one of the trees and kissed him. For a moment, remembering his rule about not getting involved with someone he would never see again, Cal thought about resisting. But as soon as Justin's tongue flickered into his mouth, any pretence that he didn't want this melted away. He'd never been kissed with such passion, such authority. The reality was even better than the fantasy he'd woven about Justin earlier, and all he could do was sigh into the man's mouth, savouring the sweetness of this unexpected kiss, while the night birds called somewhere above their heads.

Justin's body ground against Cal's, the hardness of his cock all too apparent even through the layers of clothing they both wore. He was big, impressively so, and Cal was struck with an eagerness to unzip the man's fly and take that hot, solid length in his grip.

A sharp pricking against his back distracted him, threatening to break the moment, and he let out an involuntary yelp.

'Are you OK there, Cal?' Justin asked, clearly concerned.

'Fine,' Cal assured him. 'This tree trunk's a little scratchy, that's all.'

'Well, we'll find somewhere more comfortable, then.'

Justin stepped away from the tree, taking off his footwear before removing the rest of his clothing piece by piece, laying it in a neat pile with his shoes at the bottom. He only stopped when he was down to his underwear, tight-fitting blue briefs that were losing the fight to contain his hefty erection.

'Now you,' he told Cal.

Undressing was an easier and swifter job on his part. All he had to do was shed his T-shirt and shorts. He'd gone commando beneath them, and his cock stood up hard, stimulated by the sight of Justin stripping down to almost nothing.

'Hey, that gives me an idea,' Justin said, peeling out of his briefs. 'Ever been skinny dipping in the Caribbean on a beautiful moonlit night?' When Cal shook his head in response, he continued, 'Man, you haven't lived. Come on. I'll race you.'

Whooping and yelling, knowing there was no one around to disturb with their raucous cries, the two men raced down to the water's edge. Back home in Scotland, there was no way Cal would plunge recklessly beneath the waves, as he did now. Even on the warmest days, the sea temperature was too chilly to encourage anything other than a slow, cautious submersion and a few moments splashing around before the cold defeated him. Here, though, the water enveloped him like a heated blanket, and he rolled on to his back and floated, watching Justin immerse himself completely before breaking the surface, drops of water flying from his hair as he shook himself like a dog.

'What did I tell you?' he asked, grinning broadly. 'Isn't it the best?'

'I've never done anything like this before,' Cal admitted. He wasn't simply referring to the stroll along the beach, the naked night-swimming. He'd never exposed himself so readily to a man he'd only just met, physically or emotionally. And when Justin took him in his arms once more so they could kiss again, the strong tang of salt water on his lips, Cal didn't stop to consider the consequences, as he usually did. He couldn't deny how much he wanted the resort manager, so unlike any man he knew, with the wild, reckless college boy he must once have been lurking only a little way beneath the sober, respectable surface.

'Just relax, Cal,' Justin said, breaking the kiss so they could gaze into each other's eyes. 'Go with the flow.'

As he spoke, he took hold of Cal's cock, tugging it with slow, sustained motions that concentrated on the sensitive spot just below the head. Cal groaned, giving himself up completely to the feeling of being wanked by a master of the art. They were in so deep, in more ways than one. His feet barely touched the firm, rippled sea bottom, and he knew how good it would feel to simply float, letting Justin take his weight as he continued to stroke him.

His hand moved, almost of its own volition, grasping Justin's thick length. Now they worked in synchrony, each aiming to bring the other to a satisfying orgasm. Cal had never had a circumcised lover before, and he was intrigued by the contrast between Justin's smooth, bare shaft and his own. Did he feel the sensations differently? Did he need more in the way of stimulation, deprived of the soft sheath of skin to protect his shaft? All Cal knew was that Justin seemed to be enjoying what he was doing, judging by the way his eyelids had flickered shut and his breathing was growing harsher.

Cal took Justin's lower lip between his teeth, nibbling gently, feeling his lover's breath soughing into his own mouth. They were so close at that moment, each devoted solely to giving the other pleasure. Justin's fingers moved faster, Cal speeding up the pace of his strokes in response. The come churned in his balls, beginning its unstoppable rush to be released. Unable to hold back any longer, he groaned and came, his seed shooting out in pearly swirls, to be carried away by the tide.

Spurred on by the sight of Cal in the throes of ecstasy, Justin followed moments behind, muttering a muffled curse as he came.

They held each other tight for a moment, their heartbeats gradually slowing. 'That was amazing,' Cal said at length.

'And it was only the start, if that's what you want?'

Cal nodded. Justin's fingers had given him so much pleasure, but how would it feel to have his mouth closing around the head of his cock, or to offer his arse for Justin to fuck?

'Just one thing before we go any further ...' Justin stroked strands of wet, sandy-blond hair out of Cal's eyes. 'I don't want you to think I get involved with every hot guest who comes through our doors. You're the first in the six months I've been here. I kind of had a rule about it, to tell you the truth.'

'That's funny, because I had a rule about not having sex with someone I knew I was never going to see again. But I suppose rules are meant to be broken.'

'So let's go break them again, Cal.'

Hand in hand, they walked out of the ocean to retrieve their scattered clothing. Hastily revising the mental plans he'd made to get up early and explore the island, Cal knew instead he was going to spend the rest of the night taking as much pleasure in Justin's arms as he could. If it was to be the only night they'd ever share, he wanted it to be an unforgettable one.

Cal woke alone, in a tangle of sheets. For a moment, he couldn't recall where he was, or why his body felt like it had gone through an extensive workout, then memories came surging back. When he and Justin emerged from their moonlight frolic in the sea, they'd hurried back to the hotel. Neither man had bothered to dress, knowing it was unlikely anyone would be awake at that time of night to spot them sneaking in through the terrace entrance. Justin simply slipped back into his briefs and Cal put on his shorts over his still-damp skin.

At Cal's suggestion, they went up to his room, Justin apparently relishing the novelty of sleeping somewhere other than his own bed for once. Though they had hardly slept a wink. As soon as they were through the door, the clothes they'd been wearing were rapidly discarded, the two men curling up together on the fresh white sheets so they could make a proper, unhurried exploration of each other's body with fingers and tongue.

Taking his time, Cal licked a slow path over the planes of his lover's salt-crusted torso, admiring the firmness of Justin's pecs and flat belly. He knew the resort had gym facilities on site, and Justin must take the opportunity to use them on his days off. Though there were so many great ways to get in shape on this tiny island, from running along the beach to hiking through the national park. If he were here for any longer than a day, he and Justin would ...

That thought had been buried as soon as it emerged, Cal returning to the task of mapping Justin's muscled contours with his tongue. The mat of dark hair on Justin's chest descended in an enticing trail, leading to the small bush surrounding his cock and balls. The lower Cal moved down that trail, the more Justin squirmed against the sheets, eager for the feel of Cal's lips on his most private places.

When Cal finally took Justin in his mouth, swirling his tongue over the rounded crown and licking up the salty drops emerging from its slit, he thought the man might lose his load at that moment. Even though he'd already come once, he still seemed to be on a hair trigger. From what he'd said on the beach, it had been at least six months since he'd last had sex – unless he had some lover squirreled away on the island he hadn't mentioned in the heat of the moment.

Cal wanted to believe Justin wasn't the cheating type –

though who could blame him if he was simply taking the opportunity to have a passing fling with a guy he knew he'd never see again?

'I have to know,' Cal said, gazing into Justin's eyes, their pupils dilated with desire. 'You said you didn't date the guests here, but is there anyone else you're seeing, anything I should know about before we go any further?'

Justin shook his head. 'If there'd been anyone else, Cal, we wouldn't have gone as far as we have already. And you, you're not keeping anything – or anyone – from me, are you?'

'No. There's no one in my life right now.' There hadn't been since Andy, who he'd lived with for the best part of two years. Things had been so good between them at first. Handsome, hard-working and financially responsible, Andy had been the ideal man to keep the flightier, more impulsive Cal grounded, and their sex life was hot and endlessly inventive. But gradually Andy had tired of the demands of Cal's job, and the way his flight rosters meant they might not see each other for more than a couple of days at a time. He wanted something more settled, more secure and Cal couldn't give it to him, so they'd gone their separate ways. Cal hadn't found anyone who appealed to him the way Andy had, until now.

He pulled himself back to the moment, not wanting thoughts of his ex to intrude when all that mattered was the gorgeous, naked American lying beside him, waiting to feel Cal's mouth engulfing his cock once more.

Cal obliged, planting sloppy kisses along Justin's shaft from tip to root before taking as much of the rigid length down his throat as he could. Justin clutched at the pillow beneath him, thrusting his hips up in his efforts to fuck Cal's mouth. Keeping a tight hold of the base of Justin's cock, Cal stopped him from thrusting deeper than he was comfortable with. He did his best to string out Justin's pleasure as long as possible, but the man was just too excited. With a warning cry that gave Cal enough time to pull his head away had he wanted to, he shot his come in great, sticky spurts. His mouth still clamped round Justin's shaft, Cal swallowed the outpouring before licking his lover's wilting cock clean.

Justin seemed keen to return the favour, but Cal had other pleasures in mind. 'Let me fuck your arse,' he begged, smiling as Justin nodded his assent.

Slipping away to the en suite bathroom, Cal retrieved the condoms he always carried in his wash bag, but never seriously expected to use. On more than one occasion he'd found himself lending them to Judy when her own supply ran out. In return, she'd bought him the ribbed latex three-pack he found himself opening now.

Walking back to the bed, he made a show of fitting the condom in place, stroking his cock more than was strictly necessary as he regarded Justin. His lover had rolled on to his stomach, proffering up his arse to Cal. Just the thought of sinking his dick into the tight, hidden hole between Justin's firm butt cheeks was causing his stomach to churn with anticipation.

Along with the condoms, Cal kept a few sachets of thick, latex-friendly lube. He tore one open, smearing its gloopy contents over the entrance to Justin's arse. Justin sighed. 'God, it feels so fucking good to have you touch me there. I love having my ass played with.'

In other circumstances, Cal would have filed that little snippet away for future reference. As it was, he simply concentrated on opening Justin's crinkled hole with his fingers. When he judged the man was relaxed enough to take him, he guided his cock into position and thrust home.

It was as though Justin's arse had been made to take his length, Cal thought, savouring the way the tight passage gripped every inch of him. Trying not to think about the unfairness of finding the right lover at the wrong time, Cal fucked Justin with long, steady strokes.

Sweat gleamed on Justin's broad back as Cal thrust in and out of his arse. He grunted, pushing back at Cal, urging him to go faster and deeper. Cal obliged, working up a sweat of his own as he neared his peak. All too soon, his movements grew jerky, erratic. He yelled out, unconcerned about guests in the neighbouring room hearing him celebrate his climax. His come jetted into the condom and he slumped on top of Justin, the stresses of the day and the four-hour time difference finally catching up with him.

Cal hoped Justin would fall asleep in his arms, but he'd declined the offer. 'I'm sorry, Cal, I'd really like to, but it's my day off tomorrow.'

'And why does that make a difference?' Cal pouted. 'You don't have to get up early if you're not working.'

'But technically I'm still on call,' he explained. 'If there's any kind of emergency, someone will come looking for me. And how would it look if they found me asleep with one of the guests?'

Cal supposed he had a point. He snuggled deeper into the sheets, watching Justin dress. The sun was already beginning to rise, soft light coming through the partly open drapes. 'Well, thanks for a wonderful night.'

Justin paused as he was leaving the room, one hand on the doorknob. 'What time do you leave tomorrow?'

'The flight takes off just before six in the evening. I'll have to be there an hour beforehand.'

'Great. That gives us a few hours together. We'll go into Oranjestad and I'll take you to my favourite bar. How does that sound?'

Anything that gave him longer in Justin's company was fine by him. 'OK, I'll see you in the lobby at eleven. Good night, Cal.'

Setting his alarm to give him time for a shower and breakfast, Cal managed a couple of hours' sleep. He knew he'd pay for it on the flight home, but right now he didn't care.

On his way to the restaurant, Cal bumped into Judy. Eyes hidden behind dark glasses, she flashed him a weak smile. He suspected she'd had just as busy a night as he had, but he'd catch up on all the details on the way back to Gatwick. Now, he wanted a good, filling meal before meeting Justin for their sightseeing expedition.

Breakfast was a buffet-style affair, trays full of scrambled egg, sausage, bacon and tomatoes occupying one end of a long table, fruit, cereal, yoghurt and pastries among the other options available. Piling his plate high, Cal looked around for any fellow crew members already eating. The only person he recognised was Nicki. She wasn't his ideal choice of breakfast companion, but it would have been rude not to join her.

'Have you seen the news?' she asked him, looking up from the buttery croissant she was eating in dainty bites. 'They reckon there's a big storm on the way, the tail-end of the hurricane that hit Florida yesterday.'

'I've not really had the TV on,' Cal replied. 'Does it look bad?'

'They say it'll probably miss us, but you never know.' She sighed. 'And I'd hate to be stuck here any longer than I had to be.'

'Oh, I don't know about that.' Cal's mind flashed to thoughts of everything he could do if he had more time with Justin. It was a nice fantasy, nothing more. He forked up his eggs, enjoying their creamy taste, seasoned with just a hint of pepper. 'The food's good, isn't it? We've really landed on our feet staying here.'

'Tell me about it.' Nicki rose from her seat. 'Well, I'll leave you to your breakfast, Cal. I think I may go and lie by the pool for a while.'

When Cal had finished his meal, lingering over a second cup of coffee, he headed out to the lobby. Justin was already waiting for him, casually dressed in a white polo shirt and olive chinos, sunglasses perched in his dark hair. Cal's heart lurched at the sight of him.

Justin clapped him on the shoulder by way of greeting. 'Hey, Cal, hope you slept well.'

'Fine, thanks. That bed was so comfortable.' He lowered his voice. 'But then I suppose you already know that.'

'Come on, let's make a move.' Justin led Cal out to the car park and a battered khaki-coloured open top Jeep that looked like it might originally have been US Army issue, the ideal vehicle for negotiating some of the island's more rugged terrain. Though Justin had suggested they take a trip into Oranjestad, Cal wouldn't be surprised if they found time to travel into the heart of the island too.

'I hear there's a storm coming,' Cal said, as they pulled out on to the main road.

'Yeah, apparently so, but I wouldn't worry about it. It'll pass us by. They always do,' Justin replied blithely. 'That's one of the best things about this island. Hurricanes never hit it and there hasn't been any serious storm damage here for over a decade. That's why I moved here. I used to work at a resort in Florida, and the weather there – oh man!' He grinned at Justin. 'But that's not the only reason why I love this place. And I'm going to show you.'

Chapter Three

CAL HAD NEVER SEEN anywhere quite like Oranjestad. The city's architecture was a striking mixture of Dutch and Caribbean influences. High gabled buildings decorated in ice cream shades struck him as more garish versions of ones he might see along the canals of Amsterdam, and every shop window seemed to be adorned with a multi-coloured awning, offering welcome shade from the heat of the day. Down on the waterfront, expensive yachts bobbed in the harbour, and people drank cocktails in the waterside bars. Away from the busy centre, most of the city's houses were low white brick constructions with red-tiled roofs, reminding him of similar buildings he'd seen on the Spanish Costas. Cal suspected the people who lived in those homes could only dream of earning enough money to afford a yacht and the lavish lifestyle that went with it.

As they drove from the Four Winds Resort, Justin had filled Cal in on the history of the island. Originally colonised by the Spanish, who valued it for its natural resources, its cotton crop in particular, it had passed into Dutch hands in the 17th Century. Now an official part of the kingdom of the Netherlands and a country in its own right, Aruba was still seeking full independence and all the benefits that would bring. Politics had never been Cal's favourite subject, and the intricacies of the situation would have been complicated for him to follow even if he'd had a solid eight hours' sleep, but it helped explain why the island was such a weird mish-mash of cultures. Even though he'd only moved there within the past few months, Justin spoke about Aruba with the passion of a native, and Cal realised just how quickly the quirkiness of the place had permeated Justin's way of thinking.

'And do you know the whole marina complex we've just walked through, and the marketplace over there are all built on man-made land that's been expanded out into the sea?' Justin asked. 'How amazing is that?'

Justin continued to point out sights of interest as they strolled past the candy-pink Royal Mall and down the main shopping street, but, after his exertions the night before, Cal found the place too bright, too frenetic, as though it had been designed by a hyperactive toddler. He half wished he'd followed Nicki's example, and spent the day dozing by the pool.

Seeming to realise Cal was flagging, Justin said, 'What you need is a good Bloody Mary, and the best place in town to get one is Clyde's Bar.'

When they walked into the bar, Cal wondered what kind of dive Justin had taken him to. The place was dark and gloomy after the bright sunshine outside, with rickety wooden furniture and a sputtering neon sign reading "CLYDE'S" over the mirrored back of the bar. The only other customer was an old man sitting in the corner, nursing a glass of what looked like rum.

'Hey, Justin, my man!' Clyde beamed in welcome as they approached the bar. Cal guessed the man to be somewhere in his 30s, with skin the colour of bitter chocolate and a gold tooth that glittered when he smiled, which was most of the time. As Justin made himself comfortable on a bar stool, Clyde added, 'And who's your friend?'

'Clyde, meet Cal. I'm showing him the sights of Oranjestad.'

'And how do you like our beautiful city?' Clyde asked, clearly in the mood to chat.

'It's incredible,' Cal answered honestly.

'So what's your pleasure?' Clyde asked, his words dripping with double meaning. Justin had sworn he wasn't seeing anyone at the moment, but Cal couldn't help wondering whether he and Clyde had some kind of history. Or maybe the bar owner treated everyone as though they were a past, present or future lover.

'Two of your finest Bloody Marys, please, heavy on the vodka,' Justin replied.

'Coming right up, guys.' Clyde busied himself mixing their drinks, pouring generous measures of vodka into two tall glasses before adding tomato juice and a slug of something from a small, unlabelled bottle.

'That's Clyde's special spice mix,' Justin told Cal. 'He'll never share the recipe with anyone, but it gives his Bloody Marys a kick like nothing else you'll ever taste.'

Cal was doubtful, but as Clyde presented a glass to him and he took a careful sip, he had to agree with Justin. When he served a Bloody Mary from his Celtic Air catering trolley, the only flavouring provided was a sachet of celery salt and maybe a dash of Worcestershire sauce for the first class passengers. Here, Cal also tasted a strong overtone of chilli, along with spices he couldn't put a name to. Coupled with the potent vodka, it provided the wake-up call his body needed.

'You're right, that is good,' he said, drinking more deeply from his glass. Already, Cal was beginning to revise his opinion of the bar. It might appear to be only one step up from one of the beachside shacks they'd passed on their circuit of the harbour, but he sensed the next time he walked through the door, even if that was in a year's time, the bartender would remember his name and give him a warm welcome. Though anywhere seemed better with Justin by his side. Loath as he was to admit it, Cal knew it wouldn't take much for him to fall head over heels in love with this smart, sexy man.

'Shall I set you up a tab?' Clyde asked Justin.

The resort manager shook his head. 'No, I think we'll just have the one drink here, then I'm going to take Cal into the heart of the island for a little while, before he has to catch his flight.'

Justin handed over a handful of notes to pay for their drinks. Cal noticed he used the local currency, Aruban florins, though many of the local establishments accepted US dollars or even euros, depending on whether their clientele comprised mostly of American or Dutch tourists.

A television set high up on the wall was tuned to a rolling

news channel. Remembering Nicki's mention of the report on a coming tropical storm, even though Justin had assured him he had nothing to worry about, Cal glanced up at the screen. What he saw sent chills skittering down his spine. A pretty black reporter stood on the sand, the umbrella over her head threatening to blow inside-out with the force of the wind. Rain beat down, hard enough to be seen on screen, and when the cameraman cut to a shot of the ocean, the waves were churning violently and the sky was a forbidding shade of grey, so dark it was almost black. A caption at the bottom of the image read, "STORM HITS PALM BEACH".

Interrupting Justin and Clyde, who were deep in discussion about some football game the Aruban national team were due to play in, he said, 'Uh, Justin, Palm Beach is just a bit north of your resort, right?'

'Yeah, why do you ask?'

Cal pointed to the screen. 'Well, the rain looks like it's coming down pretty heavily there. Looks like we might not escape that storm after all.'

Barely had he finished the sentence before raindrops started clattering on the tin roof of the bar. To Cal's ears, they sounded like a drunken man's attempts to tap-dance, and they were only growing louder. The old man in the corner took one look through the window at the state of the weather and decided it was time to make his move. He swallowed down the last of his rum, waved a hasty farewell to Clyde and disappeared out into the rain.

'Will he be OK?' Cal asked.

'Sure,' Clyde replied. 'Floyd only lives round the corner. But you two, now that's a different matter. If this really is the tail end of that hurricane, it isn't going to pass over in five minutes.'

So we might be stuck in your bar for a couple of hours, Cal thought. Not a problem. There are worse places to have to pass the time.

The lights in the bar flickered a couple of times, then went out. Clyde went over to the window, looking out at the parade of gaudily decorated shops across the road. Like him, they appeared to have experienced a sudden loss of electricity.

'The power lines must be down,' Clyde muttered. 'Man, this is getting serious.' A banging sound came from above them, as the fiercely gusting wind attempted to lift the bar roof.

Cal found it hard to believe how quickly the storm had intensified. Though it didn't have the power of a full-blown hurricane, it could still do a lot of damage. Looking at Justin, he realised the man was just as concerned for their safety as he was. But nothing could be gained by making a run for it; being out on the roads in an open top Jeep, with nothing to protect them should a tree fall into the road, would be even more dangerous.

It was Clyde who came up with a solution to their predicament. 'Why don't you shelter in the stock room?' he suggested. 'You ought to be protected there.'

'What about you?' Cal replied. 'Where are you going to go?'

'Oh, don't worry about me.' Clyde grinned, revealing his gold tooth. 'I know someone who'll keep me safe till the storm passes ...'

With that, he ushered Cal and Justin into the stock room at the back of the bar. With the electricity out, there were no lights in the little room, and Cal saw only the outlines of barrels and wooden crates full of bottles before Clyde shut the door on them.

It's a good job I don't suffer from claustrophobia, Cal thought, making himself as comfortable as he could on the cement floor and preparing to ride out the storm. Still, at least he could no longer hear the worst excesses of the wind and rain, and he had Justin with him. Being shut up in here on his own would have been almost unbearable.

He couldn't see Justin, but he could feel the solid, reassuring presence of his body alongside his own. With the stock room door shut, they were sitting in pitch darkness and, try as they might, Cal's eyes couldn't accustom themselves to the total lack of light.

'You're not afraid of the dark, are you?' he asked.

'Nothing frightens me,' Justin replied with a chuckle. 'Although I'm not too fond of cockroaches. But who is?'

The mention of cockroaches made Cal he wished he'd taken

a better look at his surroundings before the stock room door slammed shut. Beside him, he was aware of Justin reaching into his pocket, pulling out his mobile phone. When it was opened up, the display cast a faint bluish glow on the two of them.

Justin squinted at the screen. 'Damn, I knew I should have charged this thing up before we came out. I don't know how long the light will hold out for, and I certainly can't get a signal in here. What about you?'

Cal reached for his own phone. 'Same here.' With a guilty start, he realised he hadn't told anyone where he was going, not even Nicki when they'd been chatting over breakfast. He consoled himself with the thought that the storm would more than likely pass over in time to allow him to get back to the resort and join the others for the short trip to Queen Beatrix Airport. And if it didn't, well, the whole crew would be stranded, not just him. He couldn't see a single flight arriving or departing in conditions like the ones currently battering Oranjestad. 'But maybe we don't need any light. I'm sure we can think of some way to pass the time without it ...'

He reached out, tracing the contours of Justin's soft cheeks and strong, bearded jaw. His fingertip brushed over Justin's lips, encouraging them to part. Justin sucked eagerly at his finger, the wet suction sending a strong jolt of desire down to Cal's groin. His cock stiffened in his shorts, eager to feel Justin's mouth swallowing it.

When Cal pulled his finger away, Justin murmured, 'Let's get naked, lover.'

Never before had Cal undressed someone purely by feel. This must be what it was like to make love while blindfolded, your other senses heightened by having your sight temporarily taken away. He fumbled for and found the hem of Justin's T-shirt. Encouraging Justin to raise his arms, making the task easier, he pulled the garment over his lover's head. His fingers explored warm, bare skin, skirting over the planes of Justin's firm, lightly furred chest that he'd admired so much last night. Meanwhile, Justin had popped the button fastening of Cal's shorts and was pulling the zip down, before tugging the shorts off along with Cal's underwear. The still, humid air of the stock room caressed Cal's cock like a wicked embrace as Justin worked to strip him bare.

Spreading their clothes on the floor beneath them gave a little protection from the hard floor. Cal pulled off his own T-shirt and added it to the pile, before returning to his exploration of Justin's body.

Mapping his lover's body with his fingertips alone, unable to see the bare flesh he was uncovering, was strangely exciting. He traced the puckered indentation of a scar on the right side of Justin's abdomen. 'What happened here?' he asked.

'Oh, that's where I had my appendix removed when I was 14. The damn thing burst when I was on a hiking trip in the woods, and it was touch and go whether I'd make it to the hospital in time.'

Cal dropped his lips to his lover's belly, kissing the scar, before moving a little lower. Encountering Justin's belt buckle, he opened it before disposing of Justin's chinos and underwear as efficiently as Justin had removed his. Both completely naked, they curled into an embrace.

Deprived of his sight, Cal was more keenly aware than ever of the warm, musky scent of Justin's skin, his gentle sighs and gasps as Cal's fingers caressed a particularly sensitive spot, the faint background aroma of must and stale beer that had seeped into the stock room walls over the years. It was hardly the most romantic setting for such an intense encounter, but that didn't matter. The cramped room was their haven from the storm, a place where they could feel safe and protected in each other's arms.

Justin's lips latched on to Cal's nipple, sucking till Cal groaned with undisguised bliss. The little buds had always been exquisitely sensitive, yet Andy had so often bypassed them in his rush to suck Cal's cock.

'Mm, that feels fantastic,' Cal sighed, unable to keep his own hand off his rigid dick. The rhythmic noise of his fist shuttling along his length alerted Justin to what he was doing.

'Hey, slow down, greedy boy,' he murmured, easing Cal's fingers off his shaft and twining them in his own. 'Save some of that for me.'

Justin urged him to lie flat on his back, preparing him for the pleasure to come. He slithered along till he was crouching over Cal's groin, moving slowly and carefully – so he wouldn't scrape his knees on the floor, Cal presumed. Then Justin caught hold of Cal's cock, popping its head into his mouth, and Cal stopped worrying about the mechanics of the situation. He was utterly consumed by the feel of Justin's limber tongue, moving over his cockhead in slick figures of eight, and the tickling sensation of his beard where it occasionally rubbed against the insides of Cal's thighs. Cal had never been with a man who could take so much of his cock; Justin seemed to have mastered the art of relaxing his throat to the point where his length slipped right down it. Reaching down, he tangled his fingers in Justin's thick hair, loving the feeling of being buried so deep in his lover's gullet. The fact he couldn't see any of what was being done to him only helped to make the moment even more special. All he could do was try to picture the deliciously rude sight in his mind, as Justin breathed slowly, evenly through his nose and brought Cal to a point where he knew it would only be moments before he shot his come.

He fought the overwhelming urge to buck his hips hard, pushing his cock even deeper into the clutching hollow of Justin's throat. Instead, he managed to gasp, 'I'm going to come. Can't help myself, Justin. I'm going to come right down your throat.'

Just speaking those words, vocalising his excitement at what was being done to him, pushed him over the edge. Orgasm hit him in a series of sharp peaks, each one a little higher than the next, and when it was over, he lay back, gasping like a landed kingfish.

His cock finally slipped free of Justin's oral grasp. He couldn't see his lover's expression, only hear the amusement in his voice as he said, 'Sounds like you enjoyed that, Cal.'

'I did, thank you ...'

Working their way into a sitting position, they kissed, Cal tasting the faint traces of himself on Justin's lips. Cal grabbed Justin's cock, hard as steel and in need of its own release.

'How badly do you want to come?' he teased, brushing the

pad of his thumb across the head of Justin's cock, smearing precome along Justin's meaty, circumcised length.

'God, you can't possibly know,' Justin groaned in response.

'Maybe I should make you beg.' Cal had never considered himself to have a particularly dominant streak, but something about the way Justin's helpless, almost submissive reaction to being frustrated in this way was arousing feelings in him he'd never experienced. 'Or maybe I should just keep you right on the edge, then every time you were about to come, pull right back. How long could you stand that, d'you think, not being allowed to have the orgasm you craved until I decided you'd asked me nicely enough?'

'Please, Cal. For you, I'll do anything ...'

Why did Cal get the feeling Justin had never uttered those words with such sincerity? He was torn between making his lover beg just a little more and bringing him to the climax he so desperately craved.

'Oh please, sir,' Justin begged. 'Please let me come.'

The word "sir" acted as a magic charm. Cal's fingers no longer teased; now they applied the firm pressure that, with only a few strokes, had Justin's come arcing out to land somewhere on the stock room floor.

Though Cal knew he should keep alert, in case news came that the storm had broken, a pleasant lethargy was creeping over him. Giving up the fight to resist, he laid his head on Justin's shoulder, closed his eyes and was asleep within moments.

Cal had no idea how long he slept; all he knew was that the sound of someone pulling open the stock room door had dragged him awake. Blinking at the sudden, unwelcome influx of light, he looked up into Clyde's smiling face. Untangling himself from Justin's sleepy embrace, suddenly all too conscious of his nakedness, he looked round for his shorts. Rather than pulling them on, he simply used them to conceal his groin from the barman's curious gaze.

'Hey, don't cover that beautiful thing up on my account.' Clyde smiled. His expression bore no trace of judgement of the way Cal and Justin had chosen to entertain themselves. Indeed, it seemed to suggest that if he'd been with them, he'd have been more than happy to join in. 'Just wanted to let you know the storm's passed. And the bar's pretty much in one piece. Still no power, but that should come back on again soon enough.'

He left Cal and Justin to dress, casting one last lingering look at Cal's naked body. When they emerged from the darkness of the stock room, Cal checked his phone. Four missed calls, all from the same number. It came as no surprise to realise Rob had been trying to get in touch with him. The last thing any pilot wanted was a member of his crew going AWOL on a layover.

Cal's anxiety increased when he registered the time. He should have been at the airport, ready to commence crew check-in and security procedures, 15 minutes ago. Wondering what kind of trouble he was likely to be in, he punched the buttons on his phone to return Rob's call.

'Rob, this is Cal. I –'

He didn't get any further before the pilot cut him off. 'Cal, where the fuck have you been? Nobody's seen you since breakfast, and when you didn't answer your phone ...'

'Yeah, I'm really sorry about that. I'd gone sightseeing in Oranjestad, and when the storm hit, I had to take shelter. I wasn't able to get a signal on my phone, or I'd have rung you well before now. I didn't realise how late it was. Look, I've got to get back to the resort and pick my things up, but I'll be with you as soon as I can.'

'You don't have to worry about it, kiddo. We're all still at the hotel. I've been speaking to the airport authority. The storm's caused major damage to the runway, apparently. I've no idea what happened, but they reckon half the surface has been gouged up. Anyway, it means all flights in and out of Aruba have been cancelled till further notice. We won't be leaving until the repairs have been completed, and they don't see that happening before tomorrow at the earliest.' Rob paused. 'You're a very lucky man, you know that? In any other circumstances, you'd be getting a written warning once we got back to the UK. As it is, consider yourself verbally reprimanded.'

'Thanks, Rob. I won't do anything like this again. I

promise.'

Cal didn't know whether to laugh or cry. He'd come dangerously close to losing his job, only to be spared by circumstances way beyond his control. It seemed like fate was smiling down on him, offering him the opportunity to spend more time in Justin's company. Though that would only make the parting harder when the time came.

'Everything OK, Cal?' Justin sounded genuinely concerned.

'Yeah, I think so. It turns out we're not going to be leaving until they've carried out some repairs to the airport runway.'

'In which case, it's a good job this is a quiet week for us at the resort. It means I've got space for you all to stay tonight, otherwise you might all have been sleeping on the beach.' He grinned, making it clear to Cal he was only joking. 'Come on, let's go see what state the Jeep's in.'

They said their goodbyes to Clyde, who was surveying his bar with a measure of relief. A small section of the corrugated sheeting had been torn from the roof, allowing the rain to pour in, and though the floor was almost ankle-deep in water in places, no lasting damage appeared to have been caused. 'OK, so I have to do some mopping up,' he said, nothing able to dent his aura of relentless good cheer. 'But the glasses weren't damaged, and the booze is safe, which, as any barman will tell you, is the really important thing. We'll be partying here tonight as usual – if you want to join us?'

Cal and Justin exchanged a look. The offer was tempting, but Cal shook his head regretfully. 'I'm in enough trouble as it is right now. If I sneak away again, I think I'll be looking for a new job when I get back to England.'

'Maybe next time, then, Cal?'

'Definitely.'

Clyde clapped Justin on the back. 'See you again real soon, man. And Cal, look after yourself.'

They stepped out into the hot afternoon sunshine. If it hadn't been for the wrecked buildings and cars the storm had left in its path, they'd have found it impossible to believe the island had so recently been buffeted by fierce, howling winds and torrential rain.

The Jeep was still parked where they'd left it, sheltered by a low adobe wall, damp but otherwise none the worse for wear. When Justin turned the key in the ignition, the engine sparked into life first time.

'Man, they really don't make them like this any more,' he exclaimed.

Despite Cal's fears that the main road would be blocked with debris, they pretty much had a clear run all the way back to the Four Winds resort. Broken branches littered the side of the road, and they had to pass through more than one deep pool of standing water, but the storm had been kind. Though a couple of cars stood empty, clearly abandoned by their drivers, he couldn't see the evidence of any serious accidents caused by the weather. If Rob was right, the worst of the damage had hit the airport. Cal was torn between feeling concern that flights would soon be restored, so that passengers weren't left stranded here or frustrated in their attempts to reach the island, the delays eating into their precious holiday time, and loving the fact it might give him more time to spend with Justin. Still, he'd get a better idea of the situation when he spoke to the rest of the crew.

As they walked into the hotel lobby, Judy rushed over to him, concern marring her pretty features. She flung her arms around his neck.

'Cal! Rob told me you'd got caught up in the storm. I was really worried about you ...'

'You shouldn't have been. We found somewhere to shelter.'

At the mention of "we", Judy broke the embrace. For the first time, she seemed to notice Justin. She looked at Cal, her lips quirking, but she bit back the question she was obviously dying to ask. Cal hoped he wasn't blushing too fiercely.

'Well, things haven't been too bad here,' she informed him. 'Palm Beach took the brunt of the storm, from what we heard, but we just all stayed in our rooms, away from the windows, and kept our heads down till it passed over.'

'That must have been scary for you,' Cal said.

Judy shivered. 'Put it this way. I don't want to be around when a proper hurricane hits. Anyway, there's a crew-meeting in Rob's room at seven, then we're all going to have dinner together.'

'OK,' Cal replied. 'I'm going to have a shower, and maybe a nap. Collect me just before seven?'

'Sure thing.' Judy gave him a wink. 'And it's nice to know you had a knight in shining armour to protect you from the storm.'

With that, she turned on her heel and went to the bar, to find her own way of killing time until dinner. Cal watched her go, knowing he had so much to explain to her, but feeling he couldn't do so just yet. Not until this mad, whirlwind affair with Justin had run its course, as it inevitably would. And that was something he didn't want to think about right at this moment.

Telling Justin he'd see him later, Cal crossed the lobby and took the stairs, two at a time.

Chapter Four

JUST BEFORE SEVEN, JUDY rapped on Cal's door. 'Ready?' she asked.

'Yeah, let's go.' When he'd got back to his room, he'd taken a long shower. Tempting as it was to leave the scent of Justin lingering on his skin, his limbs were stiff from sleeping on the stock room floor. Though the power was still out across large sections of the island and would be until the electricity company had repaired the lines brought down by the storm, the resort had its own back-up generator, and Cal was able to soothe his aches under the hot spray.

He'd curled up on the bed, hoping to catch 40 winks, but he hadn't been able to drift off. Try as he might, he couldn't keep his mind from returning to events in the pitch dark confines of the stock room. Never had he known anything as exciting as the moment when Justin had begged, in the most submissive of tones, to be allowed to come. Even the feeling of being so skilfully deep-throated by the American paled in comparison. If they'd had time, they could investigate all the possibilities presented by Justin's desire to be dominated – territory Cal had never explored, but which caused his cock to twitch with excitement as he thought about it. But even with the enforced extension to their layover, Cal would be on his way back to England all too soon, his adventures with Justin nothing more than a hot memory to liven up the cold winter nights.

Giving up on his attempts to sleep, Cal slipped into shorts and a T-shirt and went to sit on his balcony, gazing out at the ocean. Its smooth, unruffled surface gave no hint that only a few hours ago, the storm had whipped it into a churning froth. If only people could shrug misfortune off quite so easily, Cal thought. Aware he was in danger of becoming maudlin, glad he hadn't poured himself a drink to accompany his gloomy musings, he was relieved to be distracted by Judy's arrival.

'So what's the meeting about?' he asked, as they made their way along the corridor to Rob's room.

'I think he just wants to give us the latest update on when the airport's likely to be up and running again,' Judy replied. 'And tell us not to go wandering in the meantime, more than likely.'

'Hey, if Jacques had invited you to go sightseeing in Oranjestad, would you have turned him down?' Cal retorted, but he knew Judy didn't mean to be unkind. She'd been telling him for long enough he needed to move on from the disappointments of his failed relationship and find someone new. It wasn't her fault the man who appeared to be a more than perfect replacement for Andy was someone who could never be a permanent fixture in his life.

Most of the crew were already assembled in Rob's room when they got there. Only Graham was still to arrive, and he slipped through the door moments after Cal and Judy. Like Cal, Rob had one of the ocean-facing suites, and there was plenty of room on the big bed and the low couch in the bedroom for everyone to make themselves comfortable while Rob outlined the situation.

'OK, people. This is the most up-to-date information I have.' He addressed them all in measured tones. 'The power's been restored throughout Oranjestad, and the people at the airport authority have told me they're working flat out to get the damage to the runway repaired as soon as possible. All the passengers who were scheduled to be on the flight back to Gatwick have been found rooms at a hotel a stone's throw from the terminal building – we've been very lucky there, as you can imagine – and as soon as we get details of the rescheduled flight we need to be mobilised to get down to the airport.'

'When is that likely to be?' Nicki asked.

'From what I've been told,' Rob replied, 'I don't see it being any time before early tomorrow afternoon, but I need you all to have your bags packed, ready to go at a moment's notice. OK?'

The assembled flight crew nodded. Used to travelling with

only the minimum of baggage, Cal and his colleagues had packing down to a fine art.

'Also – and this is very important – I need all of you to stay within the resort's grounds. It's not as if there isn't enough here to keep you entertained until we have to leave, and I don't want to find myself in a position where I can't account for someone's whereabouts if I need to.' Rob shot Cal a look that went unnoticed by everyone except Judy.

Cal wondered whether anyone else was aware he'd been missing in the island's capital at the height of the storm. If it wasn't common knowledge, it would more than likely become so before they returned to England. Fond as he was of Judy, her reputation as a gossip was well founded, and he suspected she wouldn't be able to resist telling everyone Cal had gone AWOL with the resort manager. He consoled himself that at least she didn't know the full truth of what had happened in Clyde's stock room.

'OK, so if you're all clear on that, why don't we go downstairs and get dinner?' Rob suggested. 'I understand the chef is putting on a barbecue tonight, and I did hear something about local entertainment.'

'Wouldn't surprise me if you've been enjoying some of that already,' Judy whispered to Cal, linking her arm in his as they left the room.

'Honey, I haven't a clue what you're talking about,' Cal replied.

The barbecue was in full swing when they reached the bar terrace, a calypso band was playing and what appeared to be a whole pig turned on a spit over a specially constructed fire pit. Cal looked round for Justin among the crowd of guests helping themselves to roast meat, rice and salad, and failed to spot him. Presumably his duties didn't extend to overseeing these revels.

Letting the waiting staff serve him with a big plate containing roast pork, chicken legs and baked fish, Cal found a place at one of the terrace tables and dug into his meal. Breakfast seemed a long time ago, and he was suddenly ravenously hungry.

'I got you a glass of punch,' Judy said, appearing at his elbow carrying a couple of tall glasses. Cal removed the paper parasol adorning his drink and took a sip. He tasted a warming hit of rum, mingled with orange and passion fruit.

'Quite a party they throw here,' he commented.

'Yeah, I was chatting to the cute waiter serving the bread rolls, and he tells me this is a weekly occurrence. They got really worried when the storm hit, in case the dancers couldn't make it out from Oranjestad and the event had to be cancelled.'

'Dancers?' Cal asked.

Almost at that moment, half a dozen women arrived, some white, some black and all wearing little more than sequinned bikinis and elaborate feathered headdresses. Room was cleared close to the band, and, to the calypso beat, the women went into an exuberant dance, shaking their hips and breasts in unashamedly sexual fashion. The crowd looking on clapped and cheered, moving to the infectious beat. It seemed hard to believe the people having such a good time had, only a few hours earlier, been hiding in their rooms, waiting for the storm to pass and praying nothing bad would happen to them. Like the ocean, they showed no ill-effects from their ordeal.

You're getting way too philosophical here, Cal told himself, and took another gulp of his punch.

When the dancers finished their routine, a traditional limbo pole was set up in the space they'd just occupied. 'And now, ladies and gentlemen,' the band leader announced, 'we invite you all to take part in the Four Winds limbo competition.'

Cal felt Judy tugging at his elbow. 'Hey, Cal, why don't we have a go?'

He shook his head. 'Ah, I don't know. I'm not that flexible.'

'Oh, come on, it'll be fun.'

With that, Judy dragged Cal off to join the line of guests waiting to try their hand at limboing under the pole. As was traditional, it was set quite high at first, meaning no one had to bend too far backward, but as it was lowered with each successive round, one or more of the competitors found themselves forced to pull out.

Despite his misgivings, Cal quickly got into the spirit of the game, egged on by the other members of the flight crew. His movements weren't in the least elegant, as he bent his knees and shimmied his hips in an attempt to move beneath the bar without dislodging it, but he was enjoying himself. Judy proved herself to be a surprisingly adept competitor. Though maybe he shouldn't be surprised by her skill at the game. She'd told him once that she'd been a pretty decent gymnast in her teens, with hopes of representing England at international level until a bad fall snapped her Achilles tendon and ended her dreams. It seemed she'd still kept a lot of her suppleness, and he found himself wondering whether she demonstrated the same flexibility in bed. Not that he had any intention of finding out, but …

The limbo pole was now less than three feet off the ground, and Cal was beckoned forward to take his turn. As soon as he approached it, he knew he couldn't bend far enough to sneak beneath it, and so it proved. The pole clattered to the ground, and he was eliminated from the contest, receiving a sympathetic round of applause as he departed.

It came as no shock to see Judy being declared the winner, a few moments later. She accepted her prize, a bottle of overproof rum, with a dazzling smile, blowing kisses to the crowd.

'You did pretty well back there,' a familiar voice murmured in Cal's ear. He turned to see Justin grinning at him. 'But it's always nice to see you getting down on your knees …'

'Are you allowed to flirt with the guests while you're on duty?' Cal replied, heart beating a little faster at the sight of Justin, dressed in his sober work suit.

'Only the cute ones.' Justin perched on the wooden bench beside Cal. 'I'd love to chat, Cal, but I can't really stop. There's a broken lounger in one of the beach cabañas and I need to alert the maintenance crew to get it replaced, but I just thought I'd say hi while I was passing. How's it going?'

'Fine. It looks like we'll be out of here some time tomorrow afternoon. In the meantime, we've just got to kill time here.' Cal sighed. 'There are a lot worse places to be stranded, I suppose.'

'Well, what I recommend you do tomorrow is sample the spa facilities. We've got a guy working here, Pete, gives the best deep tissue massage you'll ever experience. The spa staff will all be off duty now, but I can make sure you're booked in to see Pete in the morning. How does that sound?'

'Good.' Cal couldn't remember the last time he'd had a professional massage. With all his exertions over the last couple of days, it would be nice to have someone who knew what they were doing work on the tight knots of muscle at the base of his spine.

'OK, leave it with me and I'll get that sorted.' For a moment, Justin looked as though he might be about to make his own appointment with Cal, to pick up where they'd left off in the stock room. Instead, he put his hand on Cal's shoulder, giving it an affectionate squeeze. 'Gotta go, buddy. Duty calls. But I'll see you in the morning.'

Justin winked, and disappeared into the crowd, leaving Cal with the beginnings of a hard-on and an acute sense of frustration. He'd hoped to spend the night with his lover, but that wasn't going to happen now. Maybe it was for the best. Otherwise, he ran the risk of getting far too attached to Justin. It was already going to be hard enough to say his goodbyes when the crew were called to the airport.

Catching sight of Judy beckoning to him from the terrace for a dance, he nodded, drained the last of his drink and went to join her.

The revels on the terrace broke up early, kitchen staff moving in to clear away the remnants of the barbecue even as the last of the guests were drifting back to their rooms. Jacques and Judy left together, the co-pilot's arm round her bare, tanned shoulder, Judy still clutching her prize from the limbo competition. Watching them, Cal stifled a yawn, craving the comfort of his bed, his body clock still not properly adjusted to Aruban time. With one last backward look at the ocean, he followed his friends inside.

He'd barely undressed and slipped between the cool, cotton sheets when the phone by the side of his bed rang. It was bound to be Judy, wanting to continue the party in her room. He'd have to turn the offer down, sure she'd understand when he told her he needed his sleep. Oh, she might tease him, telling him he was turning into one of the "click-shut" tribe, but she wouldn't be offended by his refusal.

But the voice on the other end of the line belonged to someone else entirely. 'Mr Phillips, I'm calling from my office. There's something I need you to do for me.'

Justin sounded so serious, so formal that Cal wondered what might be wrong. Had the resort manager miscalculated the amount of places he'd allocated to the Celtic Air crew, or had guests unexpectedly checked in, having made it across by boat from one of the neighbouring islands? Did he need to vacate his room? It would be an inconvenience, but he ought to be able to find somewhere else to bunk down. After all, there'd be at least one bed free among the rest of the flight crew tonight; if the body language had been anything to go by, Judy and Jacques would be sharing one. 'Of course, anything.'

'Could you tell me what you're wearing right now?'

For a moment, Cal was sure he'd misheard, then a smile spread across his face as realisation dawned. I don't believe it, he thought. He's ringing me to talk dirty. 'Er – a pair of white boxer shorts.'

'That's all?'

'That's all.'

'Take them off,' Justin ordered. 'Even though I can't see you, I want you bare-assed naked. And make sure I can hear you doing it.'

'Yes, sir,' Cal replied, remembering how excited he'd been when Justin had called him "sir". Pushing back the covers, he fumbled with the waistband of his shorts. Pulling them down was no easy task, as he had to keep the phone receiver in one hand, holding it close enough that Justin would be able to make out the rustling of his underwear coming off, and the creaking of the bedsprings as he raised his rump from the mattress. Once they'd been removed, dropped without ceremony to lie on the polished floorboards, Cal said, 'Right, they're off.'

'Good. Are you hard?'

Cal glanced down at his cock; it had thickened slightly with the excitement of being made to undress, but it was a long way from being erect. 'Not yet, sir.'

'Well, we'll have to do something about that. I want you to get yourself nice and stiff. Do you have anything close to hand you can use as lube?'

A little bottle of hand cream stood on the night stand, some high-end brand he'd picked up while browsing in duty free at JFK Airport on his last trip to New York. 'Yes, sir. I've got some hand cream that might do.'

'There's no might about it.' Justin's dominant tone caused Cal's cock to stiffen further, rising up in anticipation of what might be to come. 'I want you to squeeze some into your hand and wank yourself till you're fully hard.'

'Yes, sir.' The bottle was pump-operated. Still holding the phone, Cal manoeuvred so he could push the pump down with the point of his elbow, letting a thick spurt of cream puddle in his right palm. Lying back on the bed, he stroked his slick hand along his length. Little shudders of sensation ran through him, causing his arsehole to clench and a tightness to build in his balls. From being weary and ready for sleep, his body was now on full erotic alert, craving the orgasm Justin's words and his own actions would very quickly wring from him.

'I want to hear you wanking,' Justin ordered him. 'Let me hear your hand slapping against that big, hard cock of yours.'

There was an appealing catch in Justin's voice, as though he was having a little difficulty forming the words. An image flashed into Cal's mind: Justin sitting at the desk in his office, zip down and his own cock in his hand, pleasuring himself while he told Cal what to do.

'Do – do you have your cock out?' Cal couldn't resist asking.

'I hardly think it's your place to ask that,' Justin replied, but something in his tone let Cal know that, yes, his thick length was jutting rudely from the fly of his dark business suit. 'In fact, for being so impertinent, I want you to stick a finger up your ass and keep on wanking.' Anticipating Cal's question as to how he might accomplish that, he said, 'You can put the phone on speaker function.' He gave Cal a moment to do just that, dropping the receiver securely back into its cradle before asking, 'Is it in you?'

Those four words – the dirtiest thing Cal thought he'd ever heard – almost had him shooting his load on the spot. He held himself together long enough to reply, 'Not yet, sir.'

'Well, do it, and tell me how it feels.'

Licking his index finger, wetting it enough that it would slip into his arse with ease, Cal took a deep breath. His right hand still gripped his cock just below the head, squeezing with sufficient pressure to prevent him coming before he was ready. Now he slid the middle finger of his other hand into his pucker, moaning with the sweetness of the penetration. 'Oh God!' he sighed, wishing Justin was there to see the way his hole welcomed that digit.

'Fuck ...' Justin replied. 'You're really doing it, aren't you? You're fucking yourself with your own finger.'

'Yes, sir,' was all Cal could groan in response. 'And I'm doing it for you. Oh Justin, anything for you.'

With that, he lost every last shred of his self-control. Fist pumping his cock, finger buried in the recesses of his arse, Cal succumbed to an orgasm that shook him to the very core. Slumping back against the pillows, he heard Justin on the other end of the phone, crying out in his own pleasure.

'Goodnight, lover.' Justin's voice sounded distant, but the emotion in his voice stayed with Cal after they'd cut the connection on the phone line. In the short time they'd been together, they'd reached a closeness Cal had struggled to find in relationships that had lasted years. And Cal was sure they'd barely scratched the surface of the pleasure they could have, once they'd properly got to know each other. Which was never going to happen. Come tomorrow, they'd be separated by the vast, cold distance of the Atlantic once more, and there was nothing Cal could do about it.

Chapter Five

'So,' JUDY ASKED, SPREADING honey on a slice of wholewheat toast, 'are you ready to go?'

Cal nodded, attacking the last piece of his breakfast sausage with his fork. Following a brisk shower, he'd packed his flight bag, and left it standing just inside his hotel room door, where it could be retrieved with minimal effort. Once they got word from Rob of a scheduled departure time from Queen Beatrix Airport, the whole crew would have to be prepared for a speedy departure from the resort. 'Yeah. Have you heard any more about when we're likely to be off?'

Judy shook her head. 'Not yet. I'm sure as soon as Rob knows anything, he'll let us know. It'll be a bit of a wrench to leave this place, but ...'

Won't it just, Cal thought, still not quite able to believe the lewd way in which he'd pleasured himself for Justin the night before. Though Judy had a freshly fucked glow of her own; they'd been friends long enough for him to recognise the twinkle in her eyes and the languor in her demeanour that followed good sex. Glancing round, he couldn't see the crew's French co-pilot. Unable to resist a spot of gentle teasing, he asked, 'So, is Jacques having a lie-in, or ..?'

'Cal, you're a complete beast,' Judy replied, but she didn't dodge the question. 'No, he got up about an hour ago and went for a run along the beach. He said he'd join me when he'd had a shower and – ah, there he is now.'

As if on cue Jacques strode towards them, his black hair still damp from showering, a dimple forming on his right cheek as he smiled in greeting.

'*Bonjour*, Cal – Judy ...' He dropped a kiss on each of

Judy's cheeks in turn, before placing his room keys on the table and turning to make his way to the breakfast buffet table. 'There's nothing like a spot of jogging to build up an appetite, *non*?'

Cal bit back the urge to ask whether the jogging Jacques referred to was of the horizontal variety, settling instead for a swift glance at his watch.

'Got to go,' he announced. 'I've got a massage booked, and I don't want to be late.'

'Ooh, very nice,' Judy replied. 'I did think about checking out the spa myself today, but I think I'll just stay by the pool and work on my tan instead.' She gestured to her phone, sitting prominently on the table at the side of her breakfast plate. 'After all, who knows when duty might call?'

Like the rest of the resort complex, the spa was fitted out to a standard that would rival any five-star hotel. Dressed in the white towelling robe and slippers he'd found in his wardrobe, Cal made his way to the waiting area. Haunting pan pipe music played softly, and the air held the faint fragrance of incense. He caught the eye of the blonde girl in a clinical white uniform who manned the reception desk.

'Can I help you?' she asked, her voice carrying a strong Dutch accent.

'I hope so. I should be booked in for a massage with Pete. It's all a bit last minute. Justin Holford was arranging it for me.'

The girl ran a manicured finger down the long list of appointments, and for a moment he thought he might be out of luck. At last, she said, 'Ah, yes. Cal Phillips, isn't it? Come this way. Pete's expecting you.'

She led him down a hushed corridor containing four treatment rooms. Knocking on the door of one, she waited till a deep male voice asked them to enter.

'Pete, this is Cal, your ten-thirty appointment.' She smiled at Cal. 'Enjoy yourself,' she told him, and backed out of the room.

Pete was nothing like Cal had expected. A giant of a man, he stood close to six and a half feet tall, with big, long-fingered hands. His hair was braided and caught in a short ponytail at the nape of his neck, and his white uniform coat contrasted starkly with his black skin. He smiled, and gestured to Cal to get up on the massage bed.

'Take your robe off and get comfortable, face down for me, please,' he said, his voice a deep rumble. Once Cal had done that, Pete draped a towel over him, covering him from the small of his back to just above his knees. 'Now, Cal, I'd like you to remove your briefs.'

Cal shot him a questioning look. He'd had many massages in the past, and until now he'd never been asked to take his underwear off.

Registering his surprise, Pete replied, 'I'm going to be working low down at the base of your spine. Guys who spend a long time sitting in those cramped airline seats get a lot of tension in that area, from my experience. And I wouldn't like to get massage oil on those tighty-whities.'

Satisfied by the explanation, Cal reached up under the towel and eased down his briefs, placing them on the massage bed beside him. With a grin, Pete picked them up and put them in the pocket of Cal's robe.

'Now ...' Pete gestured to the bottles of oil standing on the counter. 'Reviving or relaxing?'

Relaxing might not be such a good idea, given that he needed to be alert to the imminent possibility of packing up and heading for the airport. 'Reviving,' Cal replied. 'I think it might turn out to be a long day.'

'You've got it.' Pete poured a small amount of oil into his cupped palm, rubbing his hands together to warm it. 'Now, let's get those kinks eased out ...'

Eyes closed, face resting against the padded cut-out in the massage table, Cal gave himself up to the sensation of Pete's practised hands kneading his shoulders. Using the pads of his thumbs, the masseur chased down the knots of muscles, working on them till they disappeared.

'That feels amazing,' Cal murmured.

'Well, there's lots of tension here for me to get rid of,' Pete commented. 'Work hard, play hard, right?'

Pete had got the first part of that equation right, but Cal

barely had the strength to keep up his end of the conversation. Lulled by the warmth of the room, the gentle instrumental music oozing from the sound system on the counter and the rhythmic pounding of Pete's fingers against his back, he didn't hear the door softly open and shut. The first he knew they had company was when a voice said, 'Looks like you're enjoying that, Cal.'

Raising his head, Cal saw Justin smiling at him, mischief sparkling in his eyes. 'Hey, Justin, what is this, a visit from quality control?'

'Something like that. Or maybe I just like to watch.'

Almost without Cal being aware of it, Pete's hands had moved down to cup and squeeze his buttocks. There was nothing overtly sexual in the motion, but Cal found his cock stirring, trying to rise. He wanted to wriggle into a more comfortable position, giving his erection the freedom to swell to complete hardness, but that hardly seemed appropriate in the circumstances.

Though, looking at Justin's wolfish expression, maybe it was wholly appropriate. As if to confirm his suspicions, Pete's hand wormed its way beneath Cal's belly, seeking out his cock. When his fingers closed around its thickness, Cal whimpered with need.

'You like that?' Pete asked.

'God, yes.' The words were out before Cal could stop them. He shouldn't crave the masseur's touch, shouldn't want Pete to roll him on his back so he could wank him properly, not when Justin was in the room, but he did. And from the looks shooting between Justin and Pete, this was what Justin wanted too. Gradually, Cal realised how he'd been set up. His lover wanted to watch him being played with by another man – and what Justin wanted, Justin got.

Not that Cal was complaining. Pete's whole career was founded on knowing how best to touch his clients, and that sureness of touch was evident in the way his fingers stroked and teased Cal's hard, straining cock. It wouldn't take much of this skilful treatment to have him spunking into Pete's fist, even with his dick still trapped between his body and the massage table.

'Why don't you remove the towel, Pete?' Justin suggested. 'Let me get a really good look at what you're doing to him. And Cal, get up on your hands and knees. Make it easy for Pete to jerk you off.'

Cal didn't even think about disobeying, even as he wondered why he'd ever thought of Justin as submissive. Or maybe he was a switch, wanting to be on top most of the time, but occasionally needing to give up all responsibility for his pleasure to someone else.

'You have a gorgeous ass, Cal,' Pete commented, running his hands over Cal's taut cheeks and down into the crease between them. His finger brushed over Cal's anal pucker, making him shiver with forbidden pleasure.

If the man wasn't gay, Cal thought, at the very least he had a strong bisexual streak. He seemed to know exactly how a man reacted when a finger teased the sensitive place between his balls and arsehole, and just how to tug at Cal's tense, tight balls with a lightness of touch that had him fighting not to beg out loud to be fucked.

Looking over at Justin, he saw a prominent swelling in the crotch of his trousers. Wanting desperately to see his lover yank down the zip and play with his stiff cock, just as he'd pictured him doing when they'd been sharing that most intimate of phone calls the previous night, he bit back a sharp cry of need as Pete's oil-slippery finger probed at the entrance to his arse, worming its way inside with minimal effort.

'Mmm, lover-boy's in the mood to be fucked,' Pete said, pushing harder, finding the spot deep inside Cal's arse that held the key to his pleasure.

'Is that true, Cal?' Justin asked.

'Yes, sir,' Cal replied, not even thinking about the implications of calling Justin "sir" in front of another man. All he knew was he needed the satisfaction that only came from having a hard, excited cock thrusting into him, and if Justin wanted to watch him being fucked by Pete, he wasn't going to object.

'In that case ...' Justin reached for his wallet. Cal saw him take out a handful of Aruban twenty-florin bills, handing the colourful banknotes over to Pete. 'Thanks very much for everything you've done for us so far. Now, if you could leave Cal and me alone ...'

'Sure thing,' Pete replied. 'Though I do have a midday appointment booked, so you're going to have to be out of here before then.'

'Don't worry. If the state Cal's in right at this moment is anything to go by, I don't think it's going to take too much to have him coming on the end of my dick.'

Cal groaned, turned on beyond endurance by both the casual way Justin referred to him in front of the other man, as though he was nothing more than a glorified fuck-toy, and the thought of having Justin's cock buried in his arse.

'OK, boss.' Pete stuffed the money he'd been given into the pocket of his therapist's coat and clapped Justin on the back. 'I'll leave him in your capable hands.'

With that, the masseur left the room, shutting the door firmly behind him. Almost unnoticed, the CD Pete used to create a relaxing atmosphere came to an end, leaving in its wake a silence heavy with erotic anticipation. Cal hadn't moved from his crouching position, bare rump still raised and giving Justin a stunningly lewd view of his balls and the root of his cock from between his spread thighs.

'So how does it feel to be used as a plaything on my whim?' Justin asked, shrugging off his jacket.

Without even pausing to think about it, Cal replied, 'If you'd asked me a couple of days ago, I'd have said I'd never agree to it. Nobody's ever done anything like that to me, not with someone watching. But having Pete's fingers touching me there, knowing you were loving every minute of it – honestly? It felt incredible.'

Justin undid his shirt, giving Cal a lingering glimpse of his bare chest while he unfastened the buttons at his cuffs. 'You might not believe what I'm about to tell you, but when I booked you in to see Pete, I didn't plan for any of this to happen. I just thought you'd enjoy a massage – and he's just as good as I told you he was, isn't he?'

Cal nodded. 'He's fantastic. There's no stiffness in my shoulders any more.'

'Yeah, I can tell. It's all moved about three feet lower ...' Justin shot a look at Cal's cock, still rigid and in need of release. 'But I couldn't stop thinking about what it would be like to watch you being wanked by Pete, just the contrast of his black fingers on your white dick. So I rang him a few minutes before you were due to arrive, and asked whether he'd be averse to giving you a happy ending. I don't think I need to tell you what his answer was.'

By now, Justin was naked, his erection bobbing with every step as he walked over to join Cal at the massage table.

'Just one last thing ...' Ripping open a condom packet he'd retrieved from his wallet, he rubbered himself up, then climbed up on the table.

'Fuck me,' Cal moaned, as Justin's hands smoothed over his back, moving down towards his buttocks.

'When I'm good and ready,' Justin replied, fingers teasing and tantalising Cal's aching flesh, just as Pete's had done. 'Or would you like me to tie your hands to the table with your belt, so you don't have any choice in the matter?'

Cal stifled a moan, the thought of being bound and at his lover's mercy causing his cock to twitch with frustration. 'You can do whatever you want to me, sir,' he said, meaning every word as he never had before.

'You can't know how happy hearing that makes me.' Justin guided his cock to Cal's hole. Cal felt its blunt, latex-sheathed head press home. For a moment, his muscles fought against the intrusion, then Justin breached the tight ring and slid into his depths.

'God, yes. That's it,' Cal muttered, as Justin sawed in and out of him, his strokes strong and assured. He clung on to the edge of the massage table, so Justin wouldn't push him along it with the force of his thrusts. It was far from the most elegant position he'd ever found himself in, the narrowness of the massage bed giving Justin only just enough room to secure his shins on the padded top, either side of Cal's legs. Cal reckoned there was a strong possibility they might actually topple off it in the heat of their passion, falling to the floor in a tangle of limbs. But even before the idea had the chance to properly take hold, Justin's movements were speeding up as his excitement mounted.

'Oh, Cal, there's nothing in this world better than the feeling of being buried in your ass,' Justin grunted, reaching underneath their joined bodies to take hold of Cal's cock and pump it in his fist.

The wicked caress, fingers twisting around his overheated shaft, triggered a climax that roared through him. Arse packed full of cock, his lover's sweating torso slapping against his own, Cal felt his come explode from him, jetting out on to the table's thin paper covering. His hole clenched hard around Justin's length, bringing the man to a heaving orgasm of his own.

'You're the best,' Justin murmured in his ear, easing his cock slowly out of Cal's pleasure-sated hole. Cal almost didn't trust his legs to bear his weight as he guided himself to the floor.

Justin tossed his used condom and the massage table's paper protector, now stained and sticky, into the waste bin, then pulled Cal into his arms once more.

'I could really fall in love with you, if only I had the chance.' The words were out before Cal had time to prevent them.

For a moment, he feared Justin wasn't going to respond, or simply laugh off what they'd shared as a brief distraction from a situation far out of their control. With a sigh, Justin hugged him a little tighter. 'I'm halfway there myself, Cal.'

They kissed, long and hard, Cal trying not to lose himself in thoughts of what might have been. The sound of a ringing phone jolted him back to reality. It took him a moment to entangle himself from Justin's embrace and locate its source – the pocket of his towelling robe, still hanging on the back of his door – and he answered it to be greeted by Rob's smooth Canadian tones.

'Hey, pal, everything OK?' Rob asked.

'Sure,' Cal replied.

'Well, I've got good news for you. I've been contacted by the airport authority. The runway's fixed up as good as new, and we've been allocated a flight departure time. Taxis have been booked to take us all to the airport, so I need you in reception and ready to go in 20 minutes' time. No later.'

'Of course. See you there.' Ending the call, Cal told Justin, 'It's time to go home. I've got 20 minutes to shower, get my bag and be in reception.'

'Not a problem,' Justin assured him. 'Take your shower here. You've still got time before Pete's next appointment. As for your bag, I'll get someone to bring it down to reception for you.'

'That's great, but I'll need my uniform as well. I don't think anyone will be too impressed if I turn up to board my flight dressed in my underwear.'

Justin grinned, as though he found the image appealing. 'Where is it?'

'Laid out on the bed in my room.'

'OK, I'll get that to you too. It's all part of the service.'

With that, he was gone, leaving Cal to step into the shower. By the time he'd washed the traces of massage oil and passionate sex from his body and stepped out of the cubicle to towel himself down, his flight attendant's uniform had replaced the towelling robe on the back of the door. His phone, room key and underpants lay in a neat arrangement on the massage bed.

Muttering a silent thank you to Justin for proving as good as his word, Cal started dressing. This unexpected extension of their stay in paradise was over. Now it was time to leave this brief, sweet romance behind and return to the everyday world.

Cal's flight bag waited for him in the reception area, just as Justin had promised. Rob was already there, as were the remainder of the crew, all apart from Judy. A moment later, she bustled in, dragging her little wheeled case behind her.

'OK, everyone, glad to see we're all punctual,' Rob said.

He seemed about to launch into a little speech, until a man popped his head through the main door and announced, 'Taxi for the Milner party?'

'Yeah, that's us,' Rob said. 'If the four of you nearest the door want to head off...' Nicki and Graham, along with a couple of the other flight attendants, stood up and followed the taxi driver outside.

Soon, only Rob, Jacques, Judy and Cal were left waiting for the final taxi to arrive. Justin chose that moment to wander into reception, fixing Cal with a smile that almost broke his heart. He knew he had to speak with Justin once more before he left. If he didn't say what was on his mind, he'd always regret it.

Aware of Judy's curious eyes on him, he stood up and walked over to Justin.

'Hey,' Justin said, 'you get your bag OK?'

'Yes, thanks.' Cal dug in his pocket, and found a couple of crumpled dollar bills. 'Could you give those to whoever brought it down for me?'

'Of course.'

'And – and is there any way this doesn't have to be goodbye between us?' Not giving Justin a chance to respond, he continued, 'What I've had with you over the last couple of days has been truly incredible. I've never met anyone quite like you. You're kind, you're brilliant at your job, and the sex – well, I think you know how good that's been between us. And what I said in the therapy room about falling in love with you, I meant it. I wish there was some way I could stay here with you, but I know that's not possible, and it just doesn't seem fair that I've met the right person in the wrong place.'

Justin reached out and took hold of Cal's hand. 'Wow, that was some speech, Cal. And I'm glad you made it, because I meant what I said too. I don't usually fall quite so hard and so quickly, but you're right, there's a connection between us I never expected to find with anyone.'

'So what are we going to do about it? Cal asked, his heart beating faster simply from knowing Justin returned his feelings.

'Like I keep telling you, Aruba's a great place to come for a vacation. And with the right guide, you could get to see all the places the tourists don't know about. I mean, you never really saw Clyde's at its best, did you?'

Cal laughed, wondering whether Clyde's Bar could ever be seen at its best.

'Just think what a few days here would do for you, really give you a chance to recharge your batteries. And there's so much to do here. We could go horse riding, snorkelling, maybe take the Jeep out to the gold mill ruins at Bushiribana, or visit the Guadirikiri caves. If we ask Clyde nicely, he'll even introduce us to a guy he knows who owns his own private island ...'

It all sounded so tempting, and Cal knew he had at least a week's holiday allowance for the year still owing to him. 'I have to say that's a fantastic idea.'

'And after that – well, I've never been involved in a long-distance relationship, but I think maybe you and I could try it, see if we could make it work?'

Cal couldn't think of anything he wanted more. It wouldn't be easy, not with Justin living on the other side of the world, but who knew? He'd always regret it if he didn't at least give it a go. After all, it wasn't as though he had to work for Celtic Air forever; there were plenty of American airlines who flew to Aruba on a regular basis, and he'd always fancied living in the States. So many possibilities, so much to think about on the long flight home.

If only Rob wasn't calling his name, telling him their taxi had arrived.

'So I'll see you soon?' Justin asked.

'As soon as I can manage it.' With that, not caring they had an audience, Cal pressed his lips to Justin's, sharing a kiss so deep it left them both breathless when it finally broke. All the longing, all the love he felt for the other man, was wrapped up in that kiss, and returned to him twofold.

'Have a safe flight, Cal. I'll be waiting for you to come back to me,' Justin said, as Cal turned to leave the hotel. The expression on his face told Cal it was a promise he had no intention of breaking.

Epilogue

SOMEWHERE HIGH OVER THE Atlantic, Cal stretched and went to find a vacant spot in the crew seats at the back of the first class compartment. Dinner had long since been served and cleared away, and the handful of passengers in his charge were finally settled, most of them trying to get some sleep as the plane flew on towards Gatwick. They'd wake grumpily to a September dawn, their time in the Caribbean already beginning to seem like a distant memory. Cal could do with a snooze himself, but he needed to keep a watchful eye in case anyone needed his assistance.

What would Justin be doing at this moment? Probably one of the hundreds of mundane tasks that helped keep the resort running smoothly, like drawing up the order for cleaning supplies, or dealing with the complaints of some guest who'd hoped for an ocean view and found himself facing the ornamental gardens instead. Cal preferred to think of Justin at the end of his shift, easing away the day's stresses in the shower. As he lathered up his body, he wouldn't be able to resist reaching down and taking his cock in hand, gently stroking it to full hardness. Maybe he'd even be wishing it was Cal's fingers that kneaded him so expertly, bringing him in only a few moments to the point where he simply had to shoot his come all over the cool white tiles ....

'Oh, I need to get off my feet. These wretched shoes are really pinching me. I knew I'd packed the wrong pair.'

At the sound of Judy's voice, Cal sat up hastily, hoping she wouldn't notice the bulge that had formed in his uniform trousers while he'd been fantasising about Justin.

'So,' she said, 'tell me about you and that hot resort

manager. It looked like a pretty passionate goodbye you shared from where I was standing.'

Passionate, and only temporary. Cal's request for some holiday time would go to Human Resources on his return to England, and as soon as he could, he'd be heading back to the Four Winds to pick up where he and Justin had left off.

Smiling at the prospect, he replied, 'Well, it all started when he came into the bar to tell us to break the party up ...'

Xcite

Xcite Books help make loving better with a wide range of erotic books, eBooks and dating sites.

www.xcitebooks.com
www.xcitebooks.co.uk

facebook

Sign-up to our Facebook page for special offers and free gifts!